Her Secret Life

TIFFANY L. WARREN

KENSINGTON PUBLISHING CORP.
www.kensingtonbooks.com

DAFINA BOOKS are published by

Kensington Publishing Corp.
119 West 40th Street
New York, NY 10018

All Kensington titles, imprints, and distributed lines are available at special quantity discounts for bulk purchases for sales promotion, premiums, fundraising, and educational or institutional use.

Special book excerpts or customized printings can also be created to fit specific needs. For details, write or phone the office of the Kensington Sales Manager: Kensington Publishing Corp., 119 West 40th Street, New York, NY 10018. Attn. Sales Department. Phone: 1-800-221-2647.

Dafina and the Dafina logo Reg. U.S. Pat. & TM Off.

ISBN-13: 978-1-4967-0872-4
ISBN-10: 1-4967-0872-5
First Kensington Trade Paperback Printing: May 2017

eISBN-13: 978-1-4967-0874-8
eISBN-10: 1-4967-0874-1
First Kensington Electronic Edition: May 2017

10 9 8 7 6 5 4 3 2 1

Printed in the United States of America

Her Secret Life

JUN 17

Also by Tiffany L. Warren

Don't Tell a Soul
The Replacement Wife
The Favorite Son
The Pastor's Husband

Acknowledgments

Thank God for inspiration. I mean that. Authors must find inspiration somewhere to create these stories. My muse is spirit-led, I believe. I will see or hear something that invites a story. I am largely an undisciplined writer, I suppose, because my writing follows the inspiration. I don't try to force it.

Thank God I find inspiration just about everywhere.

The inspiration for *Her Secret Life* came from a young lady I met in Washington, DC. I was doing an assignment for work, and rushing to and fro on the Metro. The young lady had a little stand outside the train station, with books that she'd written. She was selling them because she was homeless. I had no cash to purchase one from her, so I promised to come back. When I did, she was gone. Probably went to scope out a new location.

What struck me about her was her youth. She was in her early twenties. She was a pretty and petite girl, but she was homeless. What was her story? Was she a runaway? Had someone hurt her? Was she a former ward of the state who had aged out of the foster-care system?

Or what if she was none of those?

The best stories for me begin as a what-if. I started to ask myself, what if she had fallen on hard times but was too ashamed to share it with anyone?

So, *Her Secret Life* was born.

I always have to thank my family, my complete and total support system. My husband, Brent, who was blessed (cursed?) to have a creative as a wife. My children, who have grown up with a mother who always has a deadline. They make this possible. I need them to survive. My books need them, too.

My writing team includes Tara Gavin, my editor at Kensington, my virtual assistant, Lasheera Lee, and my agent, Sara

Camilli. They keep me together. I am the author who, every year, forgets when royalties arrive and is always, always late.

I have a solid core of besties who are always there. I mean always. I never have to worry about whether or not they have my back. They just do. They are the aunties to my children, and they listen to all of my issues. Shawana, Afrika, Robin, Lulu, Renee, Tippy, Kymmie—love you!

When I start to list my writer tribe, I always leave someone out, but I love the writer community and the ones who support us. Thank you for your words of wisdom, your reviews, and your endless promotion of my books.

Enough of my rambling. Time for the story. Enjoy!

PROLOGUE

Today . . .

It was stifling hot on the Metro platform. Graham felt sweat make a little river down his cheek. He couldn't wipe it, because he didn't have a napkin or sanitizer, and the Metro was like one giant petri dish of cold, flu, and crud germs. So the little river ran.

One glance up at the monitor for the Green and Yellow Line trains told Graham he had just missed one and would have to wait eleven minutes for the next one. Eleven minutes would feel like eleven hours in this heat. A tributary started from the little forehead river.

Graham's eyes swept the train platform looking for a distraction from the heat, something to occupy his mind during the eleven-minute wait. Then he saw her. The most gorgeous distraction ever, standing right next to him.

She was petite, but not tiny. Curves filled out every inch of her jeans and T-shirt. Graham noted her shoes—flats—like every other sensible woman waiting for the train. He imagined she had business attire and high heels in her bag.

As if she sensed his gaze, the woman looked at Graham. Bright pink lips were a contrast to her caramel-colored skin. Natural curls escaped the bun on her head and mingled with the little river on her face. Graham wanted to push her glasses up on her nose. They were perched near the tip and threatened to slide even farther down.

She'd caught him staring at her, drinking her in like the refreshing beverage he wished he was holding. He had to say something; otherwise, he'd seem like a creep. And he cared what she thought.

"You waiting for the Green or the Yellow train?"

She gave Graham a confused look as if that wasn't what she'd expected him to say. Graham was similarly flummoxed. He had no clue why he had said something so stupid as his opening line.

"Which one are you waiting for?" she asked in return.

"Yellow."

"Oh. I am waiting for the Green."

"You have a longer wait than I do."

Graham glanced again at the monitor. He had nine minutes, and she had ten. Nine minutes to spit game and get digits.

"Man, it's hot," Graham said this with emphasis, and added bass to his voice. He'd read that women were naturally more attracted to men with deep voices.

She giggled.

"What's funny?" Graham asked, extra bass gone.

"I'm sorry. I was laughing at me. When you announced that it was hot, I wanted to call you Captain Obvious. But that would've been rude, so I didn't. Then I laughed, and you thought I was rude anyway. I'm sorry. I'm having a bad day. The worst, actually."

"You should've said it. I would've laughed with you. Never censor yourself."

"Oh, trust me. I am a person who needs censoring."

In that moment, Graham needed censoring, or at least his thoughts did. It had something to do with how she moved her lips while speaking. It was sensuous, and Graham was almost sure that the effect was accidental.

"I'm Graham."

He extended his hand for her to shake, and she hesitated.

She looked at his hand the same way Graham looked at random Metro riders' hands. He threw his head back and laughed.

She touched his fingertips with hers and laughed too.

"I'm Onika. Pleased to meet you."

Graham wasn't surprised that she had an exotic-sounding name. It was fitting. Onika. A rare name for a rare beauty.

Graham glanced up at the display. He had six minutes, and he was nowhere near getting her number.

"On your way home from work?" Graham asked.

She hesitated again, but this time he wasn't sure why. She glanced up at the display, too. Was she counting the minutes until he disappeared from her space?

"Um, yes," she finally responded, her tone irritated and impatient.

"I'm going to Busboys and Poets for open mic night. Have you ever been?"

"No. I don't think so."

"If you ever make it, try their shrimp and grits. It's amazing."

"I don't eat grits."

"You don't? I've never met a black person who doesn't eat grits."

She smiled. "Now you have."

He was encouraged by her smile, but he only had three minutes left, and he didn't know how to close the deal.

Graham knew his friends would be mocking him right now. They'd say he had no game. And they would be right. Graham didn't have game.

All of his long-term relationships had been woman-initiated. He had been chosen every time. He'd never done the choosing.

He knew he was good-looking. Tall, but not so tall that he towered over petite women. Dark with smooth skin, which was greatly enhanced by his goatee and dimple. Big, expressive eyes and a decent body.

He wasn't insecure about his looks at all.

It was the connecting that was hard. How to let the woman know that he was sincere, kind, and God-fearing, all in ten minutes or less without seeming like a creep.

Two minutes left. It was time for a last-ditch effort.

Graham reached into his wallet and took out a card. He placed it in Onika's hand. She grimaced. *Damn.* But she wrapped her hand around the card. She didn't throw it down.

"My train is arriving, but I would love to see you again. I know it's forward, but can I call you some time?"

"I . . . I will call you. This is your personal number on the card?"

Graham nodded, although he knew it was pointless. She wasn't going to call.

He waved good-bye as he jumped on the train. With a faint smile on her lips, she waved back.

Onika watched the train as it rolled away through the tunnel. When it was out of sight, she looked down at the card and crumpled it in her hand.

The woman standing next to Onika on the platform frowned.

"That was a handsome, polite, young man with a job. That's why you young girls don't have husbands—you turn down the nice guys."

Onika sighed but didn't reply to the woman. She was right. Graham seemed like a great guy. Polished and fine. Nice shoes and watch.

He would probably be perfect for someone, but guys like Graham didn't date homeless women.

Onika let the crumpled card fall to the floor.

CHAPTER ONE

Ten years ago . . .

Onika's hands trembled as she opened the letter. She'd done exactly as her guidance counselor had instructed. She'd taken advanced placement classes and gotten all A's. She'd joined the Key Club and was elected to Student Council. She'd even run for class secretary and won. So she wasn't worried about the response from the elite, all-women's Robinson University, the top college on her list. She was worried about the after.

What would happen after she told her mother and grandmother?

Tears rolled down her cheeks as she mouthed the first word on the page. *Congratulations.*

She kept reading, and when she got to the words "full-ride scholarship," the sobs came strong and fast. Uncontrollable.

She was going to be a Robinette. She was going to stroll on the yard wearing her sorority colors of pink and blue (because she would only pledge Epsilon Phi Beta). She was going to law school, where she'd meet her future husband. Or maybe she'd meet him at a brother college because he was going to medical school.

Onika played and replayed her fantasy in her mind as she

took the ninety-seven steps from her grandmother's mailbox to the house on the corner, where she would find her mother.

Onika made her way up the dusty path to the front porch of the dilapidated shack. One good North Carolina tropical storm could probably blow it over. Onika never remembered there being grass. It had always been only dirt, rocks, and glass. And she'd been walking these ninety-seven steps her entire life.

She pushed open the unlocked front door. No need to lock the doors to hell. No one would go in willingly, except a kindred spirit to the wretched souls already inside.

Onika knew the place well. She knew every room and, unfortunately, every corner. She knew the regular inhabitants, and she knew when there was a visitor. The visitors were dangerous. They didn't know that Judy was her mama, or worse, they knew and didn't care. After a few narrow escapes from being molested, Onika avoided the strangers in the house.

The scent in the house was hard to describe, but Onika thought it was something like melting crayons. It was a little sweet, hot, and desperate. The whole house smelled like decay. Not death, but the rotting stench of the barely living.

"Judy," Onika called, "where are you?"

Onika hoped that her mother, Judy, was either down from her high or that she hadn't taken her first puff. If she was in the middle of a full-blown high, sharing her news would be pointless. Onika wanted to see the look on Judy's face when she learned that every curse she had ever hurled at her baby girl was canceled.

"Judy!"

Onika heard a grunt that she recognized as her mother's. She followed the sound to the back bedroom.

Judy sat on the edge of a ragged, threadbare mattress in only her panties. Her breasts hung to her waist like two ebony pendulums. Judy's wig rested beside her on the mattress and next to a naked, sleeping man.

Judy looked up at her daughter. "What you doing here, Onika? Didn't your grandmama tell you to stay out from around here?"

"I came looking for you."

"I ain't got no money."

"I'm not looking for any money. I came to tell you that I got into Robinson University, and I get to go for free."

"Where's that? Raleigh?"

"Atlanta."

Judy shook her head and stomped her feet as she cackled. "You ain't going to no Atlanta."

"I am."

"How you doing that?" Judy's cackle got louder.

"I got a scholarship."

Judy slapped her male friend on the thigh. "Cole, wake up. My daughter going to college in Atlanta."

Cole grumbled and rolled over on his back, giving Onika a full view of his man parts. For some reason, Judy found this funny but threw a dirty blanket over him that she found on the floor.

"You think you something, going away to school, huh? Well, you ain't no better than me. You've always thought you were better, but you ain't."

Onika looked at the floor and dropped the hand holding the letter to her side. "I don't think I'm better."

"You do. 'Cause you're light-skinned and got that curly hair like yo' Puerto Rican daddy."

Judy always talked about Onika's father with a hint of bragging and a haughty air. Almost like she was proud of getting pregnant by him when she was a dark and overweight woman with dry, kinky hair. Somehow, she'd been able to pull a Puerto Rican pimp, and he put his seed inside her.

He hadn't stuck around to see the flower bloom.

"Mama, you need to come home. Grandma is gonna be looking for you in a little bit."

"She knows where I am. She ain't gotta come looking for me."

Onika's grandmother, Earlene, refused to accept that her daughter was a drug addict. She always just said that her daughter was sick. Whenever anyone mentioned rehab to Earlene, she'd say Judy needed a touch from the Lord. Onika watched her grandmother go up for prayer every Sunday at their church.

She'd prayed and fasted. Fasted and prayed. And then when Onika was old enough, Earlene made her pray and fast, too.

Onika remembered being on her knees at the altar, next to her grandmother. Earlene had crafted a little prayer, and she'd taught it to her grandchild. Onika knew the prayer before she knew her ABCs.

Jesus be a balm. A balm in Gilead. Heal her by your stripes. By your stripes she is healed.

For hours they'd pray. If Judy had stayed out all Saturday night, all Sunday afternoon Earlene and Onika offered up prayers. Long after service let out, the two of them would stay at the altar, saying their prayer. No. Chanting the words. Until it sounded more like an incantation than a prayer. Until the old wooden church floor splintered beneath Onika's knees. She'd wanted to cry out every time, but she was afraid that, if she broke the prayer, Judy wouldn't be healed.

Onika kept going to the altar until she was twelve years old. That's when she'd stopped believing a healing was coming.

But for some reason, now Onika whispered the words of those childhood prayers as she watched her mother examine a piece of debris on the floor, probably checking to see if it was a crack rock.

Jesus be a balm. A balm in Gilead. Heal her by your stripes. By your stripes she is healed.

She didn't know why she suddenly had the urge to pray. It was the strangest thing. But nothing had changed. The prayer was as ineffective as ever. Judy finally found a bit of the drug hiding in the filthy carpet. Long past the point of being ashamed in front of her daughter, she scrambled to her pipe to take another hit.

Onika vowed to never say that prayer again.

CHAPTER TWO

Onika left her mother feeling numb. It had been a very long time since Judy's drug addiction bothered her.

There was no reason to be embarrassed about it anymore. Everyone in town knew Judy got high. They knew she slept with men for money to feed her habit. Nothing about Judy was a secret in Goldsboro, North Carolina.

Grandma was waiting for her on the porch. Anytime Onika got home a few minutes late, Grandma feared the worst.

"Where you been, gal?" Grandma asked, hands on her hips and eyebrows furrowed.

Although Onika had inherited her facial features from her Latino father, she'd gotten her body from Grandma. At sixty-four, she still had an hourglass figure. Her perky breasts and behind defied gravity, probably because the only time she took off her bra and girdle was to bathe.

"I went to tell my mother I got into Robinson University."

"You went to tell your mother, huh?" Grandma mimicked Onika's clipped diction and shook her head. "Your mama probably didn't even know what you were saying. I done told you to stay yo' behind outta that crack house. Don't say nothing, you wind up raped."

Onika didn't argue with her grandmother. That was always a

waste of breath and energy. It was impossible to win, and sometimes dangerous when she had a blunt object in her hand.

"Robinson University. You done let that white woman at that school fill your head up with foolishness. Why are you going to college all the way in Atlanta? There are plenty good schools right here in North Carolina."

"This is the top school for young black women, Grandma. And I have a full scholarship. They are paying for everything."

Onika was careful to keep her tone nonconfrontational. She wasn't arguing. Not really. She was just stating the facts. Plus, she was going to Robinson no matter what her grandmother said.

"Everything? How you getting there, huh?" Grandma asked. "How you getting home for the holidays? How you putting clothes on your back?"

Onika knew that this would be her grandmother's reaction. Her world was consumed with Judy and making sure Judy was okay. Supposedly, Onika's father was the one who got Judy hooked on drugs to begin with. Grandma sometimes treated Onika as if she was an extension of her father. Only gave just enough so that no one could say she abandoned her granddaughter.

"I will figure it out," Onika said. "I will work hard and save my money."

"And who's gonna see 'bout your mama?"

"You."

"I ain't gonna be here forever. When I'm gone, it's on you."

Onika disagreed. The burden of having a drug addict for a mama was more than enough adversity for a young woman. She was not going to live the rest of her life pulling her mother out of drug houses when she refused to get well.

"I can't worry about that now. If I stay here, I'm gonna end up like her. Ain't nothing in Goldsboro for me."

"You ain't nothing like her. Your mama has a sickness, but she has a good heart. She loved yo' serpent father with every bone in her body. With every joint, blood vessel, and organ she loved that man. You ain't like her. You only love yourself."

"That's not true."

"Who do you love, then? Not me, not your mama. Not if you would leave me here with her when you can help. You can go to college less than an hour away. Don't nobody care what college you go to long as you get a degree."

"This school is elite."

"You ain't elite. Yo' mama on crack. Yo' daddy died from AIDS 'cause he liked men, women, and drugs. You ain't got but two bras and three pairs of panties. You ain't elite. You as low as they come. But even the lowest of the low takes care of their mama."

The words wounded Onika deeply, but she had known the conversation would go this way. She'd expected it. She'd steeled herself against it, readied her heart for the onslaught.

Onika tuned out her grandmother's ranting, and took her mind back to the day Ms. Carpenter, her guidance counselor, told her about Robinson University. Grandma was wrong about Ms. Carpenter. She wasn't a white woman. She was biracial, just like Onika. She'd gone to Robinson on a scholarship, too.

"You'll meet the most promising young black people in the country. From prominent homes," she'd said. "Doctors and lawyers for parents. Brilliant."

Initially her description had worried Onika. How would she fit in with anyone from a prominent home?

"I'll be an outcast, Ms. Carpenter."

Ms. Carpenter immediately pulled a mirror from her purse and thrust it in Onika's face.

"Look at yourself, dear. You may not have been blessed with a good home, but you are intelligent and beautiful. A smart woman can change the world. A smart and beautiful woman can change the world while wearing diamonds."

Onika remembered not being sure about Ms. Carpenter's advice. She was smart and gorgeous, but she was working at a high school in Goldsboro. Where were her diamonds?

But after that conversation, Ms. Carpenter had decided to groom Onika for Robinson. She'd taught her how to speak without a trace of Goldsboro shining through. She'd tutored

Onika in French until she was fluent. She'd helped her write essays and apply for scholarships.

No one had ever given Onika that much attention and nurturing. She wanted to make Ms. Carpenter proud.

Onika never imagined herself making her grandmother proud, nor her mother. But Ms. Carpenter made her believe she could do and be anything.

CHAPTER THREE

Onika showed up alone for move-in day and new-student orientation at Robinson University. It's not like she needed that much help anyway. All she had was a bed-in-a-bag and a suitcase.

She also came prepared with her story. She was an orphan. Raised by her grandmother. From Durham, but she was home-schooled, in case anyone asked where she went to high school. She had a Facebook account, but it was under Nikki Lewis. Of course, she was enrolled as Onika, but she'd requested that all of her student information use Nikki instead. Class rosters, dorm assignments, everything was to say Nikki. She told the registrar that she was hiding from one of her mother's abusive boyfriends and needed anonymity. It was amazing how easily the lie had been received.

Onika was too unique of a name, and the last thing she needed was for someone from Goldsboro to pop onto her page and call her out. Or say her mama overdosed. Or anything else that might blow her intricate cover.

Onika walked into her dormitory room and felt a surge of excitement. The old twin bed, desk, and dresser were nicer than any furniture she'd ever had. But what really intrigued her was the way her roommate had decorated her side of the room. She had a rug, pictures on the wall, two lamps (one a lava lamp), a shoe rack that held at least fifteen pairs of shoes, and a comforter on the bed that looked expensive. It didn't look like it came in a bag with two sheets and a pillow case. Onika imagined that the dresser drawers were filled with pretty underclothing. This was a girl who had a different bra for every day of the week.

"Hi, I'm Chelsea Richard," the girl said as she ran up to welcome Onika. She pronounced her last name *Ree-shard*. Onika wondered if it was French.

"I hope it's okay that I took this side of the room," Chelsea continued. "I wanted to wait until you got here, but my mother and father wanted to put everything up for me. Please say it's okay."

Onika was overwhelmed by the amount of sound coming from Chelsea's body. It was too much, as if she had a built-in amplifier.

"I don't really have a preference, so it's fine."

"Oh, good. What's your name?"

"Nikki Lewis."

"What's Nikki short for? Nicole?"

Onika shook her head. "It's just Nikki."

"Oh, okay. Well, do you need any help unpacking your things?"

"Nope. This is it."

If it wasn't somewhat embarrassing, Onika would've died laughing at the confused look on Chelsea's face as she looked at Onika's sparse belongings. But since it was embarrassing, Onika looked away and opened her bed-in-a-bag and removed the sheets from the cardboard.

"You aren't going to wash those before you put them on your bed?" Chelsea asked. "They're fresh out of the package."

Onika shrugged, not understanding the problem. The sheets were brand-new. Why would she need to wash them first?

"Don't you know that those sheets that come in a package are manufactured in third world countries where they have all sorts of pathogens and bacteria? You shouldn't sleep on them without washing them first."

Onika didn't know about washing them. She didn't have any laundry detergent yet, nor did she know where the laundry was on campus. She was tired from being on the bus and the subsequent taxi ride. She just wanted to make her bed.

"Here, I have some sheets you can use," Chelsea said as if she was reading Onika's mind.

Chelsea reached into her closet and emerged with a set of crisp, white sheets. They were scented with something that didn't smell like any laundry detergent Onika had ever used. When Earlene washed white sheets, they came away smelling like bleach and Borax. Onika inhaled deeply and smiled.

"It's lavender and mint linen spray," Chelsea said like it was nothing.

Maybe it was nothing to Chelsea, but Onika didn't know that there was such a thing as perfume for sheets. Or linens.

Onika quickly made her bed and stuffed the bed-in-a-bag items back into their plastic to wash later. It was warm, so the sheets would be fine for the first night.

"Are you poor?" Chelsea asked.

Onika was disarmed by the question. First of all, because the answer was obvious. Of course, she was poor. Second, who would just come out and ask a person if she was poor?

"I'm not rich," Onika responded.

There was no way she was going to tell this girl that her mama was a crackhead, and that she'd never worked a real job, so yes, she was poor.

"The good thing about being here at Robinson is that we will meet girls from every walk of life," Chelsea said. "And at the end of it all, we'll be sisters."

Chelsea sounded like the Robinson University brochure that Ms. Carpenter had given Onika her freshman year of high school. She said "every walk of life" like she had just encountered someone from a third world country and not just sheets manufactured there. But Onika guessed Goldsboro would be a third world country compared to the progressive cosmopolitan city where Chelsea was probably raised.

"I always wanted a sister," Onika said.

That was a true sentiment, and not part of her cover story. The idea of sisterhood was strange to Onika. She didn't have sisters, nor really any friends. Her high school had been full of mean girls who made fun of Onika because of Judy. And then the boys would make lecherous sounds when she wore something snug or form-fitting, and everyone thought that it was okay, because she was lower than low, the bottom of the Goldsboro caste system. They were all poor, but Judy and Onika were dirt-poor.

Onika's mother was the town crack whore. So every person who wanted to feel better about their own misery would look her way and feel lifted. Most of Goldsboro was poor; a pickle factory was the town's biggest employer. But poor was one thing. They could look at Onika and think, *It could be worse.*

"I always wanted a sister, too," Chelsea said. "I have a brother who goes to Hickman, across the street. He's a junior, though."

Onika wanted to ask Chelsea if her parents were rich. Like not upper-middle-class rich, but old-money rich. She was unable to find the words.

"My parents are on the board of trustees at both schools, so we didn't really have a choice on where we could go."

"This is where the black elite send their children, right?"

"Yes . . ."

Onika could feel the tension in the room. Chelsea didn't seem to want to admit to being rich any more than Onika wanted to admit to being poor.

"I'll tell you a secret if you promise not to tell anyone. This is, like, take it to your grave serious," Onika said.

Chelsea perked up. "Sisterhood is built on secrets. I will never tell anyone."

"Okay. So, I'm here on a scholarship . . . for orphans."

Chelsea gasped. Onika wondered if she was expecting something a little more scandalous. Or maybe just a little less depressing. And the lie was a tiny one. Onika's father *was* dead, and her mother was on her way there.

And, of course, Chelsea wouldn't keep the secret. Onika didn't expect her to. She expected Chelsea to tell just enough people so that no one would feel comfortable asking about why she never had anyone come for parents' day or why she never went home for the holidays. Chelsea and her bubbly personality would share her secret with enough of the Robinettes that Onika would never have to mention Judy.

"I'm so sorry to hear that," Chelsea said. "If you want, you can come home with me for Thanksgiving and Christmas. We always have more than enough, and my mother would just love you. You're so pretty, gorgeous really. My mother will make a doll out of you."

Onika balked at being called gorgeous by Chelsea. This girl was perfect. Her hair was silky straight and held back with jewel-encrusted bobby pins. Her cocoa-brown skin was flawless, and her lips were full and pouty. Onika felt beauty-challenged standing in the same room with her.

"I'm happy we're roommates," Chelsea said. "We're going to be the start of the pretty girl clique of our class."

Onika was happy, too, but for a different reason. She didn't care about any pretty girl clique. She cared about making a rich girl posse and meeting their rich brothers over at Hickman. One of them would probably be her husband.

CHAPTER FOUR

"Have you ever heard of a sugar baby?" Chelsea asked Onika as they carefully applied their makeup for their club night out.

"The little caramel candy that comes in the yellow and red box?" Onika said. "I used to eat them in the movies when I was little."

Chelsea burst into laughter, although Onika had no idea what she'd said that was funny.

"Not that kind of sugar baby. Well, I guess it could be little, sweet, and caramel, but it doesn't come in a yellow and red box."

Now Onika was confused. "I don't know what you're talking about."

"A sugar baby is a young girl who has a sponsor that's an older gentleman."

"A sponsor?"

"Correct. Someone to handle all of her expenses. Like tuition, books, clothes, vacations, and more."

"An older man spending money on a young girl. In exchange for what?"

Chelsea giggled. "Her companionship."

Onika's expression went dark. She knew exactly what Chelsea was suggesting. The idea was one that she knew intimately. It's just that back in Goldsboro, they called it hoeing, and Judy was an expert. The concept of hoeing didn't bother Onika as much as the fact that her newly christened sister was suggesting it to her.

"Are you a sugar baby?" Onika asked.

"What? No!" Chelsea scoffed. "But I don't have any bills."

"So are you saying that I should be one? I don't understand why we're having this conversation."

"You don't have to get offended. We've gone out a few times, and you've worn those same heels and that same skirt. They're cute, and you've switched up the top, but people will start to notice. I just want you to have money for fun. You're too beautiful to not have what you want. Especially when there are men who are dumb enough to give it to you."

Except that the men wouldn't be giving her anything. She'd be trading her body and her soul for a pair of shoes or a handbag. She wouldn't be low and in the gutter like Judy. She didn't come all the way to Atlanta to do something she could've done from a motel room in Goldsboro.

"When I'm in love with a rich man, he can buy me whatever he wants. He can take me on vacations and shopping sprees if he wants. And I'll do what a fiancée or wife does. I'll sex him until his eyes cross. Until then, it's under lock and key."

"Lock and key? Are you serious?"

"I am serious."

"Well, then, you're going to have to get a job. You can't keep wearing the same thing over and over again. Let me ask my mother if she can get you something in the office of the trustees. Then no one will have to see you in a McDonald's uniform."

Onika finished putting on her makeup, although now she was self-conscious about going out at all. Maybe Chelsea only noticed that she repeated clothes because they shared a room. Maybe no one else would know or care.

"I apologize for suggesting that you become a sugar baby,"

Chelsea said. "Please forgive me. I just want you to have nice things."

Onika didn't just want nice shoes and clothes. She wanted money in the bank. She wanted not to worry. She wanted a future.

"I'm going to find a job that pays and doesn't require me to let strange men touch me. Don't worry, I won't embarrass you with my repeat clothes. I'll stay in tonight."

"You don't embarrass me," Chelsea said in the most unconvincing of tones.

Onika knew she was correct. Chelsea had brought her around the other elite girls on campus. She'd vouched for Onika and hadn't told her secret, as far as Onika knew. But if the girls started to notice Onika's apparent lack of possessions, they'd blame Chelsea for bringing her around to taint their circle.

When they were finished getting ready, Onika followed Chelsea out to the front of their dormitory, where the rest of their pretty girl clique waited for them. Ari, with her chestnut brown weave that cascaded down her back in waves. Jennifer, with her somewhat grungy look—long locs and all black. Jennifer reminded Onika of a porcelain kitten. Tiny nose and mouth, large. expressive hazel eyes, and pale, smooth skin.

Onika slightly despised them all, with their high-end perfume and their designer clothes. All of them looked like money, even Jennifer's grunge looked better than Onika's repeat attire. It was obvious that Onika was just a cheaper version of these girls. A knockoff.

"We called a cab already," Ari said.

"Already?" Chelsea asked. "What would you have done if it had gotten here before we did?"

"We would've left you, of course," Jennifer said. "You know we don't operate on colored people time. A lady is always punctual."

All four girls giggled at Jennifer's etiquette lesson. The sisters of Epsilon Phi Beta believed in following spoken and unspoken etiquette rules down to the letter. When Onika had expressed her desire to be invited to that sorority, Jennifer had started giving her lessons.

So far, she had learned that she must be punctual, she must never buy a drink for a man, and that she must always wear a girdle under her dress (a lady's behind never jiggled—that was for whores). It seemed she had a bigger learning curve than most, because her life had been the opposite of every one of these rules so far. Judy didn't care about anyone's time clock; she bought drinks and drugs for her men if she was the one with the money, and if her behind didn't jiggle, *that* was a problem.

Instead of a nightclub, the girls were dropped off at a house in Buckhead. There was no security at the door checking identification. Clearly, if you knew about the party and where to find it, you must've been invited. Even in the entry doorway, the faint scent of marijuana made its way to Onika's nose.

"Whose party is this?" Onika whispered to Chelsea.

She grinned. "Kappa Phi Lambda. My older brother Jaime just crossed last year."

Now Onika understood. Kappa Phi Lambda was the brother fraternity to Epsilon Phi Beta. These were going to be her brothers.

"Why didn't you tell me this was where we were going? I would've gotten a new outfit for this," Onika fussed.

"They're so drunk, they won't remember what you had on or that you were even here. Let's just party."

With that, Chelsea squealed and followed Ari and Jennifer into the huge living room, where everyone who wanted to dance was bumping and grinding to the sounds of the DJ playing in the corner of the room. Onika hung back on the fringes, not wanting to dance in those close quarters, not wanting other people's sweat and bodily fluids touching her body.

She went for the punch bowl, because just looking at the dancers had made her thirsty. She took a red cup from the table and sniffed. It smelled strong. She took one sip and nearly gagged. It tasted like poison. The only thing about this concoction that reminded her of punch was the color.

A cute, ebony-skinned boy cornered Onika by the punch bowl. "You don't like the punch?" he asked.

"This isn't punch. This is straight alcohol with red food coloring."

He laughed. "You want something sweet, I can get you a can of soda."

"Yes, that would be nice."

"You have to say please."

He was beyond cute. He was sexy. Onika liked him already.

"What's your name?" she asked.

"Jaime."

"Jaime, would you please . . . pretty please . . . find me a can of soda. I am feeling a little parched."

He took her hand and pulled her into the kitchen. "Come on. What's your name?"

"Nikki."

"You're a freshman?"

She nodded. "You on the lookout for freshmen?"

"No," he said with a laugh, "but I would've remembered seeing you before. Who did you come with?"

"My roommate, Chelsea, and two other girls."

"Oh, you're my sister's friend, Nikki. Where is she? Why were you alone by the punch bowl?"

"I didn't feel like dancing. They're dancing in the living room."

"Okay."

In the kitchen, he reached into the cooler and handed her a can of Coke. "That should taste a little bit better than the punch."

Onika took the soda from his hands and cracked it open. She liked the kitchen more than the living room. It was a big kitchen, and it was quieter in there. There were only a few people milling around, and it wasn't wall-to-wall bodies.

"I think I'll stay in here," Onika said.

Jaime laughed. "The party is out there."

"This party is doing too much. I'm good right here."

"I feel you. It is pretty wild."

Onika sipped her soda, while Jaime stood staring at her. His gaze lingered on her breasts and then her hips. He licked his lips hungrily, looking just like a predator. But Onika wasn't afraid. She stood a little taller, slightly thrust her chest out, and spread her stance. It was an invitation of sorts. She wondered if he'd bite.

"You want to go upstairs?" he asked lustily.

"What's going to happen if we go upstairs?"

"Nothing you don't want to happen. No means no."

"We just met, so all I want to happen is talking," Onika said.

He shrugged. "Okay then. We can talk."

They went upstairs without going back through the dancing and noise. Slid right up the stairs and into what Onika assumed was the master bedroom.

"They don't have a den or a library or something?" Onika asked as she sat on top of the dresser. She wasn't going anywhere near the bed. "We're wasting this space. Someone else might need it."

Jaime laughed. "The other rooms are already occupied."

"So the rest of the guys who snuck freshmen upstairs tried to trick them, huh? Told them nothing was going down, so they're in the library and the office, pretending not to be trying to get the panties."

"You think that's what I'm doing?"

Jaime sat down on the edge of the huge bed. Onika shook her head. She wasn't going to join him unless she felt like it, and he hadn't convinced her yet.

"Of course it is. You want to get some, just like every other guy who sneaks a girl into a secluded area. That's all any of you want, really."

"Maybe I just want to get to know you."

"What do you want to know?"

"What's your major?"

"Education. Although I'm thinking of going into political science and law."

Jaime nodded. "I'm not going to be an educator. That's what my father wants. Our family is full of rich college professors."

"How'd they get rich to begin with?"

"Land purchases and inheritances. My great, great, great-grandfather was a white man. He gave his biracial son a huge sum of money to disappear and make his own way in the world."

"Did he own slaves?"

"Probably."

"The ancestors probably cry when they look down at y'all."

Jaime laughed. "Yep, they may, but I'm going to be a doctor. I'm going to create my own wealth."

"That's nice. You must be brilliant."

He beamed a smile at Onika. "That's what my professors tell me."

Onika pondered how far she should let this go. He was fine, no doubt, but he was Chelsea's brother, so it could get complex. Plus, he was an upperclassman, so he probably already had some girl on campus that considered herself his girlfriend.

"Where's your girlfriend?" Onika asked. "I know you have one."

"I don't. I did, but she and I broke up."

He sounded like he was being truthful. "Why? Because you were out here chasing freshman girls?"

"Because I'm a young man in college, and there is temptation all around. I don't know if I'm ready to be married yet. I still want to see what's out there."

"So . . . like I said . . . you were chasing girls."

"I don't have to chase."

"They come to you."

He nodded. "Yep. Very few are like you. You're different."

"I would never chase a man. There are too many of you to choose from. Why would I knock myself out over one?"

"You sound like a guy."

"You don't like how that sounds, do you? We girls have to hear this stuff all the time, but we just have to take it."

"I don't mind hearing it from you. Like I said, you're different."

"I'm not so different than the rest of the girls. Not even different from the ones who are behind the closed doors of these upstairs rooms. I'm just about the same."

Jaime stood from the bed and approached. Fully aware of her surroundings and unimpaired by alcohol, Onika let him advance.

"Can I hold your hand?" Jaime asked.

Onika looked at him, knowing exactly where he was headed. "Yes."

Jaime took her hand and squeezed it. Onika examined her own reaction and waited for something glorious to happen, because the boy was holding her hand. When nothing happened, she relaxed.

Jaime seemed confused. Maybe girls started to tremble and shake when he'd held their hands before. Onika was waiting for something to feel out of the norm.

"Can I kiss you?"

Onika paused for a moment before responding. She knew some boys started to get confused at the start of kissing, and she could smell the alcohol on Jaime's breath. She wasn't impaired, but he probably was.

"Yes. One kiss."

She wouldn't tell him it was her first kiss. That wasn't any of his business. If he knew, he'd probably try too hard to make it special, and then it would be awful.

Jaime pressed his lips on Onika's, and she waited for an explosion of butterflies, fairies, sparkles, and magic. Nothing exploded. His mouth tasted like the poison from the punch bowl, even though he'd tried to cover it with some sort of mint.

Jaime stepped away from her and stared like he wanted to admire his work. But she wasn't moved. She took another sip of her soda.

"Did you like that?" he asked.

Somehow, even though Onika had never been in this place before, she knew that if a man had to ask if the woman liked it, then he probably didn't want to know the answer.

"It was fine," Onika replied.

Jaime stepped in again without asking. His manners evaporated, and he stole a second kiss. This one was worse than the first. This one was angry.

Onika pushed him away this time. "I'm good."

"What you mean, you're good? Why you come up here if you was gonna act like that?"

"I'm not acting like anything. I do what I want, but now I'm good. I don't want anything else."

Lack of manners was replaced by sheer anger. He grabbed her wrists and slammed them down on the dresser, knocking the can of Coke on the floor.

"Get off of me," Onika said. "I'm ready to go."

"Not until you give me something."

He took both her small hands in one of his and used his other hand to reach under her skirt, trying to pull her panties to the side.

Swiftly, she pulled up her knee and shoved him across the room with her foot. She had not escaped being molested by her mother's johns in Goldsboro for this. She'd faced more formidable opponents.

As he tumbled drunkenly first onto the bed and then to the floor next to the bed, Onika leapt from the dresser. Her stance was a fighter's stance. She was ready to beat the rapist out of Jaime if he stepped up to her again.

He pulled himself to his feet, looked at her, and then shook his head. "You're crazy."

"Maybe I am."

He held his hand to his face and sniffed his fingers. She wanted to gag at his vulgarity.

"Next time," he said.

"Never," she spat.

She waited for him to leave the room, and she knew there would be an aftermath. She might end up being a pariah on campus, because she decided not to give one of the Kappa Phi Lambda brothers a taste.

She did not want to be an outcast here. She'd been an outcast before. This was not her plan as a Robinette. She wanted a different life.

"I'm sorry," she said, as Jaime still lingered in the room. "I'm just not feeling this. Did I hurt you?"

He laughed. "Nah. You didn't hurt me. But you're gonna get hurt playing games like you just did."

Onika ground her teeth and balled her hands into fists, digging her fingernails into her palms. This was worse than Jaime's rape attempt, but she held it together.

"You're right."

Onika had to force the words through clenched teeth. She wasn't sorry. He wasn't right. He was a predator; she was prey, but not easy prey.

"I'm gonna let it slide this time. I'll let this be between us. You probably wanna be a soror next year. If I say something, you'll never cross Epsilon Phi Beta."

"Thank you."

She wasn't grateful.

"You're welcome. Just . . . when you're ready, let a brotha know. I saw you first."

Onika's upper lip trembled from keeping her words in check. She walked to the door, unlocked it, and let herself out. Left him standing there.

She went downstairs to find her friends. She found them near the punch bowl, all with cups of the poison in their hands.

"Where have *you* been?" Chelsea asked, her words slurring as she spoke.

"Exploring the house. It's huge. I met your brother."

Ari and Jennifer exchanged glances. Onika knew what they assumed. She didn't care. She couldn't even let herself say anything, because she was still too angry about Jaime. She was close to snapping on someone, and she didn't want it to be her potential sorority sisters.

"Oh, yeah, Jaime said he would be here. I haven't run into him yet, though," Chelsea said. "This party is popping, isn't it?"

Onika nodded, although she was ready to leave. "Yeah, it's popping."

Onika swiftly stepped to the side as Chelsea vomited all over herself and on Ari and Jennifer's feet. Onika had seen it coming. The chest heave and the look of discomfort. She'd seen her mother do that same thing countless times.

"Get her to the bathroom so we can clean her off. No cab driver is going to take us with her smelling like this."

"Go find her brother," Ari said.

Onika did better than finding the rapist. She went into the bathroom and called the emergency number they'd given them on campus the very first day. The one for if they were caught out somewhere in trouble. No questions asked, they'd be delivered back to campus.

While she was in the bathroom, she wet paper towels and found disinfecting wipes for Chelsea and her friends. Onika came back to where she'd left them, and of course, the area was cleared. No one wanted to be near the vomiting girl.

Onika shoved the paper towels and wipes at them. "Hurry. Our ride will be here in ten minutes."

"What ride?"

"Our ride back to campus."

"You called the emergency number?" Ari asked.

"Yes, I did."

"You're so stupid. They will tell the dean about this," Jennifer said. "Ari, we are not riding back with them."

Chelsea started to cry. "I don't feel good."

Onika helped her to her feet and held her up as she half-walked, half-fell out of the party. One of the Epsilon Phi Beta sisters (she was wearing a sorority T-shirt) held the door open for them.

"You are your sister's keeper," she said to Onika.

Onika nodded. She understood that to be a welcome addition to their circle. She was planning to pledge Epsilon Phi Beta anyway, but this was encouraging. It salvaged the night for her from the ugliness that had happened with Jaime.

Onika helped Chelsea to the curb, and as they stood there waiting for the ride, Onika worried about what Ari and Jennifer had said. She couldn't get kicked out of Robinson or lose her scholarship and wind up back in Goldsboro because Chelsea had decided to drink.

"Don't worry about what they said," Chelsea said as if she were reading Onika's mind. "My father is a trustee. We'll be fine."

Onika stepped out of the way and sighed as Chelsea vomited again. It was going to be a long night.

CHAPTER FIVE

Lunch with Chelsea and Mrs. Richard was not how Onika wanted to spend her Saturday. The month of classes had been overwhelming, and the weekend was going to be a break. A time for Onika to breathe.

But Chelsea had insisted, promising that her mother would help Onika get a job in Robinson University's trustees' office. It was a coveted position, typically saved for upperclassmen honor students. So, as much as Onika wanted to rest, she'd accepted the invitation.

The small French café was bright and informal. Onika was glad about that, because she didn't have anything to wear to a formal lunch or tea or whatever it was that rich women did when they got together.

"Chelsea tells me that you're here at Robinson on a scholarship and you'd like to make a little extra money," Mrs. Richard asked after taking one sip of her tea.

She was an elegant and classy woman, not that Onika had expected anything different. Onika wouldn't say that she was necessarily pretty, but she was indeed flawless. Her hair, makeup, attire—all perfection.

Onika let out a nervous chuckle. "Let's just cut to the chase, why don't we?"

"Absolutely. No need for small talk and chatter when we came here to get some business done."

"My mom is always like this," Chelsea said. "It doesn't have anything to do with you needing a job."

Mrs. Richard took another sip of her tea and peered at Onika over the rim of the cup as she swallowed. Onika felt like she was being assessed. She hoped that she wasn't found wanting.

"I also attended Robinson University on scholarship," Mrs. Richard said. "My family is from Alabama. Not dirt-poor, but close enough. So I understand the need for extra finances. You don't have to have your guard up around me, dear."

"Thank you so much for helping me. I think it was a blessing that I got Chelsea as a roommate. She's been good to me from the very first day."

"It's all about sisterhood," Chelsea said. "My mother taught me well."

"Very true. My husband will hire you, but you're going to have to do the rest. You'll have to work hard, and remember to network. Every donor that comes through that office is a potential husband, father-in-law, or mother-in-law. Look stunning always."

"That won't be hard for her," Chelsea said. "Look at her."

"You are beautiful, sweetie. You'll have it a lot easier than I did when it comes to landing a husband. I had to put in effort to snag Dr. Richard. There were quite a few competitors. I wasn't the prettiest, but I was the smartest, and I was victorious."

"You make it sound like a war," Onika said.

"It is. Think about it. Do you want to go back to where you came from? Didn't you come here to start a different life?"

"I did."

This was accurate. Onika had come to Atlanta to be born again.

"Well, then, you can't be seen stumbling around drunk at fraternity parties," Mrs. Richard said.

Onika didn't reply. She wouldn't throw Chelsea under the bus, and she didn't expect the girl to tell the truth.

"I know it was Chelsea," Mrs. Richard said. "I've already spoken to her about this. But the truth is, you are not her. She can get away with it, because she is Dr. Richard's daughter."

"I understand."

"No, I don't think that you do. Anything and everything you do will be watched and scrutinized, because there are people who don't want women like us to attend college with their precious socialites. I cannot tell you the torture I endured at Robinson at the hands of some of these women."

"Will you be my mentor? I need someone to protect me."

Mrs. Richard took Onika's hand and squeezed it tightly. "I will mentor you, but I don't know how much I can offer in the way of protection. I will say this. Next time my daughter's silly ass gets drunk at a party, you leave her right there on the floor. Call me when you get back to campus."

Chelsea looked at the ground, but not before Onika could see the tears on her face. All Onika could think about was how she wished she had a mother like Mrs. Richard who cared about how she turned out. Judy wouldn't care at all about her getting drunk at a party. She'd tell the story to her friends like it was funny.

"Thank you, Mrs. Richard."

"You're welcome, darling. We're going to make Robinettes out of you both."

Onika wanted to hug her, but Chelsea looked up at her with a look of disdain. Onika knew how angry Chelsea must be, but she wanted to take her to meet Judy. If Chelsea met Judy, she'd accept every bit of criticism from her mother with kisses and hugs. To Onika, a mother like Mrs. Richard was priceless, and now she was going to start a new job because of her help.

Onika would make Mrs. Richard proud, too, just like she'd made Ms. Carpenter proud.

CHAPTER SIX

The trustees' office was enormous, but it still managed to feel intimate. Onika took deep breaths to calm her nerves as she waited for Dr. Ben Richard to interview her for an office assistant position. The opportunity hadn't been advertised on the campus jobs board. It was only for those who were referred by someone in a high place. Thanks to Chelsea and Mrs. Richard, Onika's name had found its way to Dr. Richard's desk.

Mrs. Richard had promised that she'd be hired, but sometimes men didn't always do the bidding of their wives. Onika wouldn't allow herself to believe she was hired until she heard the words come from his mouth.

Mrs. Richard did not leave anything to chance, though. She provided Onika with an interview suit as a gift. Pantyhose, shoes, and makeup, too. Chelsea hadn't lied when she said her mother would make a doll out of her. She had done exactly that.

Onika stood inside the office, unsure if she should sit. The receptionist had merely opened the door and told her to wait. Wait meant wait, but not necessarily sit, so Onika chose to stand rather than make a mistake that might cost her the job.

Dr. Richard emerged from a door on the opposite side of the office. He was wearing a fitted golf shirt and shorts, and what looked like a fresh bronze tan. The black hair on his head and face was peppered with silver strands, but even still, he was incredibly handsome. He could've been a runway model, but here he was, a trustee at a university.

"I apologize for my appearance, Nikki. I had a meeting with a senator on the golf course. We got to talking politics and it went overtime. I didn't want to keep you waiting much longer."

"Are you interested in politics, sir? Are you going to run for public office?" Onika asked.

Dr. Richard grinned as he walked toward Nikki. He shook her hand firmly, and she matched his grip, wanting to convey confidence. She desperately needed the job, but she didn't want him to feel her desperation in the handshake.

"If I did, would you work on my campaign?" Dr. Richard asked.

"I would, but not as a volunteer. As a paid staff member."

Dr. Richard's loud laughter filled the room, the acoustics from the high ceilings giving the sound more volume. He held his sides as the laughter poured out of him. Onika was happy that she'd amused him but wondered if she'd said too much. She was just being truthful. She needed a paycheck.

"I would make sure you got paid, young lady. I understand exactly where you're coming from."

Dr. Richard motioned for her to sit, and he sat on the edge of his desk, still looking quite amused.

"My wife and daughter can't find enough good things to say about you. Honors student, well mannered, and polished. So I should probably get to hiring you, shouldn't I?"

"You should, sir."

"The job entails some filing of paperwork, checking and responding to e-mails from the general mailbox, answering phones, and making appointments. Do you think you can handle that?"

"Absolutely."

"The job pays fifteen dollars an hour, and you'll work about forty hours a week."

Onika's jaw dropped. She hadn't expected fifteen dollars an hour. She'd expected minimum wage and maybe twenty hours a week. With this amount of money, she'd be able to save for a car, and for plane tickets instead of bus tickets. She might even get to go on the spring break trips everyone talked about. With fifteen dollars an hour, she could have a life.

"We'll work around your class schedule. Do you have any early-morning classes?"

"Only on Tuesdays. I have an eight o'clock class."

Dr. Richard nodded. "All right, then, you'll come every morning at seven, except Tuesdays, when you'll come when your class lets out. You'll work until it's time for class, and then you'll be off every day by four or four-thirty, leaving you plenty of time for your studies."

All of a sudden, Onika felt as if she had a knot in her throat the size of a grapefruit. No one had ever shown her so much kindness. Chelsea and Mrs. Richard, and now Dr. Richard. She didn't know how she could repay them for being so good.

"Thank you, Dr. Richard."

"You're welcome, Onika."

It startled Onika to hear Dr. Richard call her by her true name. Even though she hadn't told Chelsea her real name, it was in her school records and on her application. Dr. Richard must've read her file before their meeting.

"I know you told my daughter that you're an orphan, although your mother is alive and well in North Carolina. Isn't that right?"

Onika's heart raced. Was he going to take away all that he promised, just like that?

"It's true, sir, that my mother is alive. I wouldn't say well."

"I understand. I have family members who decided to use drugs to the detriment of their children and spouses and everyone around them. I don't blame you for walking away from all that."

Onika relaxed and exhaled.

"She didn't want me to come here and go to school, but I couldn't turn down the scholarship. I had to see what I could accomplish. I am grateful for this job, sir. I will work extremely hard."

"I know you will. And don't worry. I won't tell my wife and daughter about your mother. That can stay between us."

"Thank you, Dr. Richard."

"You do know why I'm giving you this opportunity, right? Why the pay is so good?"

Onika shook her head. She really had no idea why he was being so kind to her.

"Because there are too many brilliant young women without means who end up stripping or selling their bodies to make extra money. It's easy to do. We have girls here on campus who work at strip clubs. My daughter has taken a liking to you, and I don't want her to be friends with someone who slides down a pole at night."

Onika wanted to tell Dr. Richard that she'd never had any intention of sliding down a pole to make money. And that his daughter was the one who suggested becoming a play toy for an older man.

"Thank you for providing me with a reputable way to earn money," Onika said, not wanting to disagree with him. Let him feel like he was saving her from whoredom. Onika didn't care, as long as the job was still hers.

"Can you start tomorrow morning?"

"Yes."

"Good. You can wear something like what you have on today. Skirts, or dresses, heels and pantyhose while you're in the office. We have donors and potential donors in our offices on a daily basis."

"All right."

Onika hoped Dr. Richard didn't see the worry on her face. This was her only professional work outfit. She had a few blouses that she could match with the skirt, but there was very little variety. It seemed like the majority of her first check would end up being spent on new clothes.

Dr. Richard shook his head. "What am I thinking? Of course, you don't have a closet full of clothes."

He reached into his wallet and pulled out two hundred-dollar bills. When Onika just stared at the money in shock, he put it in her hand.

"I-I can't take your money," Onika said.

Dr. Richard laughed and closed Onika's fingers around the bills.

"Yes, you can. I won a bet today, so you're not taking any money out of my household. I do need you dressed nicely. That's not optional. So go get a few blouses, skirts, and a couple pairs of shoes. And don't forget the pantyhose."

It felt a little bit strange being instructed how to dress by a man, but Onika trusted him, and she didn't exactly know what to wear.

She got to her feet and shook Dr. Richard's outstretched hand. "Thanks again, sir," she said. "I will go directly to the store to prepare for this week."

"You're welcome, Onika. I look forward to this being a long working relationship. If it works out, you can do this all four years you're at Robinson."

Onika wanted to hug Dr. Richard, but she knew that wouldn't be appropriate, so she shook his hand again. When he pulled her into a chaste embrace and then patted her affectionately on the head, she knew she was in good. She wondered how such a kind man could be the father of a rapist. She'd have to keep her eye on Dr. Richard. That apple fell from somewhere, and she didn't want to find out too late that father and son were just alike.

CHAPTER SEVEN

Onika was running late for work at the trustees' office. She'd overslept. She cursed her cell phone alarm, because the last thing she wanted was for Dr. Richard to think she was taking advantage of his kindness. She'd worked for him her entire freshman year and definitely wanted to come back in the fall.

When she got to the office, the campus police were there, and immediately Onika panicked. Had something happened to her mother or grandmother? Would she have to leave and go to Goldsboro?

"Is everything all right?" she asked as she approached Dr. Richard's desk.

"These officers just want to ask you a few questions. I'm sure there's a perfectly good explanation for this."

"For what?"

"Come have a seat, Nikki. Relax."

It was hard for Onika to relax with her boss standing in front of her and being flanked on either side by police officers. She tried anyway, though. She sat down and eased back in the chair, although her heart felt like it was beating in her throat and temples.

"We got a report this morning," Officer Davis said (his name was on his badge). "And we just want to ask you about it."

Onika's mind raced. Did this have something to do with Jaime? Had he tried to flip the script and make it seem like she was the guilty one? If he had, Onika was going to destroy him. She had protected him and his reputation.

"All right . . ."

"A woman claiming to be your mother said that you stole her Social Security check. She said it was directly deposited to a debit card and that you stole the number."

Onika sat speechless. Why would Judy do this to her?

"I haven't stolen anything from anyone. Are you sure it was my mother?"

"She said her name is Judy Lewis, and she had all of the correct information about you. Your birthday, Social Security number, and all of your relevant contact details," Officer Davis said. His partner was silent but scribbled furiously in his notebook.

"Well, I haven't been home since school started. I don't know how to prove I didn't take her check."

"She claims purchases were made at a jewelry store and Victoria's Secret."

"I haven't made any such purchases."

"Mmm-hmm," Officer Davis said. "Well, if you don't mind, we're going to check your dorm just so we can say we followed up."

"I absolutely do mind!" Onika said. "You are not about to humiliate me in front of my roommate and sisters on the word of a crackhead. You need some proof and a warrant before you can search my dormitory."

"We can search a dormitory if we have reason to believe a crime has taken place," Officer Davis said in response.

"Please, Dr. Richard, don't let them do this," Onika pleaded.

"Calm down, Nikki," Dr. Richard said. "Listen, how much money did the woman say was missing?"

Officer Davis's partner flipped a few pages on his notebook and looked up at Dr. Richard. "Six hundred forty-two dollars was the amount."

"I'll write a check for that amount, and we can consider the matter closed."

"She's lying, Dr. Richard. Don't give her any of your money.

She's just going to use it to buy more crack," Onika said. She was beyond annoyed that Judy could call her college and get anyone to listen to her ridiculous stories.

"Inform her that if she calls the school with any more false reports on her daughter, we will file harassment charges and get a restraining order," Dr. Richard continued.

"Okay, Dr. Richard. We'll handle it," Officer Davis said. "Hopefully, we won't have any additional problems from her."

Onika broke down in sobs as soon as the two officers exited the office. She'd hardly been able to hold back the tears, but she didn't want to lose it in front of them. She didn't want Dr. Richard to see her like this either, but there was only so much restraint she could show.

Dr. Richard left his side of the desk and pulled up a chair next to Onika. He encircled her with his arms and let her cry into his chest. He stroked her hair and cooed in her ear. Wiped her tears with a tissue and rocked her until her shoulders stopped shaking.

"I hate her," Onika said. "Why won't she leave me alone? Why would she do that to me?"

"Don't hate her. Be happy that you have the opportunity to escape. She's a pitiful and sick woman, and it's not your fault."

Onika stiffened at hearing Dr. Richard repeat her grandmother's favorite excuse for Judy.

"She's sick because she chooses to keep putting poison in her body. She doesn't want to be well."

"I believe you, but you still don't need to hate her. Pray that she makes some changes, and then you be the best you can be. No matter what, you wouldn't be here without her."

Onika allowed herself to relax in Dr. Richard's arms. He was right about one thing. She wouldn't be alive without her mother's sin. If Judy hadn't been sleeping with a pimp to pay for her drugs, then there would be no Onika. Still, she found it hard to set aside her anger at Judy's antics, and she sure as hell wasn't going to pray for her.

"I don't want to go home and have to look at her all summer. I don't think I'll survive it," Onika said.

"Then don't."

"I have no choice, Dr. Richard. I can't afford to stay here over the summer."

"I am going to speak for my wife and children when I say we would love to have you join us for our summer at Martha's Vineyard."

Onika stared at Dr. Richard in disbelief. Suddenly, his embrace felt too intimate, so Onika backed away.

"Do you really mean it?"

He nodded. "I do."

Onika had never been anywhere other than Goldsboro and Atlanta. She fit in on campus, but she didn't think she'd be able to fool the Martha's Vineyard crowd. They'd see right through her. They'd know right away that she was beneath them, that she should be changing the sheets and vacuuming the floors instead of splashing in the pool with their children.

Yet she was going to go anyway. How could she not go?

CHAPTER EIGHT

A summer at Martha's Vineyard with the Richards was completely unexpected, but it was a welcome surprise. Dr. Richard even bought her a first-class plane ticket, just like she was one of the family. He could've put her on the Greyhound bus for all Onika cared. She was just happy to have somewhere to spend the summer other than with her grandmother.

On the way to the house from the airport, in their chartered car, Jaime made Onika uncomfortable with his stares. She hadn't forgotten the way he'd touched her, and the threat that he'd made if she ever told. He didn't have to worry about her telling. Onika knew better than to ruin her chance to experience their rich and fabulous life.

"Nikki, congratulations on making the dean's list this year," Dr. Richard said. "Maybe your scholastic prowess will influence Chelsea."

"Thank you, Dr. Richard. I work really hard on my studies."

"Call me Ben while we're on vacation," he said. "We are happy to have you at Robinson. I enjoy young people who value their education."

"Daddy, Nikki has to keep her grades up. She is on scholarship," Chelsea said.

"So are you. A parentally funded scholarship," Ben said.

"And as your benefactor, I'm requesting that you work a bit harder at your studies."

"Yes, Daddy. I will. I got a bit sidetracked this year."

Jaime laughed and shook his head. "You got more than sidetracked. You fell off the rails. If you hadn't passed your finals, you'd be on academic probation. Not a good look, little sister."

Chelsea scowled at Jaime. Onika hated to be the vehicle for the shaming of her Robinson sister. Especially by Jaime. If she had told about his behavior, he'd be on more than academic probation. He'd probably be expelled.

"Everyone has to make sure they stay on task," Onika said. "There are more ways to mess up than by failing classes."

Dr. Richard nodded. "That is the truth. I can't tell you how many scholars I know who have ruined their lives chasing a woman or hitting the booze too hard."

Onika glanced at Jaime and lifted an eyebrow. He scowled but was quiet. He didn't want her to go there, and she wouldn't unless he made her.

"So these two are probably pledging Epsilon Phi Beta next year," Jaime said. "I suppose I'll have to treat them nice, because they'll be my sorority sisters."

"You should be treating them kindly anyway, because they're black women. We should uplift one another," Dr. Richard said.

Mrs. Richard nodded. "I'm always torn about the value of our Greek organizations when I hear things like this come out of the mouths of our sons and daughters. They are not supposed to be about separatism and elitism. The focus is on service, scholarship, and making a difference."

Dr. Richard burst into laughter. "But you and all of your sorority sisters are one elite bunch. You'll be meeting for tea and cucumber sandwiches while we're on the Vineyard. You can't get any more elite than that."

"Girls, just remember, when you pledge, that the true spirit of Epsilon Phi Beta has nothing to do with tea parties. It's about the work that we do in our communities. How we reach back and pull other women up."

Mrs. Richard had looked at Onika when she said "reach

back." It didn't bother Onika that she was Mrs. Richard's charity project case. She didn't mind one bit. It was no worse than receiving hand-me-downs her whole life. She wasn't offended by it in the least.

"We vacation with a group of friends," Chelsea said. "The mothers of these families are all my mom's sorority sisters from Robinson. Some of the fathers are Kappa Phi Lambda, like dad. We've grown up with their kids. They almost feel like cousins."

"Kissing cousins," Jaime said.

He was so disgusting. Onika wanted to punch him in the throat every time he opened his mouth.

"Well, he's not lying," Dr. Richard said. "The young people pair off quite a bit, and even get married to each other sometimes."

"There are a few outliers, though," Mrs. Richard said.

"True. But this is a good group of people to meet, Onika," Dr. Richard said. "Many connections to be made if you network."

"Many husbands to be found if you flirt," Chelsea said.

Mrs. Richard laughed. "That is true as well. You will meet some of the best of the best here. Consider this your coming-out party."

"We need to have a cotillion just for Onika. Did you all do that in Durham?" Chelsea asked.

Onika was sure that someone in Goldsboro had tried to have a cotillion. They'd probably spelled it wrong and called it a *cuhtillion* or something crazy like that. And it was probably at the church, with all the girls wearing first Sunday white dresses and church usher gloves. Even if they had done it, they hadn't invited Onika. Here she was going to Martha's Vineyard, where presidents went for the summer, and at home she wasn't fit for any of their fake society customs.

Onika wished her grandmother could see her now and try to tell her that she was nothing. Earlene would have to shut her mouth. She'd probably marvel and call it the work of God.

CHAPTER NINE

Onika first saw him at the villas' community pool. He was all muscles and caramel, sun-kissed and god-kissed to perfection. He was already staring her way when she noticed him. She was so glad she'd chosen the white string bikini. It left nothing to the imagination but could probably stir a fantasy or two. The low-rise bottoms clung to every inch of her hips and behind, except the stubborn round tops of her buttocks, which wanted to play peekaboo.

As she neared him, she calculated that he was at least ten years older than she was. Maybe more. But she felt drawn to him, nonetheless.

Then he smiled at her and walked toward her. He took his time, didn't rush. Onika's feet stopped moving. She stood still. Waited for him to approach her.

"I'm Aaron," he said. "You're with Ben's family, correct? I thought maybe they had one-upped everyone this year and brought staff, but you're clearly not the help."

Onika's fantasy came crashing down in her mind. This guy was a jerk.

"Nah. Not the help. A friend."

Onika walked past him to the lavish pool chairs surrounding

the pristine blue water. It was an infinity pool with a view of the ocean. Onika intended to enjoy it.

Aaron followed her. She knew he would when he got a glimpse of her hips and behind, but she wasn't interested anymore. She was easy to turn on, but even easier to turn off.

"Does the friend have a name?"

"Nikki," she said, although she had no intention of conversing with him. She just knew that if she didn't tell him, he would probably never leave.

"Let me guess; you're a Robinette. You look like one. Kinda stuck up like one."

"Not stuck up at all. You decided you didn't want to know me when you said you thought I was a maid or something."

"It wasn't an insult. But then again, I don't think I'm better than the people I pay to clean up after me."

Onika felt insulted and scolded at the same time. He turned to walk away, then came back.

"You look very good in white. Wear a white dress to dinner, and we can share a glass of wine."

This time when he walked away, Onika didn't know what she felt. Intrigue? Maybe.

Onika wore a white dress to dinner.

She got the feeling that she was playing chicken with the devil, but he was too fine to resist. He said nothing to her, but stared her down the entire evening as if they were the only two people in the room. Like no one noticed him noticing her.

After dinner, out by the pool, Chelsea pulled Onika to a quiet corner.

"Are you flirting with Aaron?" she asked.

"Not really. Unless you consider flirting his ogling me like a creep."

"Oh. 'Cause I was gonna say, he's thirty."

"Ewww . . ."

Onika fake giggled with Chelsea. She knew better than to let her friend know what was going on with her and Aaron. It wasn't her business, but more importantly, it wasn't Chelsea's parents' business.

"Well, be careful," Chelsea said. "He's rich and he likes young girls."

"He wants a sugar baby, then?"

Chelsea swallowed hard. "I guess so. Yes."

"But that's not who you meant when you suggested that to me."

"Oh no! I meant someone really old, who wouldn't want to have sex with you."

"Where's the fun in that?"

Chelsea stared at Onika in disbelief. That look let Onika know that Chelsea could never be privy to her secrets. There was judgment in her gaze, and Onika had already struggled enough in life. She wasn't going to allow someone to judge her for her choices. Onika let her feel uncomfortable for half a second, and then she burst into laughter.

"I am messing with you, girl."

"Oh. You scared me. I thought you were actually considering it."

"I wish you could've seen your face. Honestly, though, there are a lot of women married to a man ten years their senior. Don't rule him out. He might be your husband."

"No thank you."

Onika bet Mrs. Richard had a different opinion on the matter even if she didn't tell her daughter about it. Mrs. Richard was a woman who'd improved her station in life by marrying a rich man.

If Onika was bold enough and savvy enough, she just might've asked Mrs. Richard for some tips on how to catch a rich man.

CHAPTER TEN

As it turned out, Onika didn't need anyone's tips or help in landing Aaron. He was all in from the first moment, and Onika was ready to be plucked like a ripe peach. Everything about their courtship was more exciting because it was secret, yet in plain sight.

Their first date was an early-morning bike ride through the State Forest. It rained, but they went anyway. They shared uncontrollable laughter when Aaron fell off his bike and into a tangle of muddy bushes. Soaked through from their adventure, they snuck back into their respective villas with no one even noticing they'd been gone.

At the huge community dinners that happened twice a week, Onika and Aaron exchanged intimate glances while having conversations with other people. It was a game they played. How many times could he look at her while talking to another person, without the other person noticing?

They were ill-equipped to play this little game, however, because their secret was discovered almost immediately.

At lunch, on their third week of vacation, Mrs. Richard cornered Onika in her and Chelsea's bedroom. She marched into the room and slammed the door.

"What are you doing, Nikki?" Mrs. Richard asked

Onika wondered if she knew about Aaron, if they'd been that obvious. Onika was absolutely in high spirits since their courtship had started. Waking early, disappearing all day, and going to bed late.

"I don't know what you mean, Mrs. Richard."

Onika backed away as Mrs. Richard advanced with her index finger pointed in Onika's face.

"If you're trying to seduce Aaron, you're making a mistake."

"I am not trying to seduce anyone, Mrs. Richard."

She laughed. "Oh, I guess you suppose that you're seeing a new boy and then what? You go together?"

"I'm not sure that . . ."

"Don't stand here and lie to my face, Nikki. I see the two of you exchanging glances and sneaking off at the same time. You're playing a dangerous game, girl. He's a grown man, and you are not ready."

"Not ready for what?" Onika asked. Maybe Mrs. Richard had forgotten that she was grown, too. She wasn't afraid of anything concerning Aaron.

"You're not ready for what comes with a man like Aaron. He is not like the boys on campus. He will have demands and needs that will be fulfilled whether you're willing or not."

"You don't know Aaron, Mrs. Richard. He's actually very much like the boys on campus. He's sweet, funny, and awkward."

"Girl, Aaron is neither sweet nor awkward. He's got you fooled, which lets me know even more that you will never survive a relationship with him."

"I'm just following your example. Trying to improve my station by marrying well."

"Oh sweetie, he's not interested in marrying you. You aren't a wife yet. Right now, you are a piece of fresh tail. If you want help in marrying well, I can help you find the right one."

"Thank you, Mrs. Richard. I welcome your help and your guidance."

"The first thing you'll have to do is cease this foolishness with Aaron. Once your reputation is tarnished, there's no getting that back."

Onika valued Mrs. Richard's opinion, more than any woman she'd ever met. She was the only mother figure she had in her life. Much more so than Judy or her grandmother. They barely kept her alive, and Mrs. Richard wanted her to really *live*.

So Onika made a choice in that moment. Several choices actually. She chose to keep seeing Aaron, because he was sexy and rich and she wanted him. She also chose to do a better job keeping the secret, and since she was no stranger to secrets, this would be easy. Aaron would be her secret man, and if he did what Mrs. Richard thought he'd do, no one would know.

"You're right, Mrs. Richard. I was flirting with Aaron, but he's way too old for me. Thank you for being there for me and not letting me make a bad decision."

"Trust me, darling, I will have you married off at the proper time. To the proper man."

Until the proper time came, Onika would settle for Aaron.

CHAPTER ELEVEN

Onika waited until midnight and found her way over to Aaron's cottage. She dressed like a ninja, in all black, and moved like one, too. She wasn't seen, and wouldn't be from now on. No stolen glances in plain sight. That part of this was over. When she was ready to go public, it would be because Aaron was claiming her before the world.

As it turned out, Aaron was more than happy to keep Onika's secret. He agreed with Mrs. Richard's words about Onika's reputation.

"She's right, you know." Aaron said when Onika shared the conversation. "I am not interested in marriage. Not anytime soon. It'll be years before I go that route."

"It will be years for me, too. I'm just about to start my second year of college. I don't want a husband right now."

"She is wrong about something, though," Aaron said.

"What's that?"

"That you're just a piece of fresh tail to me. You are not like your counterparts, Nikki. Most girls your age are just about a booty call. But you're different. You've got an edge that they don't have. It's sexy as hell, but it also means you'll make a great life partner. Maybe with me, I'm not sure. But I'm open to it."

Onika wondered how he'd feel about that edge if he knew how she'd acquired it. If he knew that she was edgy because her mother smoked crack upon rising, instead of making her a bowl of cereal or pancakes for breakfast. If he knew she wasn't shocked by his raunchy jokes, because her mother was the brunt of every raunchy joke ever written. What if he knew that her father was a pimp who died from an AIDS-related illness? Would she still be edgy or just a gutter rat that he'd pass over?

Onika feared the answers to those questions. No one had ever looked past these things about her. She'd always been judged on Judy's actions. She didn't expect Aaron to be any different from the rest of the world.

So he wouldn't know. Wouldn't get that opportunity. Her family was dead to her, and they were going to stay dead. No introductions to her grandmother would ever happen.

She prayed Dr. Richard kept her secret. No, she wouldn't just pray. Just praying hadn't gotten her mother clean, and it hadn't stopped her from being a whore. Instead of pray, Onika was going to do something that would actually work. She'd wait, watch, and then, at the proper moment, she'd take action.

"So what will we do when we leave here and go back to Atlanta? Will we keep seeing one another?" Onika asked.

"Of course. It'll be so much easier in Atlanta. It's a huge city, and I know it well."

"You've creeped all over, huh?"

Aaron laughed. "Sure I have. I am a man. I've creeped all over with many women."

"Just women?"

Aaron laughed harder. "See, that's what I mean about you. You're extremely bold, and I love it. Not many women your age would ask that question of a guy they like."

"So answer the question, please."

"I am not into men. Not bisexual, gay, or on the down low. I do, however, love women. I can't get enough of the touch, smell, and feel of a woman."

"Do you like how I touch, smell, and feel?"

"I do, but I also love the way you think and communicate.

You are mature beyond your years. They say that, when young women are as mature as you are, they've experienced something tragic, like rape."

"I've never been raped."

This was true. Earlene said it was by the grace of God that none of Judy's men or customers had ever touched her. Some people said it was because her father was a gangster, and even though he was in the grave, folks were afraid of him. No matter the reason, Onika was glad that she didn't have that particular testimony to share.

"But your parents died, so that's tragic enough."

She nodded. "I never really knew my father. He was long gone by the time I would've been old enough to remember him, but everyone who knew him says I'm his twin."

"He was Hispanic? You look Caribbean."

"I am half Puerto Rican."

"Do you speak Spanish?"

"No. There was no one to teach me."

Actually, there was. Judy was fluent in Spanish. She'd learned it from Onika's father, and they used it to speak to one another in code around the crackheads in the neighborhood. It was a random story Onika's grandmother had shared when Onika had found Judy nodding in a corner, speaking Spanish.

All of Onika's memories were fragmented. Her entire life was in bits and pieces. Shards of glass that were impossible to connect or glue back together. There was no history. No coherent narrative of her childhood. This made it easy for Onika to keep secrets. Her past was a mystery even to herself.

"I'm looking forward to knowing you better, Onika. Everything about you is interesting to me."

"I feel the same way about you. We will know each other intimately by the time we're through."

"By the time we're through?" he asked.

"Well, I grew up learning that everyone is temporary. Parents and everyone else. So I don't count on forever."

"People are temporary. That is so very true. I think that is one of the reasons why I reject typical monogamy."

"What do you mean?"

"I mean that I don't make commitments that I have no intention of keeping. I'm honest about it, because I don't want to hurt anyone," he explained.

"So you date multiple women?"

"I have in the past. Right now, I'm only seeing you."

That was good enough for Onika for the time being. She didn't know a guy who wasn't seeing multiple women at a time. The difference between Aaron and those guys was that he told the truth about it. There was something incredibly appealing about a man telling the entire truth.

Onika wished she could tell her truth, and one day she would, but not yet. Not until she was sure someone couldn't whisk this dream away, because she had no intention of waking up.

CHAPTER TWELVE

Onika sat across the table from Aaron in his Atlanta apartment, eating takeout from his favorite seafood restaurant: crab cakes and lemon pepper shrimp with whipped mashed potatoes and asparagus. One day, they'd be able to go out to dinner, but Onika didn't mind sharing these private times with Aaron.

They had continued their secret relationship for almost a year. Had gone nonstop since the summer all the way to the following spring. Her entire sophomore year at Robinson had been given to Aaron. There wasn't a guy in Atlanta who could hold a candle to Aaron. She pretended to entertain their attention, but she never went out with them. She never even let it go past the conversation phase.

Aaron looked like he had something on his mind. Onika felt her stomach do flips, wondering what he could want to say. She knew it couldn't be anything life-altering like marriage, but it seemed important.

"Nikki . . . I love you. I can't believe I am saying this out loud, but I do. I am in love with you."

"I love you too, babe," Onika said.

A declaration of love from Aaron made the night complete. Everything was perfect. Onika would cross over tonight, as an official Epsilon Phi Beta sister. They would be her sisters for life, and she'd always have someone to call when she was in need. But her sisters knew Nikki, not Onika.

No one knew Onika.

Onika was dead and buried, just like her life in Goldsboro, North Carolina. She had been reborn, metamorphosed, had shed her caterpillar body, and put on pink and silver wings.

And Aaron had professed his love. It couldn't get better than this. This was perfection.

"What does it mean for us, now that you're in love and I am in love? Do we think of a future together?"

Onika didn't want to press, but that part was important. The future part. The "'til death do us part" part. The baby carriage and white picket fence part. Or the gated community part.

"I think right now it means a deeper level of knowing one another."

"Oh?"

She was hoping for something more concrete. Maybe a designation of only girlfriend instead of main girlfriend.

"You're looking for a title?"

"Me being in love with you means that I don't want anyone else."

"We're two different people, Nikki. Do you realize how huge this is? Me saying I'm in love with you? I have never told anyone else that."

"But you won't be faithful."

"I disagree. I am being faithful to who I am, and I am being honest with you. If I stop loving you, I will tell you that, too."

"I don't see why you need multiple women."

"You can have multiple men if you want them. I don't put limits on my pleasure. If you want to limit yourself to just me, that is your choice. I don't love you with my penis, Nikki."

"So you don't make love to me. You just sex me?"

"I am saying my sexual urges are completely separate from my heart."

"Are you saying we will never marry?" Onika asked, seeking

to understand Aaron and put herself in a good place with all of this.

"I am not saying that. Marriage has legal and civil benefits. It is not a measure of love."

Mrs. Richard's voice rang in Onika's head. She couldn't tell if Aaron was sincere or had some of the best game ever played. Either way, it didn't matter. Onika's love was unwavering and solid in spite of Aaron's need for more than one woman.

"Nikki, this is me baring my soul to you. I am telling you all this, because I want you in my life, and I want you to have all the facts about me. Don't judge me for it."

How could she judge him for living his truth? She wished she could do the same.

"Aaron. My real name is Onika. Not Nikki."

"Onika is a much more unique name than Nikki. Why don't you use it?"

"I left Onika in North Carolina."

Aaron took both of Onika's hands in his. He kissed them both tenderly.

"I won't judge you. Ever. Remember that, if nothing else."

Onika nodded, but she didn't believe him. No one's love was unconditional. Everyone had a limit. She wasn't willing to test Aaron's limit any further. He could know her name, but he could never know about Judy.

And that meant that Dr. Richard could never tell either. And thanks to his appetite for one of Onika's sorority sisters, Onika knew exactly how to keep him quiet.

CHAPTER THIRTEEN

Onika called a meeting with Dr. Richard, off campus at a coffee shop. He'd honored her request and even congratulated her on taking initiative. Onika knew he assumed she wanted a raise or more responsibility. When he found out the true nature of their meeting, she doubted he'd be so congratulatory.

"Thank you for meeting me here, Dr. Richard," Onika said.

"Of course. I take mentoring seriously. Any time you need to speak with me, just put the meeting on my calendar."

"Thank you, Dr. Richard. You're also mentoring one of my line sisters, Angelica Rogers. She told me just how passionately you take your mission."

Onika stared at Dr. Richard as the words sank in. His caramel-colored face went from pale to crimson. She waited for his response. Wasn't going to say another word until he acknowledged what she knew.

"You want something," he finally said, "or you wouldn't be here meeting with me. What do you want?"

"Nothing too difficult. Mutual silence."

"I don't have anything to bargain with here. I don't have any dirt on you."

"Not dirt, but you are the only one here who knows about my mother. I want to keep it that way."

Sudden recognition appeared on Dr. Richard's face.

"You haven't told Aaron."

Onika frowned. How did Dr. Richard know about her and Aaron? They'd been extremely careful.

"Are you shocked that I know about the two of you?" Dr. Richard asked. "You shouldn't be. Aaron doesn't keep secrets. If you ask him a direct question, he'll give you a direct answer. It is one of the things I truly respect about him."

"You asked him about us?"

"I did, because my wife was concerned. When he told me he was seeing you almost exclusively, I decided not to tell her."

Onika smarted at the words "almost exclusively". She was suddenly regretting this conversation with Dr. Richard.

"I'm not going to tell Aaron about my mother. He wouldn't want me if he knew."

"You're right. As much as I'd like to think he would look beyond your family ties and continue your relationship, he would not."

"I appreciate your silence Dr. Richard."

"And I yours. I will caution you, though. No secret remains a secret forever. What will you do when he finds out?"

"What will you do with Mrs. Richard?"

"She was bought and paid for many years ago. I am not worried about what she might do. I just don't want her hurt."

Onika had no idea what she might do if and when Aaron found out. She didn't want to think about it. Couldn't.

"I am surprised, Onika, that after all I've done for you since you've been here at Robinson, you would come in and threaten me. I expected a little bit more gratitude."

"I am very grateful. I wouldn't even be dating Aaron if it wasn't for your introduction and inviting me on your family's vacation. I appreciate you more than you know."

"But you hang my indiscretion over my head."

"Never. I am not hanging it over your head."

"You could've simply come to me and asked me not to share. I am a private man anyway. I do not share other people's secrets. Look at how I've kept silent about you and Aaron. But, you chose to threaten me."

"I apologize if you took it as a threat. It wasn't meant to be threatening. It was meant to be insurance."

Dr. Richard shook his head. "You look at me as a potential threat."

"Everyone is a potential threat."

"Yes, you're definitely one of my wife's protégées. You need to learn to identify your allies, Onika. I am one of them."

Onika believed him, but she also knew that people changed. Those who were allies one day could become enemies. Having insurance was better.

CHAPTER FOURTEEN

For her graduation present, Aaron gave Onika a diamond bracelet. Her arm trembled as he clasped it on her wrist.

"Aaron, it's beautiful."

"It's to celebrate. The ceremony will be our coming-out party. As soon as you cross the stage, everyone can know."

Onika had gotten so used to keeping their secret that she didn't even know how to take it public. She'd tell her sorority sisters, of course, and Mrs. Richard. She would be angry that Onika had lied, but she'd get over it.

"We can meet each other's families," Aaron said. "My mother has been hounding me. She wants to meet you. And your family . . ."

"I told you, love, I don't have family. At least not family I know. Will your family care that I don't have a pedigree?"

"No one cares about that. They are two generations from poverty. I guess I have a pedigree, but my grandma damn sure didn't, and neither did my mother. You'll be fine."

"That makes me feel better."

"My mother will be happy as soon as you give her a grandchild."

"Which I will do as soon as I become a wife."

Aaron laughed. "You still ascribe to these old-fashioned constructs. Marriage is spiritual. Our souls are intertwined."

Onika remained silent. She already knew his thoughts on the

matter. They had discussed it at length. He didn't believe marriage validated their love. She wanted the title.

"If you found out you were pregnant with my child, right now, what would you do?"

She was about to graduate from college, with a substitute teaching job lined up. That wouldn't be enough to raise a child, and a baby's father never had to stay around if he didn't want to. A baby right now would be tragic.

"We don't have to worry about that because I take my birth control pill every day."

"What if I asked you to stop?"

"Why would you do that?"

"Because we would make beautiful babies."

"My career . . ."

He laughed. "Teaching is not a career. It's charity work. I have millions, sweetie. You don't need to work."

"I didn't go to college to meet a man. I went to get educated and then have a career."

Aaron laughed and shook his head. "Listen to what you're saying, Onika, and imagine what your mentor would say. She would tell you that you've got a great situation here, and you'd do well not to mess it up."

She would never tell him that her mentors had warned her about him. Had taken her to the side and told her he was nothing but a playboy. That he'd probably be broke by the age of forty and need to be bailed out by his parents. They were warning her to ensure she didn't make a young girl's mistakes with a debonair man.

"I am thinking of maybe going to law school in a couple of years."

Aaron's face wrinkled. "Why would you do that? Law school is so unnecessary. If you want to do something with your life, help me build my legacy."

Aaron sounded ridiculous to Onika. She wasn't helping him build anything. She was going to take her birth control and act like she had good sense. She'd give Aaron what he needed when she had what she needed. And not a moment before.

CHAPTER FIFTEEN

Onika never started her teaching job. She moved from Atlanta to Washington DC, to Aaron's main house. He gave her a ring, said it was a promise of wonderful things to come. Not of marriage. He never once promised that, but he did say that she would never have to worry about anything as long as they were together. Onika accepted that. It was enough.

Aaron was not opposed to Onika having a career, but he did have certain expectations of her. So she decided that she had no time for teaching. Her job was loving Aaron.

Loving included caring for the sprawling town house, which was within walking distance of Capitol Hill. Loving was sharing his bed, his tub, his shower, the cherrywood desk in his office, and his kitchen sink, among other places. Love was attending every networking event, every fraternity/sorority function, and every yacht party in Annapolis. This love was her career—an ever-consuming career that took all of her energy and time.

When people asked if they were engaged, Aaron dodged the question with platitudes like, "Every man needs a good woman by his side." He'd punctuate those lines with a wink and a smile, the hearer believing he or she was privy to Aaron's mysterious life. Onika knew he was avoiding facts. He had no intention of marrying her.

In the beginning, this bothered Onika. The uncertainty of her future left her feeling uncomfortable, and then somewhere along the way she got numb to it. She'd accepted that uncertainty as the price of Aaron's love. It was a love that left her feeling addicted. She was Judy's child. It was inevitable that she'd be addicted to something.

Although she felt comfortable with Aaron's love, she panicked when she saw the double line on the pregnancy test indicating that she was carrying his child. She knew exactly when she'd conceived. It was when Aaron had whisked her off to Grenada on a surprise trip. She'd forgotten her birth control pills at home. They'd used condoms for the most part, but she couldn't be sure they'd used them every time.

In Grenada, Onika had thrown caution to the wind. Staring at the pregnancy test results, she'd wept. Sat on that toilet and wept for a good two hours, because she knew she wasn't keeping the baby.

How could she have a child with a man who wasn't committed? As much as she loved Aaron and wanted to raise his children, she drew the line there. She had abandoned her teaching career for his love, but she knew she could resume it anytime. That was a temporary decision. A child was a forever decision, and she refused to make that decision without a commitment from the man. A commitment she knew was probably never coming.

Lying on that table in stirrups traumatized Onika so much that she couldn't go home to Aaron right away. She needed a reprieve. So after the recovery time was over, she left on her own, against the nurse's advice. Didn't wait for a ride. In an unsafe fog of leftover anesthesia, Onika drove, powered on Starbucks and melancholy. She kept driving south for five and a half hours until she was at her grandmother's house in North Carolina. She drove Aaron's BMW onto that little dirt driveway and immediately felt out of place, though she'd played in that dirt as a little girl.

She sat there in the car, wondering if she should get out and knock on the door. It was home. She could use the key tucked away at the bottom of her purse. Unless Earlene had changed the locks, something that wouldn't surprise Onika at all.

Then she was out of time for decisions. Earlene stepped out on the porch, looking exactly the same as she had five years ago. Solid, still, mean. It didn't stop Onika from wanting to run to her and feel something close to love.

"Who's in that car?" Earlene yelled, her view obstructed by the tinted windows.

Onika considered flight. Still had a chance to speed off and disappear into the evening, and keep the promise she made to herself to never return to Goldsboro.

She chose to get out of the car, though. Seeing Earlene made Onika want to touch the only family she had.

"My, my, my."

Earlene's three words dripped with every vile thought she must have about her granddaughter. Onika heard hatred, disgust, melancholy, and sadness. Onika heard the pain of a five-year absence.

"Hi, Grandma," Onika said as she stepped into clear view.

"I don't have a granddaughter."

"Grandma, do you realize you've never once told me you love me."

Earlene stood silent.

"Do you? Do you love me at all?"

For some reason, Onika wanted to hear the words from her grandmother. She'd heard them from Judy, but only when she was high or having a breakdown. Judy's love never came wrapped in joy. It was always packaged in sorrow.

The woman who had taken care of her, and had introduced her to God, had never felt the need to declare her love. Onika wondered if her grandmother was afraid to love again, after she'd given her entire heart to Judy and had it broken. Was that the reason Onika could only receive the minimum? Food, clothing, shelter was all her grandmother had ever given her.

"I raised an ungrateful, ungodly child who abandoned her mama when she was in need," Earlene said. There was no affection in her tone. There was spite, anger, and maybe even desperation, but there was no love.

"Your daughter sent the police after me at school. She accused me of stealing her check."

"Your mama is sick."

"She's not a mother! When has she mothered me? When has she put me before drugs or a man?"

"When she gave you over to me. When she knew she couldn't care for you. She protected you from her life, and you abandoned her. God is gonna make you pay for this, girl. Honor your father and mother. It's in the Bible. The first law with a promise. God said it would go well for you if you honored your mother. You have not."

"Your God punished me before I was even born. He punished me to be born to a crackhead. If He's up there and listening to you, let Him know He's already dealt me a bad hand. Looks like I got my consequences up front."

"Mark my words. You got worse coming to you."

Earlene turned and went back into the house. Onika could hear the door slam from where she stood. She wanted to follow. Wanted to plead for affection. Wanted to cry into her grandmother's chest and tell her that she'd ended the life of her great-grandchild. She wanted absolution.

Instead of forgiveness, Onika had gotten a curse. If the God Earlene served allowed that curse to be carried out, then Onika decided that she'd never follow Him. What kind of God cursed a child in the womb, and gave a double curse when she tried to move beyond the misery of it all? Not one she wanted to worship.

Earlene could have her vengeful God. Onika would find her way without Him.

CHAPTER SIXTEEN

O nika sat in Ronald Reagan Washington National Airport feeling worried that she and Aaron wouldn't make it to Chelsea's wedding reception. They hadn't missed the wedding, because Chelsea and her husband had eloped and told everyone after the fact. Of course, Mrs. Richard had been furious. The trade-off was a quickly planned reception without bridesmaids, groomsmen, or a wedding dress. Chelsea would wear a designer gown, but that's all Mrs. Richard could get her to agree to.

Onika had to be there. She needed to run interference for Chelsea. To protect her from Mrs. Richard's wrath, which was sure to be on expert level by the time Onika arrived.

"If they'd given people ample time to plan for this, we wouldn't be riding coach," Aaron fussed as he looked at the seat assignment on his ticket.

"Coach isn't the worst thing in the world, love. I think we'll be able to survive it," Onika said.

"You're joking, but I'm serious. I'm too tall for coach. I'm going to try again to get us upgraded."

"Honey, if they just have one seat, you take the upgrade."

"Why would I sit in first class with my companion in coach? That's just crazy."

"Because I don't want to hear you fussing the whole ride if we're in coach. I just am not here for it, and I want you comfortable."

Aaron kissed her lips. "This is why I love you. You're so practical, so drama free. We are a perfect match."

"Not quite perfect. Maybe if I had two vaginas."

Aaron's eyebrows lifted as if he was considering that possibility.

"You're gross," Onika said.

"You drew the mental picture, and I have to say, you're an artist. A regular Picasso. A Dumas."

Onika chuckled as she watched Aaron swagger up to the ticket counter. She knew what he was going to do. He was going to pull out all his sweet, good charm. He'd have that first-class upgrade, even if someone got suspiciously bumped.

Onika barely noticed when the woman sat down next to her, because she was watching the scene with Aaron and the ticket agent unfold. She didn't pay attention until the woman tapped her shoulder.

"Do you love him?" she asked. "You know about me and the countless others, but you seem to still love him. Why?"

Onika glared at the woman. She was more insulted at the audacity to ask her these questions in public than the questions themselves. Who did this tramp think she was dealing with?

"What is it to you? Do *you* love him? Clearly you know him."

"I've been one of Aaron's bed partners for ten years. I came before you. I'll be here after you're gone. I was just wondering if you love him."

"Since you're so comfortable with your position, why do you care?"

"I was actually going to warn you to get out while you can. Save your life while you can. I've completely given him mine. I wasted all my young years fulfilling his fantasies, and now I can't have children."

Onika wanted to feel sympathy for this woman, but she couldn't. Knowing that Aaron slept with other women was one

thing, but for them to come out of the shadows and into her at-
mosphere was quite another.

"I don't need your advice. I'm good. We're good."

"But you're not good, baby. I can see how irritated you are
that I'm here. It's because you love him, and you think you've
accepted his infidelity, but you haven't."

"It isn't infidelity if I know about it."

The woman laughed a hearty laugh. "You've swallowed every
single, last drop of the Aaron cherry, arsenic-laced Kool-Aid.
You're worse off than I ever was. I never accepted it. I dealt with
it, because I needed what he gave me. I need the sex more than
anything."

"Go away. If you know anything about Aaron, you know how
much he values his privacy. This would not go over well with him."

"I see why he stays with you. You're giving him everything he
wants. But what do you want? Don't you want anything for yourself?"

Onika had asked herself this question many times and hadn't
been able to come up with an answer, but she damn sure wasn't
going to try to find the answer for one of Aaron's bed buddies.
She turned from the woman and ignored her, hoping she'd
communicated that there was nothing left to say.

"And I thought I was going to get you to leave him," the
woman said as she stood. "I should've known better. You'll
never leave him."

Onika heard the words but didn't respond. Didn't feel like
she owed her a response. The woman probably wanted Onika's
life, and unfortunately she didn't have the trophy looks and
probably didn't have the education either. She had a big behind, big breasts, and a flat stomach. She looked exactly like
what she was to Aaron—a sexual fantasy.

But even though Onika had built a barricade around her
heart and steeled herself against the pain from Aaron's outside
trysts, it still hurt to be confronted with them. When the
women came out of the shadows to make themselves known, it
pained her every single time.

And every time Aaron only apologized for the women approaching her. He never apologized for putting her in the situation with his insatiable need for sex.

Onika was so weary, but also so in love with Aaron. She had no idea what she would do if he decided that she no longer suited his needs. With every additional woman, the threat was there.

He hadn't seen any of the exchange, and he walked back over to Onika with a huge smile on his face.

"I got us two first-class upgrades," Aaron said.

"Really? How?" She choked back tears, swallowing them. She didn't want Aaron to know what had just transpired.

"I can't tell you. It's a secret. But don't I always take care of you?"

Onika nodded. "Mmm-hmm. You always do."

CHAPTER SEVENTEEN

Onika hadn't met up with Mrs. Richard or Chelsea since Chelsea's wedding reception. But they were in Washington, DC, for the sorority's centennial conference, and she couldn't refuse them a lunch. They were the closest thing she had to family these days, so she wanted to see them.

They met at Legal Sea Foods in the heart of the city, near Chinatown, because Mrs. Richard wanted a lobster roll. Chelsea wanted whatever her mother wanted.

Both Mrs. Richard and Chelsea were dressed in pink and blue, the sorority colors. Onika was wearing an orange sundress, because it was spring and warm enough for her to pull out her sundresses. Plus, she was over the sorority life. The only time she put on that mantle was when Aaron demanded that she be his Epsilon Phi Beta showpiece. She'd stroll with her alumni sisters and party it up, but as soon as it was over, she'd leave it behind. She found it all pretentious now and wondered why she'd ever wanted it so badly.

Mrs. Richard ordered champagne for the table, pleasing Onika. She'd been hoping that it wouldn't be seen as too early to imbibe, because she needed a drink to deal with Mrs. Richard and her endless questions about her and Aaron's relationship.

"So, are you just loving DC?" Chelsea asked. "I always love it when I visit, but I just can't see myself leaving Atlanta."

"You should leave that country place," Mrs. Richard said. "Our family is on the East Coast. I can't believe you decided to stay there."

"My husband is there, Mama. He has a church. How can we move? Tell her, Nikki! She should be proud of me. I have everything she wanted me to have. A rich husband, a mansion, and status."

"That cretin didn't even give you a wedding. He whisked you away to get married in someone's secret chapel. Why would he do that? You're my only daughter. I was denied the chance of hosting your wedding. I will never forgive your pastor for that."

"Mother, when will you get over this? It was three years ago. You can't hold that against him forever."

"Yes, I can, and I intend to."

"Well, you still have Nikki," Chelsea said. "When she and Aaron finally decide to get married, then you can plan everything for her."

Mrs. Richard's expression turned dark. "Nikki, when are you going to leave him? Have you not grown tired of Aaron yet?"

Onika sighed. She'd known it was coming but was hoping she wouldn't have to answer the questions until after she'd gotten a nice buzz from the champagne.

"You know that I love him, Mrs. Richard."

It was funny. Onika viewed Mrs. Richard as a mother figure or, at the least, a very close aunt, but she'd never called her anything other than Mrs. Richard. Maybe because it was a title that the woman wore with pride. She was proud to be Mrs. Richard.

"I know. And I think in his warped little mind he believes that he loves you, but I must tell you he's been around the campus lately."

"What are you saying?"

"He's got some girl pining away after him. She's a senior at Robinson. The rumor on campus is that she was pregnant and miscarried. I doubt if it was a miscarriage."

"It probably was. Aaron desperately wants children. He wouldn't make her have an abortion."

"You don't seem shocked about the girl."

Onika wasn't shocked, but she was worried. He'd always had other women, but many of them were married or older. They weren't threats. He wouldn't leave her for any of them. They were merely supplements for his pleasure.

"Aaron is quite honest about his wandering eye. I know there are others. There have always been others."

"And you're fine with that?" Chelsea asked. "I could never share my man."

Onika was leery of people who said what they'd never do. She was sure her mother had said she'd never be strung out on drugs or become a prostitute. *Never* was as flaky a word as *forever*. Neither really meant anything.

"I wish that he was only with me, but he has never been dishonest about it."

"But he isn't always safe," Mrs. Richard said. "Otherwise, there wouldn't have been a pregnancy scare."

"That does concern me. I thought he was always using protection. We'll have a talk about that."

Onika knew this was a lie even as the words left her parted lips. She'd never mention this conversation to Aaron. She'd govern herself accordingly and continue to get tested for sexually transmitted infections. It was a part of her normal routine. She'd resigned herself to Aaron's ways when she'd chosen to stay with him in spite of it. Nothing Mrs. Richard said was a surprise, and Onika found that there was also no pain. She'd become numb to Aaron's actions.

"Darling, you should leave him. It's been nearly five years since you graduated, and you haven't gotten what you need from this arrangement. Can't you see how selfish he is? If he's going to have multiple women, at the very least he could give you the title. Let you be the wife with legal access to his possessions in case something happens to his simple ass."

"I don't really care about his possessions."

"You should care," Mrs. Richard said. "If you wake up one day and this is over, then what will you have to show for it?"

"I don't know."

"I will tell you. You won't have a damn thing. And don't say something stupid like you've experienced love. Get out while you still have your sanity. Don't give him every bit of yourself."

Chelsea started to cry, as if the words were directed at her.

"What's wrong with you?" Mrs. Richard asked.

"I-I just don't want to see Nikki hurt. Please don't let him hurt you, Nikki. Leave him, now."

"He won't hurt me. I'm strong. I know what he's doing. If I wake up one day and it's over, then it's over."

Chelsea sobbed into her napkin, and Mrs. Richard nudged her in the ribs.

"Stop it, girl. You're drawing attention to us. We've done all we can. We've told Nikki what we know, and she'll choose to do what she wants with the information. Don't cry. Save those tears for when your sister comes running to you when Aaron breaks her stupid little heart."

Onika wanted to get up and walk out. She came very close to doing it, but she didn't want Mrs. Richard to know how deeply she'd been affected by her words. Maybe she was stupid. Maybe her heart would be broken. But she couldn't go back now; she could only go forward.

She did know one thing. If Aaron ever did hurt her, Onika would never let Mrs. Richard, Chelsea, or anyone see her cry about it. No one would get to see her tears. No one would get to say they told her so.

CHAPTER EIGHTEEN

When Aaron asked Onika to join him in the dining room, and she saw that he'd ordered sushi and wine, she knew some sort of announcement was about to happen. And she knew it wouldn't be a good one.

He'd been in a bad mood for a few weeks. He'd picked arguments over nothing, fussed at Onika about her spending—something he'd never done. Onika had been feeling a sense of doom without any idea how to fix it.

"This isn't working," Aaron said as she sat down at the dining room table.

He hadn't even given her the opportunity to sit and prepare for his words. He dropped them on her like a ton of concrete.

Although she hadn't had time to prepare, Onika couldn't even say she was surprised. She hadn't been worried about the woman who showed up at the airport whispering in her ear, but she had been concerned about the girl at Robinson. The girl who had lost his baby. When she'd heard that story, she knew their days were numbered. But seeing the writing on the wall wasn't enough to make her plan.

Still, she wasn't ready for it to be over.

"What isn't working?" she asked.

"Us being together. We want different things. We're on different paths. You want marriage . . ."

"I'd settle for monogamy."

Aaron chuckled. "And you know I'm not monogamous."

She did know, and it didn't make this any easier. She thought that knowing would make it easier.

"Let's not drag this thing out. I'm expecting you to be gone tomorrow."

"Tomorrow? I have to get on my feet first, Aaron. Find a job, get a place."

"Not my problem. No one told you to not keep your affairs in order."

Onika stared at him in disbelief. "You told me not to work."

"I did not. I told you that you didn't need a job. I pay all the bills, so that was the truth."

"So you're going to have me jobless and penniless in Washington, DC? What have I ever done to you, for you to punish me this way?"

"Well, Onika, I've done some digging."

Onika smarted at the use of her real name. He'd never used it, even after she'd told it to him. He'd only ever used Nikki.

"And it seems," Aaron continued, "that you have a family and a home in Goldsboro, North Carolina. You can get on your feet there."

Any hope of reconciliation Onika had fizzled. She wondered how far into her past Aaron had delved. Did he know about Judy's drug abuse and prostitution?

Fear gripped Onika at her core. Not only did she not have a job; she didn't have a network of friends. The people she knew were Aaron's friends, and they would quickly envelop Onika's replacement into their fold. Onika didn't have a friend in DC who didn't belong to Aaron.

"I've bought you a plane ticket and arranged for ground transportation to your grandmother's house. She's been notified of your pending arrival."

Onika could imagine the cackling her grandmother had

done when she'd received that notification. She'd probably be standing on the front porch, legs akimbo, waiting to spit in Onika's face.

She didn't care what Aaron said or what plane ticket he'd bought, Onika wasn't going back there.

"What about my things?" Onika asked.

"What things?"

Onika owned a wardrobe of off-the-runway fashions—one-of-a-kind creations that could fetch her a good amount of cash. Shoes and jewelry, too. If she liquidated the collection she could have thousands in the bank.

"Oh, you mean my investments? Those clothes, shoes, and jewelry are listed as my assets. You had use of them. They don't belong to you."

Onika's heart sank. She did have a stash of two thousand dollars. She'd collected that money painstakingly over the years. There was rarely an opportunity for her to handle his cash. She had cards with restrictions that disallowed taking cash advances. Her stash had been built with found money in Aaron's pockets and wallet, and he was not a careless man. Those twenties and tens had been hard to come by.

Though he was very deliberate with his spending, Aaron was extremely generous. It's why Onika didn't care that she didn't exactly have her own money. She'd never gone without anything she needed. The credit cards he gave her allowed her to purchase what she wanted. He just had a record of her spending.

Still, she thought she could make do on two thousand until she found a teaching job. Her credentials were current, and she'd done her student teaching hours. It wouldn't be hard to land a job.

"I've had the clothes that you brought here cleaned, laundered, and packed," Aaron said. "Your flight for home leaves tomorrow unless you want to change it. You can stay in the guest room tonight, but you need to be gone by morning."

"Why are you being so cruel?"

"What was cruel was you murdering my child, Onika. Did

you think I wouldn't find out about that? You had an abortion. No. I'm not being cruel. I am simply asking you to leave my life now. It would be cruel to have you here when Raven moves in."

"That was several years ago, Aaron. I wasn't ready for children yet."

"You. Murdered. My. Child."

"Is your new girlfriend pregnant? Is that why you're asking me to leave now?"

Aaron didn't respond. He did this when he was angry—completely shut down. Onika knew that she could act out, scream, curse, and fall out in the middle of the floor. If she fell out, he'd step right over her and go to his cigar room to have a Cuban. He didn't do scenes or emotional outbursts. Accusing her of murder was as close as Aaron was going to get to a meltdown.

"For what it's worth, I wanted that baby. The abortion hurt me badly. I've never gotten over it," she said.

"Well, I hope you never do. You never gave me the opportunity to raise my child. I will never forgive you for that."

Onika believed him. Aaron didn't just go around making declarations like that. He fully meant to never forgive her. Again, Onika decided to save her energy, because wailing and moaning wasn't going to work.

So she'd leave quietly.

Onika was sure Aaron had left no loose ends. Her credit cards had probably already been canceled, and she was surely not going to have access to any cash of his.

"Please don't start begging or anything like that. It won't work."

For some reason, as if nothing else had been objectionable, this bothered her more than anything he'd said. Maybe, it was because her pride was all Onika had left.

"I won't be begging you for anything."

"Good. You're proud. You've learned something from me, then."

Even though Onika had no idea what came next, she stood from the table. She didn't want sushi or anything else he'd set before her as a consolation meal. She didn't think she could swallow it anyway.

"And I love you, Onika," Aaron declared again. "More than any other woman. I would've never let you go. I would've eventually given you everything you wanted. I would've married you."

"You said we shouldn't drag this out. Why are you belaboring your points?" Onika asked.

"Because when you sit somewhere and dissect everything that went wrong here, I want you to lay the blame properly. At your own feet. I've always been honest with you. You've always known that I had other women. From the beginning. But the only truth you've told me about yourself is your name."

Aaron was correct. Onika hadn't been truthful with him, and she was glad about it. He didn't deserve to know her deepest, darkest secrets. He didn't deserve her heart, and he sure wasn't about to witness her pain or see her fall apart without him.

She would leave with her head held high, dignity held intact with a tiny, thin thread. Maybe she didn't have a plan, but she knew how to survive. That was the one thing Judy had taught her.

CHAPTER NINETEEN

Onika left Aaron's town house for a cheap hotel room in DC. It was cheap by Aaron's standards, but with only two thousand dollars in the bank, the one-hundred-fifty-dollar-a-night room was actually expensive for Onika.

She had no time to waste and immediately started submitting resumes. It hurt that it was July, and most schools' administrative offices were out for summer vacation and had already hired their teachers for the upcoming school year. She applied for every teaching job that she could find, even substitute ones.

After only one day of sending out resumes, Onika had a job interview at a charter school on the southeast side of DC. Not her first choice, but she needed a check.

She showed up for the interview a half hour early, but had to stand outside in the stifling morning heat, because the door was locked and she had no way to call anyone to say she'd arrived. Aaron had shut off her cell phone and she hadn't had time to replace it with a TracFone.

Finally, someone did answer—a frantic-looking woman with hair that went in a million different directions. It looked like electricity and lightning were her styling tools of choice.

"Hello, Ms. Lewis, I'm Charlotte Wilson. Come on in. I am

sorry it took so long to answer the door. I was on the phone with our grantor."

"The school doesn't have state funding?"

"Some, but we need the grant money to stay afloat."

This worried Onika as she followed Charlotte down a long, dimly lit hall. She imagined children running through this hallway and sipping from the water fountain. But how stable was the school? She couldn't depend on a start-up. She needed her paycheck twice a month, especially now.

"When are you looking to fill this position?"

"August at the earliest."

"I thought this was a summer school job?"

"Yes, it was, but we had to cancel summer school. There was low enrollment, and the board of directors couldn't justify the expense of staying open all summer."

Onika blocked out her voice and calculated her next move. She needed to find a different hotel that had monthly rates. There was no way she was going to survive until August in the hotel she was in now.

Onika completed the interview with Charlotte. Hopefully they'd like her and she'd have a job there in a couple of months. Charlotte promised Onika would hear from her.

Onika left the interview and rode the Metro to Gallery Place near Chinatown. There were dozens of stores and restaurants on that strip. Surely someone was hiring.

She skipped the fast food places. There was no way she'd let anyone in Aaron's circle seeing her constructing a burrito or dropping fries into the fryer.

Unfortunately, every full upscale restaurant wanted someone with experience, and Onika had none. A waitress at a four-star Mexican restaurant had at least been kind.

"You're pretty and have a nice shape," she'd said. "You should go to Hooters."

Onika imagined herself in the shiny shorts, orange T-shirt, and white boots. She balked at the mental image. She hadn't gone to college for that. True, it had been five years since she'd graduated, and she'd remained unemployed, but still, Hooters was not what she wanted.

Then she thought about her rapidly shrinking bank account and applied anyway.

After pounding the pavement all day, and getting rejections and delays (most of the places she applied to wouldn't hire her before a month's time, and a check wouldn't come until weeks later), Onika realized she was in real trouble.

The only job she could think of that would provide immediate cash required her to take her clothes off. That thought simmered and festered at the back of her mind. She couldn't go there. Not yet.

Dog tired, Onika headed for the Metro station. Her mouth watered at the sight of one of her favorite restaurants, a sushi bar she had frequented with Aaron.

Then her stomach dropped. She saw a young woman who could be her twin—petite, curvy, and curly-headed. The girl was wearing a white pants jumpsuit that was an original, the only one ever produced. The black belt said NL in Swarovski crystals. It stood for Onika's pseudonym, Nikki Lewis.

That pantsuit had belonged to Onika, just like the man who purchased it.

The woman was laughing with another woman whom Onika didn't recognize, but the sound was so carefree that it made Onika furious.

This girl was living her former life. She had her lady parts pressed against the skintight pantsuit. It was obscene to steal someone's life. A criminal act.

Without thinking or caring, Onika rushed to where the girl stood. Onika grabbed the glass of red wine, made it splash all over the white. Like blood.

The girl stopped laughing.

"You bitch!" she screamed.

Now Onika laughed. Tears rolled down her face as she cackled at the top of her lungs. She hoped her grandmother could hear the sound all the way down in North Carolina.

Then Aaron emerged from the restaurant. He ran to Onika's soiled doppelgänger and tried to comfort her.

He shook his head at Onika. "So bitter. So very bitter."

Onika spit every expletive she could think of at Aaron. Her voice sounded deep and gravelly—possessed.

"Who is she, baby? Are you sleeping with her?" So doppelgänger wasn't dumb after all. Maybe she wouldn't last as long as Onika had lasted.

"No, sweetheart. She is someone I used to care for."

"Really? She doesn't seem like someone you'd go for. She's so . . . so street."

Onika's entire body shook when she started laughing this time. This girl was a carbon copy of Onika. It was like he'd stepped into a time machine and procured a younger version of Onika, although he had clearly aged himself.

"I will be sending you a cleaning bill for this jumpsuit, if it can even be salvaged."

This tickled Onika even more. Where, oh where was he going to send that bill?

CHAPTER TWENTY

Onika sat on the bed in her hotel room and cried. Maybe she'd been in denial about Aaron. Maybe, somewhere in the back of her mind or in the depths of her heart, she'd assumed they'd get past his restlessness. Perhaps she'd believed restoration was possible, because she hadn't truly believed it until she'd seen that girl wearing her clothes.

It was really over for them.

Mrs. Richard's words kept playing over and over again in her mind. *He'll never marry you.* She'd believed that she was smarter than that. That she'd be able to see the signs when they came. That she'd get out unscathed, if necessary.

She'd been blindsided. She should've been prepared.

Onika frowned when she looked at her bank account balance on the computer in the hotel lobby. Even at the cheapest Marriott she could find in DC, she was spending $149 a night. At this rate, along with food and Metro fare, her money would be gone in less than two weeks' time.

She tucked the confirmation for her flight to North Carolina in her bag. She'd called the airline, and since technically she'd missed the flight, they would allow her to fly standby to her original destination. Anyplace else would be a $200 change fee that she did not have. This was a last resort, and she tried not to think of going back there

The tears continued. Tears for the years she'd thrown away after graduating from college when she could've been in law school or teaching elementary school children. There were tears for the college girl who should've entertained many boyfriends instead of just seeing one man who was too old in the first place.

Onika cried for the time and the love that she'd wasted on Aaron. Her heart ached with the weight of it all. But more than anything she cried over the uncertainty of her future.

CHAPTER TWENTY-ONE

On day four of her hotel stay, Onika checked out of the Marriott and into an extended-stay hotel that would allow her to stretch her remaining money a few more weeks. It was on the southeast side of town, but the neighborhood wasn't too bad. There was a crappy continental breakfast with stale muffins and fruit that was hard and not ripe, but it was edible, so Onika ate it and got enough for lunch. Her dinner consisted of a hamburger or chicken sandwich from the McDonald's value menu and a cup of water. She had to preserve her cash for the Metro and the hotel.

This hotel didn't have Internet access, so Onika had to take her laptop to a coffee shop to check her e-mails. She'd spend two dollars on a cup of coffee and stay for hours.

Some of the staff stared at her with curiosity. They probably thought she was homeless, and she pretty much was. She didn't want to be kicked out, so she asked if they were hiring. Of course, the answer was no. It was summer. Teenagers had already filled whatever fast food jobs there were.

Onika opened an e-mail from the charter school. She was hired, and the pay was $38,000 a year. Aaron had taken her on vacations that cost more than that. The bad thing was that the start date was the end of August, and it was early July. What was she supposed to do for two months?

Feeling a little encouraged, Onika left the coffee shop and decided to treat herself for lunch. She'd have a whole meal instead of just a burger.

She stood at the Shake Shack counter nearly salivating at the thought of a juicy burger, fries, and a shake.

"Ma'am, do you have another method of payment? This card was declined."

"What? Swipe it again."

The girl swiped the card two more times, both with the same result.

"Okay, let me call my bank. There is money in this account."

Onika stepped outside of the restaurant, her face a crimson red. It felt like everyone in the line was staring at her.

Her hands shook as she dialed the 800 number on the back of her debit card.

After putting in her card number and PIN, the computerized voice announced Onika's balance. There was only eleven cents in her account. Panic tried to set in, but logic temporarily prevailed. She pressed the button to speak to a bank representative.

After checking that Onika was who she said she was, the phone agent asked, "How can I help you?"

"There must be a mistake on my balance. Can you review my transactions, please?"

Onika listened to the list of her last ten transactions. She recognized only two. The extended stay hotel and the coffee shop.

"Ma'am, I did not make eight of those transactions."

"Hmm . . . they were made using your PIN. Have you misplaced your card? Is the PIN written on it?"

"No and no."

"Okay, ma'am, we will file a fraud report. You will be mailed a form to the address on your account. Please return that form to us."

"I've recently moved."

"But you just verified your address."

"Well, I did because that's the address you have on file."

Onika heard the tapping of keys in the background.

"Ma'am, we must verify your identity prior to putting any funds back into your account. I just sent you an e-mail. Please follow the instructions in the e-mail."

Onika groaned. "Can I verify it some other way?"

"I'm afraid not. I need you to respond to the e-mail."

"All right. And then how long will it take to restore my funds?"

"Up to five business days."

Logic gave up the ghost, because panic put it in a choke hold.

"I need my money."

"I understand ma'am, unfortunately . . ."

"No! Not unfortunately! Put someone on the phone who can put my money back now! Let me speak to your supervisor!"

"I am the supervisor on the floor. The manager is not in, but I can send you to her voice mail."

"I don't need voice mail. I need my money returned to me."

"Unfortuna . . ."

"Do *not* say unfortunately again."

"Well, what do you want me to say?"

"*I want you to say you are putting my money back!*" Onika yelled.

"Ma'am. Unfortunately, I'm going to have to disconnect the call now."

Onika started to redial the customer service number, but then thought better of it. She'd go back to the coffee shop, log onto her e-mail, pull up the form, and then . . . Her planning paused. She needed to print the form. There was no printer at the coffee shop. The nearest Kinko's was a fifteen-minute walk. Wait . . . she couldn't print it at Kinko's. She had no money. Then it was back to the hotel. Perhaps one of the employees would be kind enough to print it out.

Onika was glad she had an all-day Metro pass. She'd used the last of her cash to purchase it, though. All the rest of her money was tied up in the bank.

Once she was back at the hotel, Onika felt a brief sense of relief. She walked up to the tiny front desk with what she hoped was a friendly smile on her face.

"Excuse me, ma'am, can you help me?" Onika asked.

"How can I help?" the front desk clerk replied.

"I have a document that I need to print, but I don't have access to a printer."

"There is a Kinko's about three blocks from here."

"I was kind of hoping you could just print it for me."

"Well . . . my supervisor is out right now. Where is the document?"

"Can I e-mail it to you?"

"Sure."

"Oh, wait, I don't have Internet. Can you log onto my Gmail from your computer?"

The clerk seemed to hesitate.

"Please," Onika begged.

"Okay, what's your room number?" the desk clerk asked.

"Oh, it's 214."

The desk clerk raised her eyebrows. "Are you Onika Lewis?"

"Yes."

"Ma'am, we had to check you out of your room."

Onika's mind shifted away from her banking situation to this new and imminent threat.

"What? Why?"

"Well, we run the credit card daily to make sure there are still enough funds to cover your stay, and your card was declined. So we checked you out. If you give us a new method of payment, we can check you back in."

"I don't . . . I don't have another method of payment."

"Hmm . . ."

"Is my bag still in the room?" Onika asked.

"Actually, no. We had to remove your belongings."

"You what? Where are they?"

"We locked your bag in the luggage room. Let me get someone to grab it for you."

Onika watched the clerk make a phone call, while her panic surpassed fear and went to full-fledged terror.

A few moments later, a young man rushed to the front desk.

"Are you sure there's a bag in the luggage room?" he asked the clerk. "I didn't see one."

"You've lost my bag?" Onika shrieked.

"It should be there," the desk clerk said, ignoring Onika.

"There's nothing in the room, or anywhere back there."

Now the desk clerk looked confused. "There should be multiple bags in there. We had to remove belongings from several rooms this morning."

"No. The door was unlocked, so . . ."

Onika felt woozy. Her stomach flipped, and her heart raced. This wasn't watching-a-scary-movie afraid; this felt like being abducted and thrown in the back of an unmarked van by a man who wanted to make a suit out of your flesh.

"Ms. Lewis, can you hold on a moment, while I go investigate this?" the clerk said.

Onika managed to nod as she watched the clerk follow the young man to wherever they were supposedly holding her luggage hostage. Onika tried not to think of the worst-case scenario, although the entire day had been the worst day ever.

The desk clerk looked annoyed and befuddled as she took her post behind the desk once more. The young man had not returned.

"Ms. Lewis, I'm going to be honest with you. I think your bag may have been stolen. We have several homeless people who hang around the hotel, and sometimes they manage to steal some food from the breakfast buffet."

"So you're telling me, you removed my bag from my locked room . . ."

"Hotel policy, ma'am. I apologize."

"You followed your policy, removed my bag from the locked room, placed it in an unlocked room, and now it's been stolen?"

"The door was locked when your bag was placed there."

It was too much now. Onika burst into tears.

"Would you still like me to print out your document?" the desk clerk asked in a kind voice.

Onika nodded and gave the desk clerk the information. She printed the form and handed it to Onika along with a pen. After she was done filling it out, Onika begged the girl to fax it over.

"There were some improper charges on my account," Onika explained. "That's why my card was declined. I'm waiting for the bank to return my money."

"Oh, well, as soon as we can swipe a card, you can go back into your room."

"The bank said it could take five business days."

The clerk drew in a sharp breath. "Oh, that's not good."

"No. No, it's not."

Without any other immediate plans, Onika sat down on the couch in the hotel's lobby. She thought about that flight to North Carolina that she could take if she showed up to the airport and flew on standby. Then she dismissed the thought as quickly as it had come.

What would be the point of going back there? There were no jobs that she'd want to do, nor anyone she wanted to see. There was absolutely no life for Onika in North Carolina, and she refused to let Aaron push her to a place past rock-bottom.

"Ms. Lewis?"

Onika was pulled from her thoughts. She looked up at the desk clerk.

"Yes?"

"I just spoke to my manager and explained your situation. He asked that you leave the premises until you can secure payment."

"Leave the premises? Have I disturbed anyone?"

"No, it's just the fact that we've had a theft. We can't have anyone who isn't a guest loitering in the lobby."

"B-but, I don't have anywhere to go."

The desk clerk looked sympathetic as she slowly shook her head. "I'm sorry."

"Will you call me if you locate my suitcase?"

"Oh, absolutely. Give me your phone number."

Onika walked back over to the front desk. Her hands trembled as she wrote the number on the note pad. She'd been trembling and crying all day. It felt like a horrible, horrible nightmare. She prayed it was, and that she'd wake up soon.

Onika took a deep breath, walked outside the hotel and wondered what she would do next. She had no money, no belongings except what was in her purse and backpack, and no place to lay her head. She needed a miracle.

A miracle didn't come.

Onika got more afraid as the afternoon melted into evening. Her stomach growled for her nightly hamburger, but she couldn't purchase it. She reached into her bag and ate part of a stale muffin. She wanted to call someone. She had her sorority chapter, but how could she tell them she was out on the street with nowhere to go? How embarrassing would that be? She'd never recover from that shame, especially since all of the members of the DC chapter were beyond elite. They'd help Onika. Their sisterhood demanded that they not leave her in trouble, but Onika would never be invited to the day parties, conferences, and special events ever again. She'd be an outcast. It was bad enough that she'd lost Aaron; she couldn't lose that part of her life, too.

No. She wouldn't call her sorority sisters. She would tough this out. Pretend she was camping out. Anything other than what it was.

She went into a McDonald's to use the restroom and looked at her face in the mirror. Her eyes were puffy, swollen, and red. Her cheeks were splotchy from crying. She looked like a domestic violence victim.

And wasn't she? Aaron had committed a heinous act of violence against her. He'd ripped her life from under her, in a week. He'd destroyed everything, on purpose—all because he had found another young girl to serve his needs.

Although Onika felt the urge to, she refused to let herself cry again. She'd grown up with a mother who smoked crack every day. She'd slept on the floor in the corner of a hotel room while Judy turned tricks. She had been through worse. She'd let Robinson University and Aaron make her weak.

She'd never make that mistake again.

CHAPTER TWENTY-TWO

With no money, no phone, and no way of getting either, Onika was, for the first time since her plight began, terrified. She had just spent her last few dollars on the Red Line train. It stayed out the latest and went the farthest. She'd ride it back and forth until someone made her get off or her bladder forced her to exit or embarrass herself.

She scored a seat in the back of the train, and leaned her body and head against the window. She allowed herself to doze off, not worried about anyone stealing anything from her. She had nothing of any value on her person. Her hair was slicked back into a greasy bun, and she disguised herself with big sunglasses, and a pair of jeans and T-shirt that she found at the Goodwill.

After she had slept peacefully for an unknown amount of time, someone tapped Onika lightly on the shoulder. She woke from her sleep a bit confused. She wanted to close her eyes again. Riding the train dressed like a vagrant (she *was* a vagrant) was supposed to be the dream—nightmare, really. It wasn't, couldn't be, real.

"Hey, girl, I just wanted to wake you up, 'cause this probably the last time they gonna run through here tonight, and we're about to pass Gallery Place. That's where mostly everybody gets off."

The woman tapping her reeked of alcohol, weed, and crack. She also had a faintly musty body odor. Onika wondered if she smelled the same. The last time she'd taken a shower was two days ago, but she'd tried to refresh herself with paper towels and hand soap in the Starbucks bathroom.

"Why there?" Onika asked the woman. "Why Gallery Place?"

"Bathrooms and always people walking around. It's safer. I'm Joyce. What's your name?"

"Nikki."

Onika had no reason not to believe the woman, but again, she had nothing to steal. What did she have to lose by getting off at a specific Metro stop? Besides, homeless women seemed to have something of a code, from what Onika could tell. They looked out for each other and protected one another from the men. If anything was dangerous being on the streets, it wasn't animals or some sort of wildlife. It was the men that women were most frightened of on the streets, even police officers. They could take a woman to jail or, worse, to the backseat of their car for a little visit.

Onika got off the train and walked slowly through the Metro station. Joyce rushed ahead, although it was two in the morning. Onika remembered how she had walked before her life had fallen apart. She'd sped through the station, not making eye contact with anyone. Especially homeless people.

More than once, Onika thought about going home to North Carolina. If she was honest with herself, she thought about it daily. Tonight, the thought was at the forefront of her mind, like a flashing sign that she couldn't turn off.

Onika's first night on the street had her rethinking all the things she thought she'd never do. Was a stripper pole really worse than this? She thought about the girls she knew in college who were strippers or, worse, had sugar daddies. She remembered thinking of them as classless whores. But as soon as things had gotten tight for her, she was thinking about going online in lingerie, and talking dirty to strangers.

Onika was the ex-girlfriend of a rich man, and there was no honor in that. There was nothing. An ex-wife had alimony. A baby's mother had child support. She had nothing to show for those years, and now she was on the streets.

She should go home.

But if she went home now, Earlene would laugh in her face. Tell her she'd reaped what she'd sown, thinking she was better than them to begin with. Earlene would take her in, but she'd rake her over the coals with guilt.

It hadn't gotten bad enough for that yet.

And plus, how would she even get to Goldsboro? She couldn't even get across town to get to the airport.

As Onika emerged from the Metro station into the night, Joyce walked up with her hand outstretched, holding a flyer. Onika didn't want to touch the dirty piece of paper, but who was she to look down on anyone now?

"What is it?" Onika asked.

"You need to go see this woman. Get off the streets. It's not for you."

Onika was immediately skeptical. "Why don't you go see her, then?"

The woman laughed. "I'm not on my meds, and if you have diagnosed mental illness, she won't take you. Plus, she has rules, and I don't like rules."

"But you think I should go there."

"Yes. She has an open bed, and she helped my friend get a job and an apartment for her and her little girl."

"Thank you. I will call her."

"Where are you gonna sleep tonight?"

Onika shook her head. "I don't think I'll sleep. I slept for a few hours on the Metro. I think I'll just find somewhere to sit and rest."

"Okay, well, I'll be over on H Street in Chinatown. There's a restaurant owner who lets us sleep in the back of his building. He's got lawn furniture for us."

Onika nodded her thanks. She folded up the flyer and put it in her pocket. She would figure out a way to call her tomorrow. Joyce was right; this life wasn't for her. Maybe she wasn't meant to be elite and live that dream, but living on the streets was not an option.

The flyer said Safe Harbor. Onika hoped it was exactly that.

CHAPTER TWENTY-THREE

Onika stared across the street at the Gold's Gym that she used to attend every day until Aaron had abruptly canceled her membership. She didn't know if she'd have enough guts to do what she planned, but she knew that she couldn't show up at Safe Harbor looking dirty and grungy. It had already taken her all day to get her nerve up to go to Safe Harbor, and she definitely wasn't going there stinking.

Yes, she was homeless right now, but she was still a lady. She had at least one shred of respectability left.

Well, maybe a half shred, because she was about to sneak into her former gym's locker room and steal her ex-boyfriend's new girlfriend's clothes. And maybe her purse. She needed a shower and some clean clothes, and since Aaron probably paid for everything the girl had, he was going to give Onika one last gift.

But first she'd have to get past the front desk staff.

Onika crossed the street and held her head up. She slung her bag over her shoulder onto her back, held her shoulders back, and thrust her chest forward. She was just going to walk straight inside. Before anyone stopped her, she'd have exactly what she needed.

As she walked through the front door, she grinned. Mrs. Owens was at the front, complaining about the towels, like she always did. If Onika hadn't had a short window of time to complete what she needed to do, she'd stand there and laugh her head off. No one paid attention to Onika as she slipped by and into the locker room.

Once she was inside, Onika found her former locker and then turned and faced the mirror. One of these lockers had to be Aaron's girlfriend's.

Onika tried all of the lockers in that area and came across a clean pair of jeans and a T-shirt. She wasn't sure if the clothing was hers, but she swiped it anyway. It looked about her size. She didn't find a purse or wallet. Not even a cell phone. But there was forty dollars in the pocket of the jeans.

Onika hurried to take a shower and wash her hair. She used the body wash and shampoo that was provided for the gym's guests. At first, she resisted the urge to take a long shower, but finally she did, and she enjoyed it. Onika felt like all the Metro crud was washing down the drain, and she was finally clean after her paper towel baths at Starbucks.

She dressed very quickly, trying to make sure she was out before the girl finished her workout. The jeans were somewhat tight, and the T-shirt hugged Onika's full breasts, but she made it work. She felt bad for the girl when she finished her workout and found her clothes missing, and vowed she would return them later.

That hot shower gave Onika a fresh perspective on her day. It's amazing what hot water and clean clothes can do. She was embarrassed that she didn't have clean panties, but she'd use part of the forty dollars for that.

How could Aaron, after all the love she had given him, be so cold to her? She'd chosen him over law school. Over everything. And he'd thrown her away like a bag of trash.

Onika took one glance in the mirror on the way out of the locker room. At least she didn't look as desperate as she felt. Her ponytail, though a utility hairstyle, looked sleek. Her glasses (Gucci frames, thanks to Aaron) made her eyes pop. She looked okay, sort of pretty.

Too bad the only person she was going to meet was the director of a homeless shelter for women.

CHAPTER TWENTY-FOUR

Today . . .

Onika stood in front of the brick town house, contemplating whether or not she should go in. She didn't really have much of a choice—her only other option was sleeping on a Metro car until it stopped running and walking around Gallery Place in DC for the rest of the night.

Why today, of all days, had she finally met a guy who might be worth getting to know? Today had been the worst day of her life. The day she stood on the Metro platform wearing stolen clothes and carrying stolen cash in her pocket. The day she was thinking she'd go back to Aaron, if he'd have her. God, if He was watching, sure had a sense of humor.

Onika regretted balling up and tossing his card. What were the chances that she'd ever see him again? And if she did, he'd probably think she was a jerk for never calling him. He seemed like a regular guy, and Onika had never dated a regular guy. She'd never dated any man besides Aaron, and maybe that was a tragedy all by itself.

When Graham had asked her name, she'd told him the truth. She'd said Onika and not Nikki. She wondered if that meant anything, or if he had simply caught her off guard with his friendly demeanor. Onika was used to men in DC being standoffish and rude. Some of them waited for the woman to make the first move. She hadn't cared really, because she was seeing Aaron and hadn't wanted anyone else.

She felt a wave of sadness come over her. Survival mode was exhausting, maybe as tiring as grief. Her body, soul, and spirit felt weary. Broken. Yes, God sure had a sense of humor to send a seemingly good guy her way, when she'd just been broken.

Onika sighed, knocked on the door, and waited. She wondered what it would be like on the other side. She'd seen stories about homeless shelters on TV. They were full of drug addicts and the mentally ill or women who had been beaten and abused by their spouses.

Onika was none of those, but she was homeless. She had no money, no paycheck coming anytime soon, and nothing that Aaron hadn't given her.

The woman who opened the door looked pleasant enough. The first thing she noticed was her beautiful smile. She had long, thick hair—the kind black women ooh'ed and ahh'ed about when it was as natural as this mane appeared to be.

She was wearing yoga pants and a snug T-shirt that showed off her curves. She was what the boys called thick these days. Well, maybe she was a little more than thick. She probably was more plus-sized, but very fit.

"Hi. You must be Onika. I was starting to think you weren't going to show up. You want dinner?"

"Yes, please."

Nikki's mouth watered, and her stomach rumbled at the smells coming from the brownstone. She hadn't had a real meal in days.

"I don't know what you like, but we're having spaghetti and meatballs tonight. There is also leftover fried chicken, macaroni and cheese, and collard greens. What would you like?"

"All of it?"

Charmayne laughed out loud. "Oh, we are going to get along great, honey. You can go and wash your hands in the bathroom right down the hall."

Onika found the bathroom easily. Once she closed the door, she burst into tears. This woman was already being too kind.

She didn't know her, or that she'd even show up, and now she was feeding her dinner. She hadn't watched her walk to the bathroom to make sure she wasn't stealing. The clothes she had on were stolen, and this woman never suspected her.

Onika opened her eyes and looked at the bathroom walls. They were covered in words. She squinted to read some of the sentences.

I am a gift.
My body is sexy, and beautiful, and healthy.
I have a purpose.
I am mine.

Onika whispered the words the way she and Earlene had whispered Judy's healing prayer at the altar.

She washed her hands and face. Took a damp paper towel and dabbed at her eyes. Her stomach grumbled again, reminding her of the food on the other side of the door.

Onika walked back into the kitchen, and Charmayne pointed to her seat.

"I started making your plate. Or plates. I couldn't fit it all on one."

"You're going to think that I'm greedy."

"No, I won't. I don't think anything about anyone based on their actions. Cream and sugar in your coffee?"

"Yes, both. Thank you."

Onika thought about Charmayne's words and decided that Charmayne was fooling herself. Everybody made judgments about people. People had been judging Onika her entire life.

"I don't believe you," Onika said.

Charmayne's eyebrows shot up. "What don't you believe?"

"You have to form opinions of people. Everyone does."

"I used to."

"What changed?"

"One day I broke all the glass in my home because my husband left me for a man."

"Wow."

"If you had seen me that day, what do you think you would've thought about me?"

"That you had lost your mind."

Charmayne nodded. "Mmm-hmm. I wound up in a psychiatric ward, and I was broken. Stressed to the limit, but my mind was intact. I decided after that to not judge people on their actions. They might be having their worst day."

This broke Onika's floodgates. She was right in the middle of her worst day. In the last twenty-four hours she'd slept on a train, walked outside all night, and stolen someone's clothing from the gym. The sum of those actions painted a horrific picture in Onika's mind.

Charmayne gave her a sad smile and a tissue.

"You're getting tears on your fried chicken."

Onika looked down at her plate and sighed. Suddenly, she no longer had an appetite.

"Eat, honey. I know how it feels for everything to be shattered. If you let me, I can help you put it back together."

Onika didn't see how Charmayne could help other than giving her a roof over her head. The broken things in her life were irretrievably broken. She didn't even want to put that life back together.

She wanted to throw it away and start over from scratch.

CHAPTER TWENTY-FIVE

Charmayne gave Onika a tour of Safe Harbor. It was a fairly large town house with four bedrooms and a finished basement.

"I am surprised that you're not full," Onika said. "There are a lot of women out here who . . . who would need a place like this."

"You mean women who're homeless and abused?"

"Yes, that's what I mean."

"Then why don't you say it?"

"I guess I'm not ready to accept that I'm homeless. My life wasn't supposed to go like this. I got into an elite school and sorority, and got a rich man. I was living the dream. Or I thought I was. I wasn't supposed to end up like this."

"You're exactly where you're supposed to be, and this is exactly the right time."

"Oh, lord. You sound like one of those preachers on television. So God wanted me to get kicked out by my boyfriend and not have anywhere to live? He wanted me sleeping on the Metro? And what about the homeless woman who gave me the flyer for here? God wanted her sleeping on a train, too, and she was old?"

"She gave you a flyer?"

"Yes. Her name was Joyce." Onika reached into the pocket of her jeans and handed Charmayne the balled-up flyer.

"Hmm . . . I've never seen this flyer before. We typically work on referrals only, but when you called, you sounded so distraught that I had to let you come."

"That's very strange that someone would be making flyers for your shelter. Don't you think that's strange?"

Charmayne shook her head. "No, I don't think anything happens by accident, so you're here because you're supposed to be here. Let's go meet Tyshonna. I think she just came in."

Onika followed Charmayne upstairs. She could hear Tyshonna's voice through the bedroom door. It sounded like she was talking on the phone, and the conversation was pretty heated. Charmayne knocked lightly.

Tyshonna threw the door open, gave Onika a quick up-and-down glance, and then smiled.

"Hey, somebody close to my age. You moving in here?"

Onika nodded. "For a little while, until I can get on my feet."

"Girl, that's why we're all here," Tyshonna said with a laugh. "I'm Ty. Don't call me by my whole name like Charmayne does."

Charmayne laughed. "She's a little older than you, but you're right, she's close to your age."

"I'm twenty-six," Onika said.

"Oh dang! You're almost thirty. I'm twenty-one."

Onika had to check herself to keep her jaw from dropping. This girl looked like she was in her early thirties. She had tiny lines around her eyes, the kind that came from smoking cigarettes and spending too much time in the sun. Her teeth were stained and yellow, and she had gray all through her thick black afro.

Ty also had more curves than Onika had ever seen on a twenty-one-year-old. Her hips and behind looked like they'd borne multiple babies, and her heavy breasts looked like they'd nursed a village. Not that anything was sagging or drooping, though. She had a dangerous body. The kind that made a man act like a fool.

"I'm almost thirty, but I still like to have fun."

"Aye!" Ty did a little dance in which she swiveled her hips from side to side. "Finally, a club partner."

Charmayne laughed. "I said I would go to the club with you."

"No. You said you would go to the club if I would go to church with you the next day. That is not a fair exchange."

"I think it is. I would be going somewhere I didn't want to go, and so would you."

Onika considered church. She wasn't in the mood for it. Too much had happened for her to believe there was someone on a heavenly throne looking out for her. She hoped Charmayne's help wasn't contingent on attending a church.

"So is that part of your help?" Onika asked. "Do I have to do the whole church thing?"

"It's not," Ty answered for Charmayne. "If it was, she woulda put my butt out months ago."

"How long have you been here?" Onika asked.

"Ty has been here six months, and she can stay as long as she needs to stay. Maybe she'll tell you her story."

Ty was suddenly sheepish and looked at the ground. "I don't want to keep telling that story."

"One day, when you're on the other side of this, you'll tell that story to anyone who will listen," Charmayne said. "You know what happened to me."

Ty nodded. "And you got past it."

"Yep. It's a process. You'll make it too."

Ty perked up a bit and grabbed Onika's hand. "Well, I might as well show you our room now. Since we got all sentimental right then."

"Yes, you did. Next time give me a warning when that's going to happen."

Charmayne laughed. "We don't always know when we're going to have our moments."

"You just wait," Ty said. "You're going to be having moments, too. You can't live here and not have epiphanies and break-throughs."

Onika smiled but didn't reply. She didn't want an epiphany or a breakthrough. She just needed a little help until she started her job. She wasn't at rock-bottom. She'd just lost a man in whom she'd placed too much trust.

She wasn't broken. Judy and Earlene had made her unbreak-able.

CHAPTER TWENTY-SIX

Graham had spent the entire weekend checking his phone for a missed call or a text from Onika. She hadn't reached out. Not once. Something deep inside had told him she wouldn't.

"What's wrong with you this morning?"

Graham looked up at his friend, Lorne, who had probably stopped at his desk for their morning coffee run. Graham checked that he had his wallet and work badge, then got to his feet.

"Nothing. I'm ready."

On the way to the elevator, Lorne smiled, winked, or spoke to at least five women. They all gave him call-me-maybe glances. Graham didn't know how Lorne did it. Lorne was an all right looking dude, but nowhere near as polished as Graham. If Graham had to guess, Lorne probably hadn't been to the gym since the first day of January, when he'd made a resolution to work out.

Lorne whistled contentedly on the elevator. He was probably counting up all the tail he was gonna tap.

"How do you do it?"

Lorne laughed. "You always ask me this, but then you don't believe me when I give you the answer."

"'Cause that answer is not the truth. You have a secret cologne you spray on in the morning? A voodoo ritual you do at the house? What?"

"I told you. I look at every one of them like I want to take them to bed. Fat, homely, skinny, old, and young."

"But that's because you do want to have sex with all of them."

"True. But never let a woman tell you she doesn't want to be the object of a man's desire. She just doesn't want to be disrespected."

"I'm not like you. I don't want to sleep with every woman I see."

"You ought to get your testosterone levels checked. That ain't normal."

Graham shook his head and laughed as they exited the elevator in the lobby, where their other friend, Craig, was waiting for them.

"I was about to leave y'all," Craig said. "Y'all know Pat be on my case these days."

"She should be on your case. You don't do any work," Lorne said.

"Neither do you, but some of us aren't lucky enough to have a frat brother for a manager."

"Don't hate," Lorne said. "Just ask me for help."

"You hear this fool?" Craig asked. "I'm gonna help you to a knuckle sandwich."

"Violence in the workplace," Graham said. "I won't be a part of it."

"So Lorne texted me and said you were looking destitute this morning," Craig said. "What's up?"

The story was embarrassing, but they were all friends. Plus, maybe they could help.

"Met a girl on the Metro platform. Fine as all get out, sense of humor. Gave her my card. She didn't call."

Lorne and Craig erupted in a cacophony of sounds. It was a mixture of laughter and scorn as they clowned him at full force.

"You gave her your card?" Lorne asked. "You were supposed to get her number, fool!"

"No chick is about to call you first."

"Y'all think I don't know that? I was working up to it. There wasn't enough time. The train was coming."

"So you continue talking on the train, then."

"I was getting on the Green. She stayed for the Yellow."

"So you got on the train, while she stood on the platform? My brother . . ." Lorne shook his head like all of their African ancestors were disappointed in Graham.

"You should've waited until she got on her train. Maybe even changed courses and got on her train."

"That sounds like stalking and menacing."

"It sounds like she wasn't all that fine," Lorne said.

"She was. I wanted to propose right there on the platform."

"What did you just say about stalking?" Craig asked. "You sound creepy as heck."

"Forget I mentioned it."

"Did you get her name?"

"Onika."

"Onika what?"

"I didn't get her last name."

Lorne and Craig groaned. Graham wished he had a time machine. Then he could go back and conquer the way he should've conquered. Slay the way he should've slain. Maybe he did need his testosterone levels checked. His inner caveman was nowhere to be found.

"That's why he's gonna end up with Leslie's thirsty self," Craig said. "You might as well go on and take her out on a second date."

Now Graham groaned. Leslie was their office's desperado. She wanted a date at all costs. Graham had run into her at a church men's conference. She said she was volunteering, but Graham thought she was shopping. He'd had coffee with her afterward, and they did some PG-rated flirting on their Facebook accounts. It wasn't much of anything in Graham's opinion, but she told her friends at work that they'd gone on a date.

"I'd do her," Lorne said.

"We already discussed this," Graham said. "You and I are very different."

"For real, though. She isn't bad looking. A little bit beyond thick, but not sloppy. No kids. Good job. She's doable."

Graham was sure Lorne would have a field day with him saying he didn't just want to do someone. Well, sometimes he did, but recently he'd been wanting more. Leslie wasn't bad; she just wasn't more.

"Maybe you can find Metro girl. Onika is a weird name. You might luck out and find her on social media."

"Already looked. Vapor. Zilch."

"Maybe she was a mirage," Lorne said. "A figment of your lonely imagination."

Or maybe he just had to find her. DC was big, but he had time. If it was meant for their paths to cross again, they would. And next time he'd conquer and slay. Or at least get her phone number.

CHAPTER TWENTY-SEVEN

Graham sat at his desk, staring at the computer screen, try-ing to make sense of the report that he was supposed to brief his manager on at their morning meeting. He couldn't concentrate because he couldn't stop thinking about his dream from the night before.

He'd dreamed about Onika.

And it wasn't one of the dreams he usually had after a very long dry spell. It wasn't X-rated at all. He dreamed about spend-ing time with her. They were at a baseball game, eating hot dogs and cheering on the Nationals. He remembered her laughter, and the warm kisses she placed on his cheeks. It had felt so real.

And now he couldn't stop thinking about it. He had to find her but had no idea where to start. He had her first name.

He'd done the obvious already. After he got off work on Monday, he went to the same Metro station, hoping to catch a glimpse of her. He would chase her down, run behind the train if he had to, but he was getting her number. But she wasn't there. He'd waited for hours, even sending up little prayers that God would send her back his way.

Graham felt a little obsessed about Onika, and he wasn't sure if that was a good thing. But he couldn't help it. She'd made a tremendous first impression on him. The mother of all first impressions.

"Graham. Graham!"

Graham looked up from the computer screen. Leslie stood there, holding a plastic food container. A strange scent came from the little plastic bowl. It smelled vaguely of food.

"Leslie. Good morning."

"Good morning. Did you have breakfast yet? I made a hash-brown casserole, and I thought you might like some."

Leslie tilted the bowl toward Graham so he could see the brown, greasy, cheesy gelatinous blob of something. It didn't look like a casserole. It looked like something a hazmat team would need to dispose of.

"Oh, I did have breakfast. I had a green smoothie on the way to work."

"A green smoothie? That's not food. You're a grown man. You need sustenance to get through the work day. Try it."

Graham cringed as Leslie scooped some of the goop into a spoon and thrust it in his face. She didn't seem to be planning on moving until he took the bite, so he did. It tasted worse than it looked. Like cold Crisco and flour with too much salt and too much pepper.

"It's good," Graham lied. "Just leave the rest here, and I'll finish it up."

"Or you could come and join me in the break room. We can have breakfast together."

"I wish I could, but I've really got to get this briefing ready for my meeting at nine. Maybe another day this week, okay?"

Leslie let out a frustrated sigh. Graham knew she was tired of him avoiding her, but he'd never told her that he wanted to date. He wasn't interested in hurting her feelings, but he wasn't interested in her. At all.

"I know what it is. You don't really want our coworkers in our business. I get that."

"We don't have any business."

"Graham. You were the one in my Facebook inbox. Don't try

to act like I'm delusional and making this stuff up. You were trying to holler at me, and as soon as I said yes, you started tripping."

"Leslie, I'm sorry. I really have to get ready for this meeting, but let's talk about it later. Maybe go to happy hour or something."

"Really?"

Graham cringed at the excitement in her voice, but it also made him sad that she was that eager. That was really messed up.

"Sure, but as friends. Don't go telling everyone we're dating. I don't mind us being friends and hanging out."

"You're saying you're not interested in me?"

Crap! Graham watched tears well up in Leslie's eyes. He didn't have time for this. Hadn't asked for this.

"I'm not saying that. I'm just saying we don't know each other well enough for all that."

"Okay. I'll text you later. I'm gonna just leave your breakfast right here. You can eat it while you get ready for your meeting."

"Thanks."

Leslie walked away with a little bounce in her step. It made Graham shudder to think that his non-promise put it there.

Graham's computer chimed indicating an instant message from Lorne.

LOOK AT YOU. GIVING WATER TO THE THIRSTY.

Graham frowned and clicked the message closed. Lorne wasn't funny, and he didn't have time to verbally spar with him this morning.

Graham peered again at the report and came up with a few talking points from the information. If his mind wasn't a hundred other places, he would've been able to write something stronger. Actually, his mind wasn't in a hundred other places, it was only in one place, with only one subject—Onika.

He had to find her.

CHAPTER TWENTY-EIGHT

Onika sat in Charmayne's office having her one-on-one session. It was one of the rules Joyce had warned her about. Three sessions a week to talk about her goals, plans, and dreams for the future. She wasn't thrilled about it, but she'd do whatever it took to keep a roof over her head for the next few weeks.

"So you've got a job lined up."

"I do. It doesn't start until the end of August. I wish I had more options, but I was stupid and didn't start my career right out of school when I should've. It was probably the only job I could get."

"So how many paychecks do you think you'll need before you're able to get an apartment?"

"I'll be bringing home about three thousand dollars a month gross, so probably no more than a month or so."

"Where do you plan to live? DC?"

Onika shook her head. "Probably not. I may have to commute in from District Heights or Hyattsville. Somewhere I can afford."

Charmayne smiled. "You do have it all planned out, don't you? It's like you don't even need me."

"I wouldn't say that." Onika remembered that harrowing night on the Metro. She didn't want to relive that.

"Well, I know one way I can help. Let's get your wardrobe together for your first month at work. We can't have you looking crazy in front of the children."

Onika smiled. She wondered what kind of clothing Charmayne could procure. Surely not the designers she was used to, but she no longer cared about that.

"I'm a size two, and I'll take anything you've got."

"A two, huh? Well, I may not have much of a variety. It seems like the majority of the stuff that's donated are clothes for bigger women. The women at my church always donate after they go on diets and lose tons of weight."

"Nobody donates when they gain weight, though."

Charmayne burst into laughter. "No, they don't. You know how we do. We save the small clothes until they go out of style."

"You know, I had a huge wardrobe when I was with Aaron. Huge. My closet was the size of this room."

Onika was surprised at herself for offering that information. It sounded strange saying Aaron's name out loud. It sounded like a demon's name. Maybe she wouldn't say it again.

"Is that your ex-boyfriend?"

Onika nodded. "He asked me to leave. We'd been together since the summer of my freshman year of college."

"He asked you to leave. You lived with him?"

"Yes. I couldn't believe it, but I had no choice. Everything was his."

"You didn't have to leave right away. He would've had to have you evicted. Whether your name was on anything or not. He didn't have the right to just put you out of his house."

Onika hadn't even thought about the legalities of what Aaron had done. She just knew that he was moving the next chick in, and she didn't want to be there when that happened.

"It's okay, now, I guess. I've found you."

"Did he hurt you, Nikki? Abuse you in any way?"

She shook her head. "No, it wasn't like that. Aaron had issues, but I had something to do with it, too."

"What do you mean? What were his issues? You take blame for what happened to you?"

Onika frowned. "Is one of the rules here that I have to tell you all my business?"

"No, that's not a rule."

"Okay, good, because I don't really want to talk about what happened with Aaron. I loved him for many years. We loved each other. I still love him, I think, but it's over now. I just don't want to talk about it."

"You don't have to do anything you don't want to do. If you don't want to talk about your relationship, that's your business, but I'm here to help you. I don't just run a shelter. I'm a licensed counselor. I know that when I was going through my worst time, I leaned on my counselor, and she helped me see the light at the end of all that darkness."

"Like you're helping Ty."

"I think I'm helping Ty, but God is doing most of the work."

Onika cleared her throat and stared straight ahead. She didn't want to go there about prayer, and God.

"Do you have a problem with God, Nikki? Every time I bring up church or God, you get quiet."

"I don't have a problem with what anyone believes. I went to church when I was little. I'm just not into it now."

"Really? Why?"

Onika wasn't about to sit up there and tell Charmayne about all her unanswered prayers, so she remained quiet. She wasn't going to tell her anything about Judy, Earlene, or Goldsboro, North Carolina. That was not her business. All Charmayne needed to know was that she was a girl who was down on her luck and with nowhere to go.

"I see," Charmayne said. "Let's just keep the focus on getting you into the workplace and into an apartment."

"Perfect."

The sooner Charmayne realized that Onika didn't need fixing, the better. She needed present help, and that was all. Other than that, she was okay. She'd survive Aaron, just like she'd survived growing up with Judy. No need to bring church or anything else into the mix.

CHAPTER TWENTY-NINE

Onika woke up with one thought on her mind. Restoration. She did not want to have Aaron back, but she sorely missed her life. She looked over at Ty sleeping in the other full-sized bed in the room and immediately got annoyed. She was *not* supposed to be living like this. She was supposed to be living fabulously. She was doing that when she was with Aaron, but it was his money that provided that life. Her mistake.

She lay in the bed, strategizing about her future. The teaching job wasn't going to get her where she needed to be, not at all. There would barely be enough money to live. It would not be enough for vacations, clothes, and jewelry. She deserved those things in her life. She'd had them once, and she'd have them again.

When she'd left Goldsboro for Robinson all those years ago, she'd wanted to be a lawyer. Being a teacher was a suggestion from Aaron, probably because he didn't want her to continue in school for another two or three years.

Onika made a grunt-like sound and then wished she hadn't. She didn't want to wake Ty. She didn't feel like talking.

She'd been so dumb, falling into Aaron's trap that way. Onika wondered if the trap had been set since the first day. No. She couldn't believe that there hadn't been love there. They had had too many good times. It was the abortion that had done it, and that couldn't be taken back.

She threw off the light comforter, used the bathroom facilities, and then went downstairs. She made herself a cup of tea and booted up the computer in the library, entering the password Charmayne had given her.

The first thing she did was check her e-mail. She had a message from her bank, stating that she had been the victim of a cyber-attack and that her money would be back in her account in twenty-four hours. This time she did make a loud noise. She shrieked.

Onika shook her head when she heard the patter of feet running down the hall. What was she going to tell Charmayne? Would she make her leave if she found out that she had nine hundred dollars in the bank? Maybe, but Onika settled on telling her the truth. Not the whole truth, but this truth.

"Are you all right?" Charmayne asked as she poked her head in the office door. She was still wearing her morning head wrap and robe.

"Yes, I'm great. The bank is giving me my money back. I can buy some clothes for work."

"Oh, perfect. If you want, we can still check my sources first. You'll need your cash for emergencies, or if you just want to have a cup of coffee. You don't have to spend it on clothes if you don't want to. We can figure that out."

This felt too much like when she was a little girl in Goldsboro. Everyone had teased her for only wearing hand-me-downs. All of her clothes had been donated at the church. Her first-day-of-school outfit, no matter how cute, had always already been worn by one of her classmates, and they made sure to point it out.

But what choice did she have? Charmayne was right. Onika couldn't be down to zero cash, ever again. That had left her too destitute.

"You're right. I'll check out your leftover fashions."

Charmayne tilted her head to one side and furrowed her

eyebrows. "They are nice things, Nikki. I wouldn't give you something that I wouldn't wear myself, and I am quite stylish."

"I know. That is usually how every hand-me-down is presented. These are *nice* things. It doesn't change that someone owned it before. Someone else wore it, sweated in it, and shed their skin cells in it."

"You've got a thing about hand-me-downs, then."

Onika scoffed. "Told myself I'd never wear them again when I started college. I know better than to say never, though. So here I am. Hand me the hand-me-downs."

Charmayne stepped into the office and sat on the small love seat. Onika's upper lip trembled with irritation. She didn't feel like having a one-on-one right now. It was the middle of the night, and she wanted to keep strategizing.

"What do you want out of your life, Nikki?"

"Right now? I want to get some paychecks under my belt and get my own place."

"No, I mean, take yourself out of survival mode. What do you *really* want? What would make you feel joy?"

"I guess having all the things I thought I'd never have. Enough money so that I never have to worry. Property. Status."

"Those things will bring you joy?"

"Not having those things will bring me the opposite of joy."

"I know people who are joyous and fulfilled without any of those things," Charmayne said.

"I am not them."

Onika felt her anger rising. Charmayne had everything she wanted and needed. Onika did not. Why was it so hard to understand that Onika wanted her finances in order and, more than that, to have a life of abundance?

"There's nothing wrong with wanting to be rich."

"No, unless you have to sacrifice your values to get there."

"Is this lecture time?" Onika asked.

Onika was not trying to get sassy with Charmayne, but the woman needed to understand a few things about her newest resident. First, that she wasn't like these other homeless strays she'd taken in.

"Am I bothering you? I don't mean to. Typically, when a woman finds herself in your position, she wants someone to listen and help. I'm just trying to be there for you."

"I can't tell you how much I appreciate what you're doing for me," Onika said. "I didn't have anywhere to go. You saved me from sleeping on the Metro, but I already have mentors."

"But you didn't call any of them when you got in trouble?"

Onika closed her eyes and exhaled slowly.

"I haven't told anyone about this. No one in my circle knows what's going on with me."

"Listen to what you're saying, Nikki. You have mentors, but you've not let them in to help you at your lowest point. Are they truly mentors? Do you truly have anyone guiding you?"

"I am an adult. I guide me."

"Baby, you're here. Let me keep reminding you of that. You're *here*. You need help whether you want it or not."

"And I am accepting the help that I need. I just don't want you to think that this is some sort of intervention, because it's not."

Onika knew people like Charmayne. They'd visit her at her grandmother's house when she was a girl. They felt better about themselves when they did something for the poor and unfortunate. It wasn't about doing good; it was about them feeling gratified. At this point, she didn't mind how Charmayne felt about what she was doing. All she needed was three hots and a cot and to be left alone.

"When you're ready for someone, maybe God, to intervene on your behalf, you let me know," Charmayne said. "Be ready to go to the clothing storage this afternoon."

"Are you angry with me?" Onika asked. "I didn't mean to make you upset."

"No. Not angry at all. Prayerful."

Onika gave Charmayne a fake smile as she pulled her robe tightly around her body and left the library. She wished she could tell her to save her breath, because nine times out of ten, those prayers wouldn't be heard or answered. She was wasting her time.

CHAPTER THIRTY

Graham stood on the Metro station platform where he'd met Onika. It was Friday, and the same time. Maybe lightning would strike twice and she'd appear before his eyes.

He'd dreamed about her every night since he'd met her, and in every dream they were laughing and having a good time—something he rarely experienced with the women he dated. Not that he didn't try to have fun. They were either too saved, too serious about getting married on the first date, or too concerned about how he could help them.

Graham had no problem with salvation, marriage, or helping, but when these things were too evident from the first date, it usually spelled trouble.

"Hey, Graham!"

It was Leslie's voice booming across the platform. She thought he didn't know, but she had taken to waiting around for him to leave, even though she came in a whole hour earlier than he did. Instead of walking out at the same time, she'd let him leave first and then speed out to catch up with him. He knew she was doing this, because Lorne had spotted her sprinting toward the Metro station three nights in a row, and all three nights she'd cornered him on this exact same platform. He'd thought about changing his station, but this is where he'd met Onika, and he dldn't want to risk not getting a chance to see her again.

Graham turned slowly to face Leslie. "Hello."

"Why'd you speak all formally like that?" Leslie asked between huffing and puffing.

"I wasn't being formal," Graham said. "I was just saying hello."

"Oh."

"You know, you don't have to sneak up on me at the Metro station. If you want to walk over with me, I don't have a problem with that," Graham said.

He knew this was basically an invitation for her to walk with him every day, but he didn't want her making a fool out of herself in the office. She already had a reputation for being desperate. No need to add anything to that.

"You want to walk me to the train? You carrying my books, too?" Leslie asked.

Graham guessed she was supposed to be flirting, but she was so confused. He had just saved her from looking stupid, but now he was the one chasing?

"I won't carry your books or walk you to the train, but I don't mind walking over with a coworker."

"Coworker? That's all?"

"You're my sister in Christ."

Leslie's jaw dropped. "Thanks a lot, Graham. I'm sure God is pleased with you."

Graham wasn't sure how pleased God was with him. If He was happy with him, then why didn't he send Onika his way again?

"So, did you hear Chrisette Michelle is doing a show at Fourteenth and Park next Thursday? We should go." Leslie casually said this, like Graham hadn't just brushed her off.

"I already have plans. Maybe next time."

Leslie opened her mouth like she had a rebuttal, but then didn't say anything. The silence became tense and awkward because Graham wasn't saying anything, and Leslie stared at him like she wished he would say something.

Finally, Graham ended the torture.

"Leslie, it is really okay that I don't want to date you. It doesn't mean there's anything wrong with you. I just am not interested."

"I know there's nothing wrong with me. Why wouldn't you be interested in a beautiful woman who has no children, loves the Lord, and is single? I should be asking what's wrong with you."

There it was. Graham knew the accusation would come at some point. He didn't want her, so he must be gay. He wanted to start with, *"First of all, you are nowhere near beautiful . . ."* but of course he didn't. That would be cruel and uncalled for, even though she'd been cruel to him.

"There's nothing wrong with me, either. I love beautiful, single, and saved women. I don't really care whether they have children or not. I just don't feel that way about you."

Right on schedule, her eyes filled with tears. After the gay accusation and then the rebuttal, this is what usually comes next. Tears of desperation that result in guilt, and the guy taking the girl out on a pity date. Sometimes at the end of the pity date, there is some awful guilty sex, and then the awkward, not-gonna-call phase.

Graham handed her a tissue and prepared to stand his ground. He noticed that they'd garnered a little audience on the Metro platform, mostly because Leslie's theatrics were pretty obvious. He scanned the crowd for a coworker. Dang. There was one. She worked on the fourth floor, maybe Human Resources. She was watching intently.

"Leslie, tears won't work, and you don't even need to shed them. I'm nowhere near the only guy on the planet, and I'm not the guy for you. Stop it."

"Now you're trying to act like I'm desperate for you or something."

"I'm not trying to do anything. Actually, I am. I'm trying to catch a train. Or I was. I'm outta here."

Graham fled up the platform stairs. He'd walk a few blocks to a different station, even though it was as hot as the devil's armpit. Everyone thought it was easy being a single man with no kids, good credit, and a good job. He was supposed to have his pick of women

But no. His luck always sent him women like Leslie. Super sanctified, holy, saved, single and…crazy.

No one like Onika had ever crossed Graham's path. She was a lightning strike, a rare phenomenon. Graham had to stop thinking about Onika. He had to put her out of his mind. Rare phenomenon that she was, chances were she wouldn't strike again in the same place.

CHAPTER THIRTY-ONE

Charmayne watched Nikki move around the kitchen, silently fixing her breakfast. The foods she put on her plate—eggs, a slice of avocado, and fruit—were probably the reason she had such a nice body. But Charmayne went ahead and enjoyed her shrimp and grits while she silently prayed.

Charmayne knew that God had sent Nikki to her for a reason, just like he'd placed a crack addict named Letha in her recovery room at the psychiatric ward so many years ago. She'd been able to help Letha not just see Jesus, but get clean and free from drugs. Letha was a testimony now. A cashier at a grocery store, and a mother.

Nikki was different. Stubborn. She was unwilling to admit that she needed anything except a roof over her head. There were some wounded places there, but Nikki wasn't letting anyone near enough to help fix them.

Charmayne kept praying for the right words as Nikki sat down at the table.

"Those grits look good," Nikki said.

"Have some."

Nikki raised an eyebrow and smiled. "That food will stick to me and have me out here looking like a video vixen."

"I don't see a problem," Charmayne said with a laugh.

"Well, that's how it starts, and then I'm on high blood pres sure medication and diabetic like my grandmother."

"Is your grandmother still alive?"

Nikki sighed but did not respond. So the grandmother was a sore subject.

"You don't talk about your family much."

"I don't have any family," Nikki snapped.

"Oh. I have my mom and my sister, and they are crazy. We have our good times and bad times."

Silence again from Nikki. She chewed her food and stared, like she didn't care how much talking Charmayne did. She wasn't biting.

"So your guy was your family, then. He was everything to you."

"Charmayne."

"Yes?"

"What are you doing? Is this another one-on-one? Are you trying to fix me again?"

"I'm trying to get to know you. You're living in my home for a while. Can't we be friends? This is what friends do. They ask questions about each other."

"Okay. You're right. Friends do get to ask each other questions, but you don't get to give any advice. I don't want advice."

Charmayne inhaled sharply. This would be a challenge. Giving advice was in her DNA. It was her nature. It had made her a shrewd businesswoman in her life before Safe Harbor, and it made her an anchor for all of her friends. Not giving advice would be like not drinking water.

"I will try my best not to give you any advice. I get that you don't want it."

"The times you do slip up and give me advice, just know that I probably won't follow it. Or if I do, I won't let you know that I did."

So, not just issues with her family. Issues with control and autonomy. Did that come from her childhood or from what happened with the boyfriend? Charmayne couldn't tell which and, of course, she couldn't ask. Nikki couldn't stop Charmayne from analyzing her for the sake of prayer.

"Do you mind if I pray for you?"

"You mean like put oil on my head, hold, and squeeze my hands until I get a breakthrough? Yeah, I mind."

Charmayne laughed. So, some sort of Pentecostal upbringing then. This was important. Nothing wrong with being Pentecostal, but maybe she needed a different take on Jesus to get through this time in her life.

"No, I meant pray for you in private. Not with you. About you."

"I can't stop you from doing that, can I? That's between you and God."

Charmayne nodded. "It is. I guess I just wanted you to know I was doing it."

"Why? So that when everything turns out all right, I can give God the glory?"

This might be harder than Charmayne thought. "You do believe in God, right?"

"I do, but I don't think He cares what happens to me or to you. He's got plans, and He's a creator, but as far as my little life, He doesn't care. Life is about what you get out there and do for yourself."

Charmayne had absolutely nothing to offer. She'd never been so far removed from God that she thought He didn't care about her. And what was worse, Nikki seemed to really mean this and not be troubled by it.

"So, you're just going to work harder? Hustle harder?"

"I haven't been working at all these past five years. This is where I've made a mistake. I trusted a man to take care of me, like an idiot. He was already rich. I should've gotten mine first and then spent his."

"You're going to get rich being a teacher?" Charmayne asked.

"Of course not. But right now, I need money, and teaching is what I can do. I will figure the rest of it out later."

"Well, I guess you have a plan then."

"You keep making me have these sneak one-on-ones."

Charmayne chuckled.

"Let me ask you some questions now," Nikki said as she popped a bite of avocado in her mouth.

"Okay. Ask me anything."

"Why do you do this? The shelter thing? I was expecting this to be run by a church, or maybe a social worker, but it's just you, letting women live in your town house. Why?"

A simple question with a complex answer. "Because we all make bad choices sometimes. I just want to be a help."

"So go work at a shelter. Go volunteer somewhere. You don't have to open up where you live to a bunch of strangers. What if one of these women has mental illness? What if they're criminals?"

"I've had both. I told you, all of the women who come through my door are by referral. You're the first to show up, and no one sent you."

"The homeless woman who was on the train with me—she sent me."

"Right."

"You still haven't answered the question," Nikki pressed. "Why not volunteer? Why do you do this extra part?"

Charmayne cleared her throat. "You're going to think this is stupid, because you don't think God cares about what we do."

"Try me."

"I opened Safe Harbor because God told me to."

Nikki rolled her eyes. "Oh my goodness. I was hoping for a real answer. God opened up his mouth and told you to open a shelter and let anybody come live in your house?"

"Yes, He did. It came to me in a dream. Even the part about moving to Washington, DC."

"So you had a dream about it, and you up and did it? Are you kidding me?"

"No. I wasn't doing anything else really. I was running a little job-placement program that was doing some good, but all of my clients were placed, and I was just a ball of energy with no one to help. When God told me to move, I sold my house in Ohio and bought this town house."

"You bought a four-bedroom town house in DC? This place must've cost you a grip."

"No, it didn't. A woman who attended my church owned it, and she died. Her family was happy to sell it to me. I only paid two hundred and fifty thousand dollars."

Nikki's jaw dropped. "You have got to be lying. You should sell it right now. You could get a million dollars for it. That would be a come up for real."

"I don't want to sell it. God blessed me with it so I can help people."

Nikki scarfed down the rest of her food. "I don't understand you right now, Charmayne. You are a different kind of person. Never met anyone so crazy, but I'm glad I met you. Maybe some of your good luck will rub off on me when I get ready to go apartment hunting."

"Not luck. God. He can rub off on you and Ty too. Go to church with me on Sunday, and you'll see."

Nikki jumped up from the table and rinsed her plate in the sink. "No thank you, but if you hear of any more old ladies selling town houses, let me know."

"I sure will."

Charmayne was worried that she had her work cut out for her with Nikki, and that she'd have very little time to accomplish anything. Then Charmayne corrected her thinking.

Nikki wasn't her work at all. She was God's work. And He had all the time in the universe to accomplish exactly what he wanted.

CHAPTER THIRTY-TWO

"**S**o do you want to go out or not?"

Ty had been pestering Onika about going to a bar, and Onika had successfully avoided giving a response until now. It was Friday evening, and both of them were in their shared bedroom that Onika hated. Onika had almost asked Charmayne to give her a room by herself since, at the time, she and Ty were the only girls living in the house.

"Go out where?" Onika asked, knowing it would be somewhere she didn't want to go.

"We could bar hop on U Street. I just need to get out of here and let my hair down."

"U Street isn't really my cup of tea. Too much walking, and the crowd is sketchy at times. No thanks."

"Well, where do you like to go?"

Onika couldn't reply without sounding like a snob, but where she liked to go were places Ty had probably never been. She liked to go to yacht parties in Annapolis and private parties in hotel penthouse suites. Bars and clubs were for people trying to be seen. Onika preferred parties where people didn't need to be seen. They were already known or had been properly introduced to the circle.

"Why do you like bars?" Onika asked, instead of responding

to Ty's question. "Hot, sweaty, bodies all grinding on one another. Weak drinks and men who pretend to like you all night so they can dance up on you and then don't ask for your number? What's so good about that?"

"I like dancing. I like having a few drinks and flirting. I don't want to give anyone my number anyway."

Onika considered going. She was sure she wouldn't see any of the social climbers she'd known for the past few years at any bar on U Street, and getting out of the house would be better than staring at the walls and whispering affirmations to herself.

"I don't have anything to wear," Onika said, remembering that she'd just gotten work clothes from Charmayne's leftover treasure chest. She'd bought a few pairs of sweats. Nothing she'd ever wear in public.

"Maybe I have something you can wear," Ty said, which made Onika burst into laughter. Nothing that fit on Ty's dangerous curves would fit on Onika's slim ones.

Ty went into the closet and emerged with some jean leggings—they didn't even look like Ty could fit one of her thighs into them—and a cut-off baby-T that said "juicy." Neither were items that Onika would ever be seen in public wearing.

"This is cute," Ty said when she noticed Onika's apprehension.

"I'm not saying it's not cute. I'm saying it's not me. It's not my style."

"And we aren't going to any of your bougie hangouts either. This works perfectly for where we're going."

Onika took the clothes from Ty and looked at them again. "I can't wear this. Let me look and see what you have for myself."

Ty stepped out of the way so that Onika could look into the closet. "You sure have a lot of clothes for a homeless girl."

"I wasn't really homeless when I came here. I was in trouble. Needed to hide."

"But you want to go out to a bar?"

Ty closed her eyes and exhaled heavily. "I am going crazy. I've been inside for six months, hiding from my pimp. Well, he used to be my pimp. He's not anymore."

Onika could tell that Ty had had a rough life, but she didn't look like a prostitute. She looked like she should be attending a community college or auditioning for a play on Broadway. She had an edgy, grungy look, but not the same desperation that Onika had seen in her mother.

"How did you end up with a pimp?" Onika asked, still feeling a bit of disbelief.

"Started out stripping. I was eighteen and making a few hundred dollars a night. Up to a thousand on a good night. D'Angelo promised me at least five thousand a week. He delivered on that promise."

"So you just decided one day to become a stripper? How'd *that* happen?"

"You're super nosy for someone who doesn't share anything about herself."

"You're right. I'm sorry."

"You tell me something, and I'll tell you the rest."

Onika shook her head. "That's okay. You don't have to tell me your secrets. I was out of line for even asking."

"Come on. The rest is the most interesting part."

Onika turned to face Ty, holding a red miniskirt and black blouse. It was the most conservative outfit she could assemble from Ty's wardrobe, and still it was risqué. The blouse had a deep V in the front that would show every inch of Onika's cleavage.

"I'll tell you something," Onika said. "I had an abortion behind my boyfriend's back."

Ty stared at Onika for a long, silent moment.

"That's it?" Ty said, breaking the silence.

Onika frowned deeply. She'd never admitted that to anyone, not even Aaron when he had proof.

"Yeah, that's it. Sorry, I don't have anything more shocking."

Nothing that she'd tell Ty or Charmayne, anyway, no matter how hard she pressed her for the information.

"Well, I guess if that's all you have, it's a big thing for you."

Onika nodded. "It is. Never told another soul about it, but somehow my boyfriend found out."

"Your boyfriend or your ex?" Ty asked.

Onika shuddered. Had she said boyfriend when referring to Aaron? Of course, it was a habit. They'd only been broken up a few weeks.

"My ex-boyfriend. He's definitely moved on."

"Well, I started stripping because I was a runaway. Left home at fourteen."

"Really? Where's home?" Onika didn't want to imagine why Ty ran away, and she wasn't about to ask. Onika wasn't going to share any more of her story to hear about it, and she was sure that it was depressing anyway.

"Cleveland. That's how I got connected with Charmayne. My auntie knows her from way back. They used to go to the same church."

"Well, no wonder Charmayne thinks you're going to visit her church."

"I don't have a problem with going to church. I just don't want to go right now. I'm not ready."

"I'm never going," Onika said. "When I get my life together, it's not going to have anything to do with God. It's going to be because I handled my business."

God had never answered any of Onika's prayers. He hadn't dropped any spiritual guidance down on Judy, and she'd never gotten off drugs. No matter how many prayers they'd sent up, nothing had happened.

"Well, I'm not like you. I need help getting my stuff together," Ty said.

Onika clutched the borrowed clothing to her chest and sighed. She didn't even have an outfit to wear on a night out, but she was bragging about how she handled her business.

"Are we going out or not?" Ty asked. "Stop looking all crazy and sad. Go get dressed!"

"We're going. Let me get dressed."

Onika wasn't feeling much like partying, but she hoped she'd be good company. It wouldn't hurt to see some new faces. And maybe she could help Ty forget her troubles even if she couldn't forget her own.

CHAPTER THIRTY-THREE

Graham didn't know what he was thinking, letting Lorne talk him into going out, especially to the bars on U Street, which were frequented more by college students than by career-minded folk. The bar Lorne had picked out felt like a basement. It *was* a basement, complete with big pipes in the ceiling and in the middle of the dance floor.

The music was all over the place. When they first walked in, eighties rap was playing, but then it quickly switched to nineties pop and some light rock from an unidentified decade. No matter what the DJ played, the dance floor stayed packed, making Graham think that these partiers probably had had some pills dropped in their weak cocktails.

"It's jumping, right?" Lorne asked as he sipped his third vodka and cranberry juice in less than an hour.

"It's something," Graham replied. "I don't see any women I'd talk to, though."

"Man, you're crazy. There are plenty of women here for me."

"Enjoy. I'll be over here. At the bar."

Lorne downed the rest of his drink and slid back out to the dance floor, where a group of three barely legal girls pulled him into their circle. Graham laughed at his homeboy, but wished that he'd stayed home.

Until he looked up and saw Onika. Her hair was different. In a little bun on top of her head. But the glasses were the same. The curves were the same.

He nearly dropped his drink. Was she real or a mirage? The tall tattooed girl with her was real. He couldn't imagine Onika being friends with a girl who looked like her. Then he realized he had no idea what kind of friends she might have, because he didn't know anything about Onika, outside of the fact that he was inexplicably drawn to her. Maybe that's why she hadn't called. He wasn't her type. She was probably into guys with tattoos, ballplayers, and rappers. Not a square government employee.

Graham tried not to stare at her. He kept looking away, but then couldn't help but look again. She laughed at something her friend had said. He wanted to make her laugh.

Should he send her a drink from the bar? Guys always did that in movies. Old guys or rich guys, and it always worked. The girl was impressed. Would it be creepy in real life? Probably.

Graham was about to just chalk it and convert his fantasies about Onika into fables. Tall tales. Fairy tales.

But then Lorne swooped in like the villain that he was. He was holding another drink, and his damn pinky was in the air. Graham growled under his breath. She couldn't fall prey to the Lorne Ranger.

Graham slammed his now empty cocktail glass onto the bar. He moved quickly, closing the space between himself and Onika. He focused. Forgot about Lorne and the tall tattooed friend.

He only saw Onika.

Graham stopped in front of her and panicked for a moment. He hadn't thought of anything to say. The picture in his mind crumbled and was replaced with a video reel of Lorne cracking up laughing.

Then Graham relaxed. All she could say was no.

"If I was you, I'd stay away from this guy. He's here for all the girls."

Lorne threw his free hand into the air and frowned. "Really? You putting a brotha out there like that?"

Onika and her friend giggled for a bit, and then she recognized Graham. He could tell because her laugh faded and she looked uncomfortable.

"Onika, right?" Graham asked. "I thought I'd never see you again."

Lorne's mouth formed an O shape, and his eyes widened. "This is her?" he asked. "I thought you made her up."

"I was starting to think maybe I did, too."

"Good seeing you again, Graham. This is my friend, Ty. We were just about to leave, though."

"No, we weren't!" The friend clearly wasn't loyal. Onika bit her bottom lip when her girl threw her under the bus.

"We were until you started talking to this guy, but maybe now we're staying," Onika said. "How have you been?"

Graham didn't know if he wanted to reply. He didn't want to force her to have a conversation or make her feel awkward. But another part of him wanted to never let her out of his sight again. God had let them cross paths twice. It couldn't be an accident.

"It's cool if you don't want to talk to me," Graham said. "I get it. You didn't call, so I get it. I just wanted to let you know I noticed you again. I'm happy I laid eyes on you twice in a lifetime."

Graham turned to walk away.

"Wait," she said.

He turned to face her but said nothing. She could do all the work. He'd already embarrassed himself enough.

Onika's friend took Lorne by the hand and dragged him toward the dance floor. It was great timing too, because he was definitely about to say something and probably spoil the moment.

"I am sorry I didn't call."

"Why didn't you?"

She glanced at the ground and then back up at Graham.

"I kinda threw your card away right after you gave it to me."

Graham stared at her, unblinking, his jaw somewhat slack. She hadn't just not called; she'd dismissed him from jump. Graham shook his head. He wasn't about to beg this girl for anything. Her loss.

"But now I'm thinking I shouldn't have," Onika continued. "Out of all the people in DC, I ran into you again? That's not random."

"So you're going to give me your phone number this time?"

"Um . . . see . . . I don't have a phone."

Graham shook his head and started walking away again. "Yeah, right."

This time she grabbed his arm. "I promise I'm telling the truth. My ex turned off the phone when we split up, and I haven't put any minutes on the TracFone I bought."

"So I can't call you. You can't call me."

Graham wondered what kind of joke God was pulling on him. Then he asked himself, what would Lorne do?

"Why don't we go out now, then?" Graham said. "Let's have our first date right now."

"Here?"

The smile on Onika's face encouraged Graham a bit. "No, this place sucks. Let's go over to Ben's Next Door."

Onika's smile faded a bit.

"You don't like that place?"

She shook her head, but gave no further explanation.

"Let's just go anywhere other than here, then. We can walk down the street until we find somewhere good."

"What about my friend?"

"We can leave her with my friend. She'll be okay. He's one of the good guys."

"I need to check."

Feeling a bit irrational about letting her slip out of his grasp once again, Graham followed Onika over to Ty and Lorne.

"Graham wants to take me out on a date. Right now," Onika said to Ty. "Are you okay, or do you want me to schedule another time?"

Ty stared Graham up and down. Her piercing gaze made him want to check and make sure his fly was zipped.

"I will be fine," Ty said. "Will *you* be okay? What about getting home?"

"Oh, I got it. Nothing to worry about at all," Onika said.

A glance passed between the women, and then Onika smiled and nodded. "Okay. Date time," she said.

Lorne jumped up from the bar with a look of alarm on his face. "Hey, I know you ready to get out of here, but let me holla at you for a second."

Once again, Graham felt nervous about letting Onika out of his sight. She still felt like a flight risk, and Lorne was probably about to say something crazy.

When Graham didn't move from his place next to Onika, Lorne said, "Man, this is a little bit personal. Can we talk over there? We'll be right back. Promise."

Graham followed Lorne to the other end of the bar, with every step fighting the urge to turn around and check if Onika was still there.

"What?" Graham asked.

"Man, be careful. I have a bad vibe about these girls. Why she want to go out with you all of a sudden? And when they were talking just now, it was strange. I think they're scammers or prostitutes. Maybe worse."

"A prostitute? She is not a prostitute."

"Ask yourself why she's hanging with this girl, Ty. Don't they seem mismatched? Where in life would these two girls be friends?"

Though Graham cringed at the thought of agreeing with Lorne on anything, he could be right. Onika seemed like a woman who'd gone to college, probably pledged a sorority and had a decent career. Ty, with all of her tattoos and piercings, gave a different impression.

But Lorne didn't know about Graham's dreams.

"I just don't think it's a coincidence that I found her again."

Lorne shook his head. "Let me guess. God sent her fine self your way. Or maybe fate. Perhaps it was the universe."

The mocking tone in Lorne's voice was unsettling, but not enough for Graham to be dissuaded.

"I'm not stupid, man. I've got my doubts, too, but I would be crazy to pass on this opportunity."

Lorne sighed and signaled the bartender. "Just watch yourself, man. As tempting as it might be, don't sleep with her."

"She doesn't seem like the type to give it up on the first date."

"Maybe not, but her friend is the type to get you off in the bathroom at the club."

"Did you . . . ?"

"Naw, but I could hit that tonight."

Lorne's opinion on this point was pretty useless. He thought he could get in every woman's panties at any time.

"I hear you. I won't lose my mind or track of my wallet. I'm good."

"Okay, man. You're my little brother, so I want to make sure you're okay."

"I'm older than you."

"With women you're like a college freshman. I have a PhD."

Graham shook his head and laughed. Lorne was probably correct, so Graham would keep his guard up, but not high enough that Onika couldn't get inside.

CHAPTER THIRTY-FOUR

Onika narrowed her eyes and stared at the two men debating at the end of the bar. She wished she could hear what they were saying. Lorne's wild hand gestures and Graham's defensive stance told her that Lorne was trying to make a case about something, but what?

When Graham had walked up to Onika, her initial thought was to blend into the crowd and disappear. Partially because she hadn't wanted to be put on the spot for not calling Graham, and partially because she'd thought the conversation would be awkward even if he didn't mention her not calling.

As soon as she'd made the decision not to run away from the moment, Onika had also promised herself that she'd tell him the truth if he asked about her calling. Surprisingly, he hadn't run away.

Onika doubted that he was desperate. He was, by no means, an unattractive man. If it wasn't for her living situation, she would never have thrown his card away.

Graham was so darned nice that he couldn't be true. Most gorgeous men were cocky and arrogant. Like Aaron. No one would ever confuse Aaron with a nice person. He was, at his best, a brilliant alpha male and, at his worst, a condescending jerk.

Onika had never dated a nice guy. She'd only ever dated one other guy.

"He doesn't trust you." Ty said with a chuckle. "He probably doesn't want Graham to leave with you."

"What? Why not? It wasn't my idea to leave. It was his. I should be the one who's worried."

"No you shouldn't. Graham is as square as they come. Back in the day, me and my girls would've run all the game on him."

"Really?"

"Girl. Would've promised him a ménage a trois, and when we got to the hotel, would've knocked him out cold with a pill. Then we'd take his cash, credit cards, and everything else. If he had his Social Security number on him, it would've been the mother lode."

"Wow."

"And as easy as Graham would've been, Lorne would be easier. He thinks he's street smart, which makes him a challenge and a more rewarding takedown."

"You sound like a predator."

"I was. In another life."

Onika wondered what Graham thought of her. It annoyed her that he might think she was a predator, like Ty used to be.

"What are you going to say when he asks to take you home? Are you going to bring him to Safe Harbor?"

"No. This is a first date anyway. He doesn't need to know where I live."

"Not tonight, no, but he will."

"And by then I will have my own spot."

"Hopefully."

"I am not staying with Charmayne past September. I am done sharing a bedroom with another girl like I'm still in undergrad."

"Forget you too, heffa."

Onika laughed. Ty had been trying hard to stop cursing. *Forget you* took the place of another *f*** you*.

"Here he comes," Onika said as Graham and Lorne made their way back.

"You ready?" Graham asked. "I'm in the mood for tapas and wine."

"Yes."

"Are you sure you don't want to make it a double date?" Lorne asked, just as Graham touched her arm.

"If it will make you more comfortable," Onika said, "I don't mind."

"It'll make me more comfortable," Lorne said.

Onika didn't care what Lorne thought. She stared at Graham, waiting for his response. Her last few weeks had been too much. She was heartbroken and homeless.

What she did not need was one more affront to her character. She wasn't some black widow scammer, and if Graham couldn't look into her eyes and see that, then she didn't want to waste any time on him. Her life was already complicated enough.

It was probably too soon for her to be looking at a man anyway. The breakup with Aaron was still fresh. She was still reeling from it and trying to find her footing. A man would throw her off her game again.

"A double date?" Graham asked. "We aren't in high school. I don't need a buddy. Let's go."

Onika smiled. And they went.

CHAPTER THIRTY-FIVE

Graham thought they'd never get out of that crazy little bar and away from Lorne, who didn't even try to hide his displeasure at Graham's decision to leave with Onika. Graham would check him once they got to work on Monday, because that wasn't cool.

"So the tapas spot I like is near the Verizon Center. You want to go there? We could hop the Metro to Gallery Place."

Onika shook her head. "No, not there."

"So no to Ben's Next Door, my favorite restaurant in DC, and no to tapas? Where do you want to go then?"

Onika concentrated for a moment, and then said, "What about the place you were in a hurry to when we met? What did you call it? Poets and something."

"Busboys and Poets. I can't believe you've never heard of that restaurant. There's a few of them."

"I'm not from DC. I moved here after college with my boyfriend. What I know of this area is what he showed me, so I'm really just now starting to explore. I've never even been on U Street."

"What? Every twentysomething in DC knows U Street. You have been deprived. What were you doing for fun? Karaoke in Laurel or something?"

She seemed a little bourgeoisie to Graham, so he wouldn't be surprised if she'd spent her time with the other upwardly mobile black people of Prince George's County in Maryland. She'd be perfect for that scene.

"Karaoke? No. I went to parties in Potomac and on yachts in Annapolis, and I spent my summers since freshman year of college on Martha's Vineyard."

Potomac? Yachts? Martha's Vineyard? Graham wished he could turn back time and take Onika right back to where he'd found her. He'd never be able to live up to any of that on his government salary. Her ex-boyfriend must've been a millionaire.

The silence had become a bit awkward, so Graham blurted, "You want to Metro or Uber over? It's not far."

Onika chuckled. "Or we could just get a cab over."

"Uber is cheaper."

Onika was quiet as Graham pulled up the app on his phone to request a pickup from the independent car service. When he was finished, he looked up at Onika, and she was staring at him.

"What's wrong?" he asked.

"Nothing. How long will the Uber car take to get here?"

"Four minutes."

"Cool."

Onika gazed down U Street and watched a few people walk by. Graham's mind raced. What had he done? Had he made a fatal mistake five minutes into their first date? Of course he had. Her ex-boyfriend, the millionaire, wouldn't have cared to spend a few extra dollars on a cab.

"We can take a taxi if you don't want to wait," Graham said.

She shook her head. "I don't have a problem saving money."

"Okay, so we wait. You said you're not from the DMV. Where are you from? Let me guess. Atlanta? You look like a Georgia peach."

Onika smiled, and Graham felt himself relax a little. All was not lost. Not yet.

"I went to college in Atlanta. Robinson University. It feels like my life began there anyway, so I say correct. You get a gold star. Georgia peach all day."

Graham wanted to venture further and ask where she'd been before college. But she hadn't offered, and he didn't want to make any more mistakes.

"What do you do for the government? Is it top secret?" Onika asked.

"Not secret at all. I write the budgets for my division and several others. Write justifications for spending the taxpayers' dollars."

"That sounds pretty boring."

"You wouldn't be wrong. It's excruciatingly boring. What do you do?"

"I am a middle school teacher. I start a new job at the beginning of the school year."

"So you've got a few weeks of vacation left, huh?"

"I do. If I could afford it, I'd go on a trip."

Graham's eyebrows shot up. Was this part of the con? Was this the first part? Damn that Lorne for planting this seed in his head.

"I haven't gone on a real vacation in a while. I have done a series of staycations, though, and they've been great."

"What's a staycation?"

"When you don't travel far from home. A one-tank trip."

Onika nodded slowly. She seemed to be appraising him again.

"What would you be doing if you weren't at the boring job? If you didn't need money."

He answered without hesitation. "I'd spend more time teaching black kids how to swim."

"That's what you do when you're not working?"

"Yes. Too many black children die every year from drowning."

"I never learned myself. I stay in the shallow end of the pool and right near the sand at the ocean."

"But what if you get caught in a flash flood and get trapped in your car? Or what if you fall off a yacht into the Chesapeake Bay? What are you gonna do?"

"Die."

Onika said the word so matter-of-factly that Graham didn't have an immediate response.

"Or you could let me teach you how to swim."

"I did fall into a lake once when I was a little girl. It scared me pretty badly. Haven't wanted to swim since then."

"What if I told you I could make it fun?"

"There's nothing fun about not being able to breathe."

"But . . ."

"What kind of car does the Uber driver have? It seems like four minutes should be up by now," Onika said.

Graham guessed she was trying to close the swimming topic, but he'd never be able to drop it completely. For the sake of their first date, though, he'd let it go for now.

"That's the driver now. In the blue Corolla."

Onika smiled. "Okay. Let's go hear some poetry."

"And eat. Their food is dope."

When the car stopped in front of them, Onika waited while Graham opened the car door. This shocked him a little, but not much since she wasn't from the DMV. A lot of women he knew would look at a man as though he were crazy for opening a door. He was glad Onika wasn't like them.

Well, he didn't really know what Onika was like at all, but he was going to spend the rest of the evening learning.

CHAPTER THIRTY-SIX

In the car on the way to the restaurant, Onika's mind was full of thoughts. Mostly questions. When Graham had decided to take the Uber car and there was a cab waiting *right there,* she wondered if she'd be able to do this. Date a man who wasn't rich.

Aaron had ruined it for anyone coming behind him, and she'd come upon a millionaire as a college freshman. Most women had their poor boyfriends in college, but Onika had never been on a struggle date. She'd only dated one man, and his pockets were deep.

And why had he brought up swimming? Onika hoped he kept that particular hobby to himself if she decided to ever see him again. She was never going to stand in water that went above her waist, much less purposely put her face under.

That was a sport that Judy and Earlene had ruined for her. She'd only been seven when she'd almost drowned at the church picnic. They'd watched those mean little boys from the church harass her and pull her hair. Thinking about it made the scene replay in her mind.

Rowdy Gerald had said, "This ain't yo' real hair. It's a white lady's wig."

"It is not!" Onika had screamed helplessly as Earlene watched. Judy

was as high as a kite, but Earlene had brought her to the picnic anyway, because July loved barbeque.

"Yeah it is. Look at how nappy her mama hair is," Jerome had said. "How her hair straight and her mama hair so nappy, look like it'll break a comb."

Onika had hurled a small rock at Jerome; he'd artfully dodged it as he continued laughing at her cries and tears. Those two brothers thought they could do anything and say anything, just because they were the pastor's nephews.

"Her mama don't comb her hair," Gerald chimed in. "Crackheads don't comb their hair."

Even at seven, Onika knew exactly what a crackhead was. Her mama was someone who sat around in the corner half the time, and the other half, she sat scratching her arm or asking Grandma Earlene for money or food, or anything that came to mind.

Onika knew it was an insult. And she also knew that none of the adults who were standing around were doing anything to help her or stand up for her. She knew she'd have to stand up for herself.

This time she hurled half a brick at Jerome and caught him right upside his head. He made a noise that sounded like a wounded puppy. Then both boys had rushed her at the same time.

"Wonder what her wig will do when we dump her in the lake? You think it'll fall off?" Gerald asked.

Jerome replied, "Not sure, but let's try it out."

They lifted her into the air, struggling, screaming, and crying. Right in front of her mother, grandmother, and the entire church. No one stopped them.

Well, one person had tried. One of the church mothers had screamed for them to put Onika down, but the boys had laughed.

Maybe no one had expected them to really throw her in the lake. Maybe they'd thought the boys would only scare Onika. It had all happened so quickly, and the events were now dull and blurry in Onika's mind.

But she remembered the terror of water rushing into her mouth, and her not knowing how to push it back out. She remembered the splashing and the feeling of helplessness. Then she remembered hands pulling her from what felt like a dark abyss but was just a small lake.

They'd done CPR on her right on the grass next to the lake. They were still pressing on her chest when she'd regained consciousness. Judy had been standing in the crowd of spectators, like she didn't have anything to do with her own child.

Onika had turned her little head toward Judy and stretched her hand out in Judy's direction. Judy hadn't even acknowledged the gesture.

And Onika, for the rest of her life, would probably remember the words Judy had said as she'd stood there scratching her arm and her head.

"Why don't she know how to swim?"

No one had answered Judy's question, because the answer was absurd. Onika didn't know how to swim because her crackhead mother hadn't ever been sober long enough to teach her.

Now, Graham wanted to teach her to swim. Well, he'd have to get her in the water first.

CHAPTER THIRTY-SEVEN

Busboys and Poets was packed more than usual for a Friday night, and the hostess told Graham they'd be waiting half an hour for a table. This seemed to annoy Onika, as Graham watched her go from expressionless to a peeved grimace. He glanced down at her feet. Heels, of course.

"Why do women do this to themselves?" Graham asked as he led Onika to the waiting area, since there were no open seats at the bar either.

"Do what?"

"Wear shoes that pinch your feet. Then you have an attitude when you have to stand for a long time."

Onika looked down at her feet and let out a little laugh. "I have always hated heels. I would much rather be wearing flip-flops right now."

"Let's go over to CVS. There's one right down the street. We'll be back before they call our names."

Tears of laughter pooled in Onika's eyes. "You want me to wear drug store flip-flops?"

"No, I want you to stop making that face."

Graham took Onika's hand and led her to the door. He told the hostess they'd be right back. The store was less than a block away, which was probably for the best, since Onika was already wobbly.

Inside the drugstore, Graham grabbed a red basket from next to the door.

"Why do you need that for one pair of flip-flops?" Onika asked.

"We may see more things we need."

Giggling, Onika asked. "Like what, Graham? We came here for flip-flops."

"Like this. Cough drops." Graham grabbed a bag of lozenges and dropped them in the basket.

They walked down the aisles searching for flip-flops, but finding all kinds of interesting things to add to the basket. Onika picked up a pink bell with a picture of a cherry blossom on it and WASHINGTON, DC, painted on the bottom.

"This is pretty, right?"

"It is. Let's get it," Graham said.

Graham was happy they were laughing. She'd seemed incapable of merriment after that somber ride over to the restaurant. He thought it had something to do with her learning how to swim, so he'd stay away from that topic until she was his girlfriend.

"There they are. The flip-flops." Graham pointed down the aisle with summer and picnic supplies.

Sure enough, there was a discount pile with leftover American flags, water toys, and noisemakers for the Fourth of July. And there were red, white, and blue flip-flops with stars and stripes. Patriotic, plastic, and huge.

"These are a men's size ten," Onika said as she picked them up.

"Is that the only pair?"

They looked all over the shelves for another pair, but that was it. One enormous pair of flip-flops for Onika's tiny feet.

"What size shoe do you wear?" Graham asked.

"Six. A women's size six!"

"It's either these, the heels, or we walk to another drugstore. There's a CVS or a Walgreen's on every other corner. I'm sure we won't have to walk far."

Onika shook her head. "See, the thing is, I already got my feet prepared to go into flip-flops. They won't last another block. They might not last to the front of this store."

"Well, put them on now, then. You can carry your heels around."

Graham held Onika steady while she ditched her sparkly heels and slid her petite feet into the flip-flops. Graham was surprised that her toes were just neatly cut and buffed, but plain. He'd expected polish as sparkly as her shoes.

"Don't look at my toes. I didn't polish them because I was wearing closed-toe shoes."

"No judgment from me," Graham said. "Maybe our second date can be pedicures."

"Two things. Second date? And you get pedicures?"

Graham nodded. "I know you're going to say yes when I ask. And yes, I get manicures and pedicures. And I hate when people say it's metrosexual. I think it is just personal grooming."

Onika simply smiled. She didn't say yes to the second date. But she also didn't say no. Graham felt encouraged.

"Let's pay for this stuff, so we can make sure to get our seat at Busboys and Poets."

Graham placed all of their random items on the counter. Cough drops, the bell, some chopsticks, and a bag of peppermint puffs.

"She's wearing flip-flops, too," Graham said to the cashier, a young guy who stared at Graham and Onika like they were on drugs.

After Graham paid for everything, he handed Onika the bell wrapped in a bit of newspaper.

"Put this in your purse," he said, "so you don't forget to take it home."

Onika swallowed hard and took the bell from his hands. All of a sudden her good humor seemed to fade away. First, the swimming thing, and now mentioning what? Home? Graham bit his bottom lip and wondered if Onika was too high-maintenance for him. He didn't know if he could deal with a girl who was up, down, up, down, then up again, and then back down in the dumps.

When they got outside the drugstore again, Graham asked, "Are there certain things you don't want me to talk about? I mean, we'll be having a great time, and then all of a sudden you're quiet and not laughing anymore."

"I don't know what's wrong with me this evening. I'm not usually this dramatic. You brought up a bad memory about the swimming. Honestly, I was just wondering where in my place I'm going to put my bell. There was nothing to it."

"Are you sure? I don't want to trigger anything else except fun."

"Trigger? You think I'm nuts, don't you?"

Graham shook his head. "No crazier than the last woman I went on a date with. She's definitely crazier than you."

"Well, as long as you know it could be worse."

"Absolutely. And you're way hotter than her, anyway. Hotness goes a long way."

"You'd date an unstable girl if she was gorgeous?" Onika asked.

Graham pulled the door to Busboys and Poets open for Onika before he answered the question. The answer was complex, and he was trying to think of a way to deliver it without sounding like a Neanderthal.

"In the past . . . I may have spent time with an unstable girl a time or two, but I wouldn't call it dating."

"What would you call it then?" Onika asked. Her face shone with curiosity.

"It was just sex. I'm not proud of it, though. That was when I was a much younger man."

"You're not that old now, are you?"

"Thirty-one," Graham said. "Do I look younger?"

"You do. I turn twenty-seven this year. So I'm closing in on that dirty thirty."

The hostess alerted Graham that their table was ready, so they followed her through the insanely packed restaurant to their seats. Although it was only a few steps, Graham got to enjoy the sway of Onika's hips in her red miniskirt. He could watch that movement all night. Those hips could hypnotize him, have him saying "your wish is my command" and then spending all he had to make those wishes reality.

He pulled out the chair for Onika, and she gave him an appreciative smile in return. Her smile was just as hypnotic as her body. Her laugh was an opiate. He'd been high all night long.

Graham was smitten.

"I think we should plan our third date, too. I want to get on your calendar before the school year starts," Graham said.

"So pedicures for the second date. Which needs to happen quickly, because you already saw my feet," Onika said.

"Tomorrow, if you want. I can come and pick you up."

"Send me the spot and I'll meet you there."

"You don't want me to know where you live?" Graham asked.

"Not particularly, no. We just met."

Graham processed this for a moment and then just accepted it. He wasn't a woman. He didn't know what it felt like to not feel safe all the time. So he'd let that one go.

The waitress came to the table, and without even glancing at the menu, Graham knew what he was having. He'd had the shrimp and grits dozens of times and had never been disappointed.

"What's good here?" Onika asked.

"Depends on what you like," Graham said. "Are you a meat and potatoes girl, fried chicken, or seafood?"

"All of the above, but tonight I think I'm in the mood for seafood."

"The shrimp and grits is very good," the waitress said. "It's my favorite."

"Then I'll go with that," Onika said.

"I was going to order that, too. It's also my favorite," Graham said.

"Well, then give me something different. The pan-fried catfish," Onika said.

The waitress nodded and walked away to put in their orders.

"Why couldn't we eat the same thing?" Graham asked.

Onika smiled. "Well, that's a waste. You only ever need three bites of food to experience a meal. We should experience two different entrées."

"Three bites of food to experience a meal? Did your nutritionist tell you that?"

"Nah. My grandmother used to watch Oprah. I heard a guest on the show say it, and then I tested it out. It's true. After three bites, I really don't need to eat any more."

"Did you live with your grandmother?"

Onika paused. Oh man, had he brought up another sad situation?

Finally, she nodded. "I did. Never met my dad. My mom died when I was little."

"I wish I had known my grandmothers. They were both gone by the time I was born," Graham said, trying to get the focus off of Onika's situation. He didn't want her to become somber again.

"Do you have any kids?" Onika asked.

"No. Do you not date guys with children?"

"It's never come up before. I've only ever dated one guy. But I don't think I'd like to be with a man with children."

Onika was still talking, but Graham's eyes had glazed over. Her lips were moving, but the sound wasn't making it to Graham's ears. Did she say she'd only ever dated one guy? That didn't make sense at all. As fine as she was, she had to have had guys lining up as soon as she hit puberty. How could a pretty girl make it to twenty-seven and only have had one boyfriend?

"Are you leaving out the boyfriends you had in high school? You're talking about you've only been in one adult relationship?"

Onika shook her head. "No. I mean I've only ever dated one guy. Met him in college. None before that, and none after. My grandmother was strict. Church of God in Christ strict."

"Oh, now I get it. I was about to ask you if you were born a woman."

"You went way left, didn't you?"

Graham shook his head. "No, I didn't. I would like to think I would be able to tell, but . . ."

"I know some transwomen that you wouldn't know were born with the same parts you were. I went to school in Atlanta. I've seen it all."

The conversation was starting to make Graham uncomfortable.

"You go to a COGIC church here in DC? There are quite a few good ones."

Onika laughed out loud and almost choked on the water she was sipping. "I don't go to church, Graham."

"Oh, are you an atheist?"

Graham wished he hadn't asked the question as soon as it came out of his mouth. He had no idea what he would do if the answer was yes. He was unapologetically Christian and had never dated a woman who didn't believe in God. He definitely couldn't marry one, and his fantasies about Onika had carried him all the way to their wedding day.

"No, not an atheist. I just don't do church."

"Do you think it's just because you haven't found the right church?"

"I don't think I need church or a preacher to believe in God. I believe there is a higher power, because this universe is amazing, but I don't think we can pray to Him and get what we want."

"I believe when we pray we don't necessarily get what we want, but we get what we need."

Onika said nothing else. She sipped her water and gazed at Graham. She didn't seem to be bothered by the lack of conversation, but Graham panicked. He'd come across yet another touchy subject on the first date. He would be lucky if he made it to the second. He'd be lucky if she didn't get up and walk out.

But she wasn't moving.

"You know, you're not even my type, but I like you," Onika said, breaking the silence.

"How do you know what your type is if you've only dated one guy?"

"It takes me a while to choose, but when I do, I stand by my choice. The guy I dated was my type in every way but one."

"What was the one thing?"

"He needed more than one woman at a time. He was poly-amorous."

"Is that the new word for it now?" Graham asked. "I thought it was just called being a player."

"Except that he wasn't. He didn't lie about it."

Graham sat back in his chair, astonished. He got the feeling that he was in over his head with this woman. She seemed damaged and complicated, yet enlightened. She was insecure and maybe a little arrogant. She was modern and sophisticated, but the southern charm shone through. She was a series of beautiful contradictions.

And he wanted her.

After dinner, Graham and Onika moved from the table to one of the more comfortable couches to enjoy the spoken word. None of the poets moved Graham more than the feeling he got from having Onika's thigh graze his on the love seat. Onika cozied up against Graham, and her perfume intoxicated him. He wanted to kiss her neck, which was elegantly exposed, but he restrained himself, unsure if the touch would be welcome and not wanting to extinguish the new flame.

"This is nice," she said after the third poet shared words about love and loss. "I'm glad I came."

"Me too."

Graham's words came out throaty and rough, because it had been a long time since he'd been pressed against a woman he liked this much. He didn't want to do anything to ruin the moment or embarrass himself.

"You okay?" she asked.

He only nodded and pulled her closer. Instead of kissing her, he settled for inhaling her hair. The curls smelled like coconut oil.

When the set was over, Graham sighed. He didn't want the date to be over. He wanted to keep cuddling with Onika until the sun came up.

They left the restaurant, and although it was late, they strolled down the street. Not hand in hand, but close enough that their arms grazed every few moments.

"It's late. I should probably be heading home," Onika said after a few minutes of peaceful silence.

Graham hailed a cab for Onika and opened the door for her. She gave him a chaste, sweet hug before she climbed into the backseat. Graham reached into his pocket and pulled out thirty dollars.

"This should be enough to get you anywhere in the DC area, plus a tip."

"Thank you. I need your number again, though. I will call you as soon as I put minutes on my phone."

"Last time I gave you my number, you threw it away. How do I know you're going to call me this time?"

"You just have to trust me."

Graham took another business card out of his jacket pocket. He grinned, kissed it, and handed it to Onika.

"Don't on purpose lose this one."

She didn't reply. She kissed it back and tucked the card into her cleavage.

Graham's heart raced; it threatened to burst right out of his rib cage as he watched the cab take off down the street.

CHAPTER THIRTY-EIGHT

Onika was in the greatest of moods when she went into Charmayne's library to check her e-mail. She'd woken up late and was still in her pajamas and bunny slippers. She'd woken up with Graham on her mind.

He was everything she wanted except that he had a normal job with a normal income. This wasn't everything, but it was something. Onika had become accustomed to a certain way of life, but how long could she hold onto that without sounding and seeming ridiculous? She was in a women's shelter with a roommate who used to scam men when she needed money. Onika didn't know where she found her audacity to dismiss Graham because of his lack of baller status.

The first e-mail was from her new job. Time to get into work mode. She was ready to know she had cash and a regular paycheck.

Onika nearly dropped her coffee mug when she saw the words "We regret to inform you."

They had rescinded their offer. Through a haze of tears, Onika read that they had lost their grant funding and had to make budget cuts. She was welcome to apply again next year or try for a substitute position later in the year.

Onika didn't realize how loud she was sobbing until Ty poked her head into the library.

"What's wrong?"

Onika shook her head. She couldn't articulate how desperate she felt. The job was her way out. With the beginning of the school year about to start, there was no way she'd be able to get a teaching job.

What was she going to do for a whole year?

Onika opened her mouth to speak, but Ty had disappeared. She returned a few moments later with Charmayne, who was still in her robe and head scarf.

"Honey, tell me what's wrong."

"The job fell through."

Charmayne threw one hand in the air. "Is that all? I thought someone had died, the way Ty came running into the kitchen."

"It sounded like someone died," Ty said.

"Is that all? This job was everything! I can't leave here without that job."

"I know. We can work on that. It's not the end of the world. You are still sitting here with activity in your limbs, so you still have time to figure it out."

"Activity in her limbs?" Ty asked.

"Yeah, they say that at church. It just means you're still alive," Onika said. "Church folk love talking in riddles."

"Do we? Well, riddle me this. Who isn't getting any of these Belgian waffles I'm about to make?"

Ty laughed. "Her. I want food from the kitchen ministry. I'm not mad at Jesus."

"I don't want any," Onika said, "and not 'cause I'm mad at Jesus. I have to find a job."

"That can wait," Charmayne said. "Come eat first."

Charmayne's tone was loving instead of mocking. Deep down, Onika knew she was right. It wasn't the end of the world, but it sure felt like it. Although she was tempted to stay right there at the computer, Onika got up and followed Charmayne and Ty into the kitchen.

The ingredients spread out on the counter didn't look like any kind of waffles Onika had ever had.

"I thought you were making Belgian waffles," Onika said.

"I am. They're my gluten-free, sugar-free, banana waffles."

Onika rolled her eyes. She didn't want anything healthy right now. She wanted something decadent. She wanted a crispy, golden, flaky, buttery waffle. Not this organic thing that was about to be assembled.

"I should've warned you," Ty said. "She's a health nut. She ropes you in on the first day with all that yummy food. When you get here, she gives you pastries, shrimp and grits, and all that, and then out come the vegan meat crumbles."

"I'm not that bad, but I do it mostly for me. I used to be over three hundred pounds."

Onika looked at Charmayne's solid frame, which wasn't thin but nowhere near fat. Onika couldn't tell by looking at Charmayne that she used to be extremely large. It made sense that she was such a good cook then. All the big women Onika knew were good cooks.

"Sit down while I make the waffles. I want to tell you about a job opportunity that just came across my desk that is probably perfect for you, with your background in teaching."

A job opportunity? Charmayne should've opened with this news. Then Onika wouldn't have been so averse to the breakfast.

"What is the job?" Onika asked as she sat at the kitchen table.

"It's a tutoring job, and it could turn permanent," Charmayne said.

Onika's spirits sank again. A tutoring job wasn't going to pay enough money for her to move out of Charmayne's house.

"How much does it pay?"

"Twenty dollars an hour, but you'll have to tutor anyone who walks through the door. School kids, adults, some homeless . . ."

"Homeless people?" Onika asked with a bit of contempt in her tone.

She was contrite before she could even inhale her next breath.

She was homeless. For a moment, the comforts of living in Charmayne's home had made her forget her own plight.

"There but for the grace of God, go I," Charmayne said.

Tears formed in Onika's eyes. "What is wrong with me?"

"You forgot," Ty said. "It's easy to forget here with Charmayne. We're not on the street. She's an angel."

"No. Not an angel," Charmayne said. "Just someone who's been broken before."

Onika pulled herself together and wiped her eyes. "So, a tutoring job? What would I be expected to teach?"

"Some of the adults are studying to take their GED, and the children need help with their homework. A lot of the children are homeless, too. They live with their mothers in a hotel across the street that the city runs."

"That sounds like a *good* job," Ty said. "Let's trade."

Ty worked as a dishwasher in a church-run soul food restaurant. She worked from breakfast until early evening, and sometimes she didn't just do dishes. She also cleaned the bathrooms and vacuumed the dining room.

"That would be a negative," Onika said.

Ty sucked her teeth. "You're a hater. I can tutor people. I know how to read and do math."

"Not sure they'd hire you for this one," Charmayne said.

"I know. My felonies are gonna haunt me forever, it seems," Ty fussed, with her arms folded tightly across her chest. "Sometimes it just seems like it would be easier to go back to hustling. I'm not gonna do it, but I think it sometimes."

"You don't ever have to go back to that. And, I told you, we're working on your record. You weren't a juvenile, but you were so young. The lawyer said she may be able to convince the court that you were basically being trafficked and you did everything you did to survive."

"That's not a lie," Ty said. "D'Angelo would've killed me if I didn't run every scam I could on every john."

"I'm praying about it, and God hears me when I pray," Charmayne said. "You won't be in that kitchen for long, but since you're in my kitchen now, can you hand me the cinnamon out of the cupboard?"

As Ty reached on a high shelf for the spice, her baby T-shirt rose up in the back, exposing an ugly, ropelike scar. Onika shuddered at the thought of what might've happened to Ty when she was selling her body. It made her think of Judy, which depressed her all over again.

"So you two went out last night, but came back separate. What was that about?" Charmayne asked.

"Nosy," Ty said.

"She sure is," Onika quipped. "We don't ask her what she does with her time. Where she goes every Thursday night for a few hours. I suspect something boring like prayer time at the prayer house, but it could be a secret rendezvous."

"A rendezvous with Jesus. You're right, except it's not prayer service; it's women's Bible study."

"So you say," Onika said. "I prefer to believe you have some hot, muscle-bound twentysomething providing you with the ul-timate in stress relief."

"No ma'am." Charmayne waved a spoon at Onika and frowned. "There is nothing a man that young can do for me."

"So her muscle-bound man is in his fifties then," Ty said, joining in on the fun. "Is he fully gray or does he have salt-and-pepper hair?"

The corners of Charmayne's mouth twitched with a faint smile, but she didn't respond. She started loading ingredients into the blender.

"Oh, shoot. Ms. Charmayne has herself a church boo. Is he a health nut like you? If he isn't, please don't make him anything with twigs and berries. Make him some of those shrimp and grits."

"I don't have a church boo," Charmayne said.

Onika nodded slowly. "Oh. She has a church crush, then. He just doesn't know about it."

"Enough of this. What happened with you two last night? My mama used to always tell me to stay with my girlfriends at the party or the club."

Onika sighed when she could tell Ty was getting ready to tell Charmayne what went down. She wasn't sure if she wanted to have Charmayne analyzing everything yet. Or if she wanted her to know about Graham at all.

Graham might be nothing. He could be an anomaly she'd never see again. She thought about his card tucked away in her purse. She wanted to call him but didn't want to seem too pressed about it, so she'd decided to wait until the afternoon.

"I think Onika might have a new boyfriend," Ty said. "She met the perfect guy in the Metro and ran into him again at the bar. He took her on a date right then. He wasn't about to let her get away."

"Really?" Charmayne asked.

"He was fine, too. All chocolate and buff. When he was walking up to us, I was hoping he was about to holla at me, and then he came through and swooped her up. Left me at the bar with his ole busted friend."

Onika couldn't help but laugh at Ty's recollection of events. She still felt a little bad for leaving her with Lorne, but it worked out fine anyway.

"You didn't like the friend?" Charmayne asked.

"Um, no. These two dudes don't even seem like they should be friends. Graham, Onika's guy, was super polite. She said he didn't even try to kiss her at the end of the night. The one they left me with tried to get me to give him some in the bathroom."

"Ugh, that's disgusting," Onika said. "You didn't, right?"

"I can't believe you just asked me that. Of course I did."

"What?" Charmayne dropped her spoon on the floor.

Ty laughed so hard she cried. "I'm just playing y'all."

Charmayne scowled at Ty as she retrieved the spoon from the floor and rinsed it. She sprayed oil on the waffle iron so that it could preheat. Onika was still skeptical that the bananas, eggs, coconut flour, and oats was going to make a good waffle.

"I'm not talking to her for the rest of the day," Charmayne said. "Onika, what happened with your date?"

"It was nothing major. I met him in the Metro on the same day I came here. I was actually on my way. Threw his card away, because I really wasn't in the mind-set for meeting a man. Then it was so weird to run into him again, so I gave it a shot. Nothing else to tell."

"Are you going to see him again?"

"He says he's taking me for pedicures. I haven't called him yet, though."

Ty shook her head. "Why haven't you called him?"

"It's morning. I had to check my e-mail, and now I have to figure out my life. I don't have time to call a man."

"That's a pretty odd coincidence—to run into the same guy like that, in all of DC," Charmayne said. "What does he do?"

"His business card says program analyst. I don't know what that means, but he works for the government."

"It means he probably gets paid a decent amount of money to do absolutely nothing. If I didn't have these felonies, I'd try to get a government job," Ty said. "Maybe he can hook you up."

"Maybe."

Onika hadn't thought about Graham helping her get into government employment. She really did prefer to teach, but if he could get her a job to tide her over until the next school year, she'd gladly accept it. Especially if it paid more than substitute teaching and tutoring.

Charmayne poured some of the batter onto the sizzling waffle iron. "Did you like him, though? Would you care to see him again?"

Onika shrugged. "He was nice and everything, and we had a great time. I just . . . wouldn't want to date him seriously right now. I have nothing, not even my own roof over my head."

"Funny, he came along at this time, though," Ty said. "You can't ignore that. It could be the universe pulling you together."

"I don't know if I believe any of that. I just know that I enjoyed his company, and I haven't decided if I'm going to call him. End of story."

"No happily ever after?" Charmayne asked. "It would be nice to hear one of those for a change."

"It would, wouldn't it?"

Onika drew circles in a little pile of coconut flour that had landed on the counter. Her life probably wouldn't have a happily ever anything, because it hadn't started with "Once upon a time." It had started with, "It was a dark and stormy night in the crack den."

Calling Graham would just be inviting her catastrophic situation into someone else's world. She'd be bringing her struggle into his boring, albeit peaceful life. Why should she do that to him? No, she wouldn't call him.

Then she thought about how much fun they'd had in the drugstore picking out flip-flops. It was the dumbest thing ever, but it was so hilarious. She'd been so at ease with him in that moment. And he didn't even flinch when she said she didn't go to church, even though clearly he was a churchgoer. She didn't feel the same judgment she felt with most Christians.

Graham was different. But even if he didn't judge her for being homeless, Onika was embarrassed about it. A homeless Robinette. The alumnae circle would be ashamed of her. Mrs. Richard would probably faint right before going straight into cardiac arrest. Onika didn't want to even think about her sorority. Her sisters would help her find a place to stay, because it would be the right thing to do, but then they'd shun her and suddenly stop inviting her to events.

"You do need a pedicure," Ty said. "Your feet are busted. Maybe you should call him. He's paying, right?"

Charmayne chuckled as she sat the first waffle in front of Onika. "Try it."

Onika poured syrup on the waffle and dug in. She didn't know what to expect when she put the first bite in her mouth. Actually, she did know what she expected. She'd thought it would be edible. Instead, it tasted like a coconut-flavored foot. A human foot that had been in a gym shoe for too long. Probably after it ran a marathon. Yes, it tasted like both feet of a marathon runner who'd just crossed the finish line.

Reflexively, and instinctively, Onika spit the mouthful of food back onto the plate. Her body knew it was being poisoned, and it threw all manners out the window to save her life.

"Why does it taste like that?" Onika asked.

Charmayne gave Onika a worried glance. "Like what?"

"Like feet. Foot fungus. Why?"

Meanwhile, Ty was cracking up again. "I'm glad you were the guinea pig this time."

"I'm sorry," Charmayne said. "This was my first time making them. It was an experiment. Maybe it was the buckwheat. Maybe it was the lemongrass."

"Didn't you have a recipe?"

"No. I just went based on another recipe I had and did a couple substitutions."

Ty took a fork and cut a piece of the waffle off for herself. When she bit it, her reaction was the same, if not worse.

"That waffle was an epic fail," Ty said.

"No. A fail is never trying out something new. A fail is me sitting in my bed and wondering how a banana lemongrass waffle might taste without ever making it. An epic fail is doing nothing, but expecting your life to be incredible."

"I feel like she's turning this into a sneak lesson," Ty said.

"I'm not sneaking at all. I'm telling you the truth."

True or not, Onika was annoyed by Charmayne's constant dispensing of mother wit. It seemed to be the price paid for living under this roof.

"Do you have children, Charmayne?" Onika asked, feeling sorry for the lectures they must've endured if she did.

"No, I'm afraid I don't," Charmayne replied.

This was the first time Onika noted a dejected look on Charmayne's face. What was the story there? Had she given her child up for adoption? If she had, running her shelter must be penance for that. Onika had encountered very few people, if any, who were kind just for the sake of kindness. Most of them were making up for something. Repenting for something. Doing penance for their sins, and hoping their God forgave them.

"You've still got time," Ty said. "You're not that old."

"I'm not old, but I'm too old for babies. I don't want to be chasing around a teenager in my sixties. There's no telling what kind of technology they'll have then. I can barely keep up with Facebook."

"So we're it, huh? Or women like us who find ourselves in the most unfortunate circumstances," Onika asked. "You've got a savior complex."

Charmayne chuckled. "I know a savior, that's all."

Onika got up from her barstool and took a loaf of bread from the pantry. "I'm making peanut butter and jelly for breakfast, if that's okay."

"That's fine. I think these waffles can't be salvaged," Charmayne said.

"You calling or what?" Ty asked. "Do you think we've forgotten since you sneakily changed the subject?"

"Charmayne is sneaking with her lectures, and I'm sneaking and keeping my business to myself. Quid pro quo."

"Well, I don't care if you call the man or not," Charmayne said, her tone snippy. "I was just making conversation. You need to care about getting a job and being able to sustain yourself, not about having a social life. You can keep that other business to yourself. I don't care about it."

Onika became quiet. Charmayne had been so kind since Onika had shown up on her doorstep that she almost *did* think of the woman as some kind of a saint. She had gotten out of pocket with Charmayne on more than one occasion, and the last thing Onika wanted to do was get on her nerves to the point where she ended up back on the street. Her stomach flipped at the thought of sleeping on the Metro again.

"Charmayne, I was just being a sarcastic jerk," Onika finally said. "You can give me whatever lecture you want. Just please let me stay for a little while longer. I-I don't want to be back out there again."

Onika hated her voice cracking and her eyes filling up with tears. She despised feeling so utterly helpless. Her well-being literally depended on Charmayne's goodwill and mercy, but Onika had been taking it for granted and, crazy enough, almost feeling like she was entitled to kindness. Like, if there was a God, then He owed Onika a miracle after dealing her the worst hand ever.

Charmayne's anger, no matter how mild or how small the infraction, reminded Onika of her vulnerability. If Charmayne woke up one day and decided that running a house for misguided women wasn't her calling in life, then Onika would be out of luck and out of time.

Charmayne stepped from around the kitchen counter and pulled Onika into a hug. "You don't have to worry about leaving here until you're ready."

"I'll interview for that tutoring job," Onika said. "And let me know how much I have to contribute to the household."

"I don't want you to contribute anything. You should save all of your earnings."

"Okay, thank you."

Onika broke the embrace with Charmayne and started to walk out of the kitchen. She wanted to be alone to lick her wounds. Then she realized what had been troubling her and turned around to face Charmayne.

"Out of all the homeless women in DC, why do I get your help? Why me? It's been bothering me since the first day. That one full night when I was out there, and the day before, I saw so many women who looked like they'd been homeless for years. And then, after one night, I end up in someone's home with job opportunities."

"Do you want to trade places with one of them?" Charmayne asked.

"No, of course not."

"Then I don't understand what you're asking."

"My boyfriend broke up with me because I had a secret abortion and he found out about it. Terrible, right? That I could choose to end the life of a child he wanted."

Ty made a "humph" sound. "Is that the real reason, or is that what he told you?"

"It's what he told me, but I always knew he had other women. That was part of our relationship."

Charmayne shook her head. "I have no idea why you ended up here. I already told you that I'm not even sure how you got the information, because I don't know the woman or anything about that flyer. What I do know is that now that you're here, you're welcome."

"I just want to . . . I don't know . . . pay a bill or something."

"This is a gift," Charmayne said. "All you have to do is accept it, and be thankful."

"I am."

"Do you think Graham might be a gift, too?" Charmayne asked. "Maybe you don't think about why or how you met up twice. Your being here is a coincidence as far as I'm concerned."

"He sure looks like a gift," Ty said. "No. He looks like he's gifted. You should find out."

The mood in the room lightened considerably once the fear of returning to homelessness was lifted.

"It's not my birthday, but I'm open to gifts any day of the week," Onika said. "I'm gonna call him."

CHAPTER THIRTY-NINE

Onika called.

She agreed that with so much wrong happening to her, Graham could be something right. But as the phone started its fifth ring, she became doubtful. Maybe he wouldn't answer.

He picked up right as she was about to disconnect.

"H-hello?"

Onika heard scuffling and struggling in the background.

"What's all that noise?" She asked.

"Onika? You called."

"I did. Good morning. Did you think I wouldn't?"

"I was sure you wouldn't, but I am so glad I was wrong. What are you up to today?"

Onika's first thought was to share her problems with him. To tell him about her job situation. She restrained herself, though. She wanted him to bring his weightlessness to her day.

"I'm just sitting around, looking at my feet, wondering if I was gonna get that pedicure anytime soon."

He laughed. "We can go later today, if you want. I am teaching a swimming class at the recreation center. You want to meet me here and we can ride over?"

"You stopped your swim class to answer the phone?"

"Of course. You're the only one who would be calling me. I am glad you put some minutes on your phone."

"Oh, I still haven't gotten around to that. I am calling from the house phone."

"You have a house phone? You could've given me that number."

Onika heard the skepticism in his voice. He still thought she was playing him, and she understood why. He had no reason to think she wasn't.

"I didn't know the house phone number."

"Oh. Okay."

That was true, but Onika imagined how it sounded to him. Of course, it sounded like a lie, but she couldn't tell him that she hadn't known the number that day on the Metro platform because she hadn't moved into Charmayne's house yet.

"When is your class over?" She asked.

"In an hour. Then I have to shower and get dressed, so an hour and a half."

"What's the address?"

Graham told her, and Onika jotted the address down, then smiled. She would change his mind about her. It surprised her that she cared so much about what he thought. It was too soon to care.

Graham was just a regular guy, but he had made her laugh. She felt like she was on an even footing with him, and not that he was in a position of power. That had been the difference when she'd met Aaron. He was a prize and not a gift.

Onika dressed carefully for her outing with Graham. Not that she had a huge wardrobe to choose from, but she settled on the nicest of her sweats. She couldn't very well put on business attire. For a moment, Onika thought about her lost luggage and the cute outfits she'd painstakingly put together. She didn't let herself dwell on that too long, though. It was depressing. She focused on what she did have—a date with a nice guy—and finished getting ready to leave.

Instead of a cab, she forced herself to take the Metro over to the southeast side of town. She had to save every additional penny, so cabs, Uber rides, and pedicures wouldn't be in her budget until she had a job and somewhere to live.

Graham was waiting for Onika outside the recreation center when she arrived. She took in the dressed-down version of him in a crisp white T-shirt and basketball shorts, and decided that she liked it. He was unquestionably handsome and seemed to glisten with a fresh coat of whatever he'd used to moisturize after he'd taken a shower.

"You're shining in the sun, like an onyx-colored warrior," Onika said as she approached Graham.

He cracked up laughing, and so did she. That was the corniest greeting she'd ever given anyone.

"And you're looking like a caramel-coated, melanin-infused, confection sprinkled with black girl magic."

Onika snapped her fingers in the air, appreciating his poetic ramblings more than her corniness.

Then, unexpectedly, Graham hugged Onika. He said his hello with an embrace, and she closed her eyes and received it. It was ninety degrees outside, but the warmth of his touch added about five degrees.

"Let's get food first, then pedicures. You like sushi?"

"Yes."

"I know a great place. It's walking distance from here."

Graham hummed as he walked, which made Onika smile. Was he happy because she called?

"You're jolly," Onika said.

"Oh, well one of my students finally got her dive correct. She can join the team now."

"That sounds like a big deal." Actually, it didn't sound like too big a deal to Onika, but she went along with it anyway.

"It is. She's a great swimmer. Excellent form and a powerful stroke, but for some reason she couldn't make herself go head-first into the water. She could jump, but not dive."

"And you have to dive to be on the team?"

"Yeah. She'd never win a freestyle race without diving. Wouldn't make it off the starting block."

"How'd she get over her hang-up?"

"Practice, and lots of it."

"That's cool. You know, I thought you were jolly because I called."

"I am pretty darn jolly about that, too. I was surprised at first, and then I was happy you felt the connection as I did."

They crossed the street, giving Onika a chance to think of a response. She didn't know if she felt a connection. It was something, but as far as Onika could tell, they didn't have anything in common.

"Are you in a fraternity?" Onika asked when they got to the other side. Graham seemed like a black Greek. He had the appropriate amount of good looks and swagger.

"No. They didn't have fraternities or sororities at my school. Plus, I only have an associate's degree."

This was a minus. If he only had a two-year degree, he couldn't be making very much money. Onika felt bad about thinking this way, but with her money situation being so tight, she didn't know if she needed a man who was strapped as well. Someone had to be doing well.

She had to admit that the only sign she'd seen of Graham being frugal was when he chose the Uber ride over the cab. Outside of that, he'd seemed generous with her meal and drinks, but he definitely wasn't rich. Onika had been around enough rich men to know.

"Fortunately, I got into federal service. At the time, my skills were more in demand than the piece of paper."

"That's good."

"What about you?" Graham asked. "Are you in a sorority?"

For her response, Onika did a portion of her stroll and did her sorority call. Graham seemed amused and entertained.

"Epsilon Phi Beta," Onika said. "I pledged my sophomore year."

"Sometimes I wish I had done the whole black college thing. Everyone I know who did it seems to have fond memories."

Onika did have fond memories of her time at Robinson, but almost every one of those memories included Aaron. She wondered if there'd come a time when she'd want to forget.

Graham looked at two women walking down the street toward them and frowned. He turned on one heel.

"Let's go for burgers instead."

"Okay."

As soon as they started in the other direction, one of the women started yelling.

"Graham!"

He cringed. Closed his eyes and balled his fists.

"Just act like you don't hear her," he said.

"But . . ."

"Come on! She is crazy. My coworker, Leslie."

Onika followed but laughed every time the woman called out, because her voice was getting louder and closer.

"Should we run?" Onika asked, even though she was laughing too hard to have enough wind for any real speed.

"No. Then she'll know we hear her."

"Of course we do. She's screaming at the top of her lungs."

Graham stopped walking and slowly turned like he was facing a firing squad. Onika did the same, trying to compose herself the best she could.

"I know you heard me calling you," Leslie said.

"I heard someone yelling. I didn't think someone would be screaming my name on the streets of DC."

"Mmm-hmm . . ." She turned her attention to Onika. "Who is this? Your girlfriend?"

"Hi, I'm Onika, and you are . . ."

"My name is Leslie. I thought I was Graham's friend. But we don't run from our friends when they're trying to say hello."

"I wasn't running from you."

"Anyway, I'll let you and your girlfriend enjoy the rest of your day."

She turned and walked back up the street in the direction she had come from. It was a little silly, in Onika's opinion. Leslie's exit was so undramatic, with her having to walk away and all.

"That would've been so much more effective if she had had a car," Onika said.

Graham stared at Onika, his face frozen and his mouth slightly ajar. After a few seconds in this pose, Graham started laughing. He laughed so hard that he had to hold himself up on the side of the building they were standing next to.

"Shhh!" Onika said. "She's gonna hear you and think you're laughing at her."

"I can't help it. That was hilarious. Especially the way she was trying to stomp away."

He started laughing again. This time he slid his body down the building until he was sitting on the ground cracking up.

"I'm walking away. I don't want her to turn around and see both of us laughing."

"She's long gone," Graham said.

"You better hope she doesn't try to get back at you at work what with all that noise you're making."

"She won't. I don't think she will."

Onika started walking, and Graham jumped up to follow her.

"So what's the story on her?" Onika asked. "She's obviously butt hurt to see you out with a woman. What went down with you two? Did you sleep with her?"

"Not at all. She just decided that we should be together because she likes me. I'm not interested."

"Why? Because of me?" Onika didn't want Leslie coming after her. Not that she was afraid. She just didn't want anyone else's drama following her around.

"Not because of you. She's not really my type."

"Are we walking toward a restaurant?" Onika asked. "I'm just walking. I have no idea where I'm going."

"We can go this way."

"Okay, so why wasn't she your type?"

"You ever go out with someone who, on paper, seems like they should be everything you want, but they're just not? I really think falling for someone is a series of chemical reactions to pheromones. If someone doesn't smell right to a person, then on a primitive level, they're not interested."

"So you're saying she doesn't smell right to you?" Onika

chuckled, because she couldn't relate, seeing that she'd only dated two guys and she'd been attracted to both.

"She smells fine. It's just that there's nothing that attracts me to her. She's not a bad-looking woman, and she's educated and she's saved. I'm just not interested in her."

"Is there anything she could do to change your mind?"

Graham shook his head and laughed. "Are you trying to get rid of me?"

"No. I guess I'm just trying to understand men. I feel like I don't."

"I don't think I understand myself."

CHAPTER FORTY

They had two dates down, and Graham wanted another. Onika knew she wouldn't be able to hold him off forever. He'd want to see where she lived, and he would ask to take her home. Then it would all be over.

Onika was so concerned about it that she didn't even want to get out of bed. It was almost eleven, and she'd only crawled out of the bed to go to the bathroom, and then had tucked herself back into the blankets.

"You like him, don't you?" Ty asked. She hadn't yet gotten out of her bed either.

"Why does she have to have that big sign outside that says Safe Harbor? If she didn't have that, no one would think this was anything other than a house."

"I think she has that sign up there so that people can find her. The building is a little bit hard to see."

"Oh, I know her purpose and everything, but that's not helping me right now."

"Did he ask you to go somewhere today?"

"He did, but I pretended to have plans, because I didn't want him to ask about bringing me home."

"Did y'all do it yet?"

Onika gave Ty a dirty look. She sounded like a middle-school-aged child. Onika hoped she was joking with the way she phrased that question.

"Did we have sex? I don't talk about that type of thing with my girlfriends. I never have."

"That means y'all did. After two dates, you must be really feeling him."

Onika made no reaction to deny Ty's assumption. She really didn't care what Ty thought, so it wasn't necessary. If Charmayne asked, she might tell her the truth, but Charmayne wouldn't ask.

There was a knock on their bedroom door. Ty jumped up to answer it. Onika always marveled every time she saw Ty in the tiny shorts she wore as pajamas. There were so many tattoos on her thighs that you could barely tell the color of her skin.

"I'm on my way to church," Charmayne said. "Anyone want to come with me?"

"Maybe next week I'll meet you there," Ty said.

"What do you mean you'll meet her there?" Onika asked. "Why not just go with her?"

Charmayne smiled. "She hasn't shared her news with you yet."

"What news?" Onika asked, starting to get annoyed.

"I'm moving out on Saturday. Charmayne got me into a rent-subsidized apartment, and my ex-boyfriend is finally in prison for trafficking. It's time for me to leave the nest."

Onika wanted to say congratulations, but she couldn't form the words. Maybe because she didn't want Ty to leave.

"I've been here way too long," Ty added when Onika remained silent. "It is time. I'm ready for my own space again."

"There are a couple new residents coming next week, too," Charmayne said. "It's going to be packed in here."

"New residents?" Onika asked.

"Yes, a mom and her three kids, and a runaway," Charmayne said. "Back to school time, we usually get at least one family."

"It's been pretty quiet for these three weeks that you've been here," Ty said. "It almost doesn't feel like a homeless shelter right now."

"She came at a good time, and I think that was God-ordained," Charmayne said. "I don't think she would've stayed if she had to sleep on a cot in the living room."

Charmayne was wrong, but Onika didn't let on that she was. A cot in Safe Harbor's living room was much better than a corner of the Metro station.

"You may be rooming with the runaway," Charmayne said. "But I'm not sure. I have to find out her entire story before I make that happen. You two sure you don't want to go to church?"

Ty shook her head, and Onika sat there in silence, trying to figure out an escape strategy. She absolutely couldn't bring Graham here when it was teeming with homeless people. He was kind and would probably let her down easy, but Onika was sure he'd move on. Without question.

Charmayne closed their bedroom door, and Onika slumped down into the blankets again. As much as she hated to admit it, she wanted to close her eyes, fall asleep, and wake up back in the town house with Aaron.

"I think Charmayne purposely makes it uncomfortable to be here. I would've moved the last time we were full if I'd had the money together," Ty said as she walked back over to her bed.

"What happened the last time you were full?"

"She had accepted a drug addict who was coming out of rehab. The girl stole from Charmayne and everybody else, then she disappeared."

Onika drew in a sharp breath. If Charmayne brought a drug addict in here, she would leave. She'd have to. She'd figure something out, but she wasn't going to go through life with Judy again.

"Charmayne is too free with her home. Does she even lock stuff up?" Onika asked, thinking of the damage Judy could do.

"She didn't at first. I think she had only been doing this for a few months when I got here. She'd just moved to DC from Cleveland. Then, when all that happened, she got a safe for her important papers. She doesn't want anyone to feel uncomfortable here, though."

"I would feel uncomfortable with a drug addict."

Ty shrugged. "I've seen it all. Actually, I'd rather have a sweet drug addict than a violent person. I mean, they're really only hurting themselves when they take drugs."

Onika held her peace, because if she started talking she wouldn't be able to hide her own history. But addicts didn't only hurt themselves. They destroyed their children. In fact, their kids and parents and other family members always got the worst of it, because the addict stayed high all the time and didn't have to deal with the damage they did.

"If you're going to bring Graham here," Ty said, "it should be this week, before she moves all the people in."

"You're right. Can I spin it? Can I say that I'm helping here with the program?" Onika asked, forming a plan as she spoke.

"Why even say you're helping? Why can't it be your own place? If you have him come when Charmayne is gone, then you could say it's yours."

"When is she gone for more than thirty minutes?"

"Her Thursday night Bible study. You could cook Graham dinner or something."

Onika chuckled, although she did like the idea. "I don't cook well. I don't know how to make anything fancy."

"We can order food, then. It'll be fun."

"So you're gonna help me? I thought you'd be packing up and getting ready to leave."

Ty waved one hand in front of the closet. "I've got about two suitcases worth of stuff to pack. I don't think it'll take that long."

"Are you going to be able to afford your apartment?" Onika asked.

Ty nodded. "That job at the restaurant isn't going to cut it, though. I don't want to just have barely enough for rent and utilities. I want to live my life, too."

"So are you going back to school for something?"

Ty burst into laughter. "School? For what? Do I look like an accountant or computer professional? I'm going to go back to stripping."

Onika gasped. "But . . ."

"Listen, I'm not going to turn any tricks. I'm just going to strip."

"Did you tell Charmayne?"

Ty shook her head. "Of course not, but Charmayne isn't always living in the real world. She's so positive all the time that she doesn't realize she can't fix everything. She helped me get on my feet and get out of a bad situation, but at the end of the day, I don't have that many ways to make money."

"But what about when you can't strip anymore?"

"You don't think I've thought about my future? I know I only have a few good years left on the pole. If I don't have any babies I might be able to extend it. That's why I am going to work hard and bank my money. I think I want to open a beauty bar."

"Do you do hair and nails?" Onika asked. "Why not build your brand doing that? Why do you have to go and strip?"

"Because I need cash. Capital. Do you understand how much money this body makes me on a good night? I have brought home thousands for a few hours of work."

"And what do you have to show for it?"

"Nothing right now, but my mind-set has changed. I don't care about a thousand-dollar pair of shoes or a handbag anymore. I'm going to save and invest my money. One thing I have learned from Charmayne is that money in the bank and a good credit score are worth more than a few items in the closet. She's rich—you know that, right?"

"I thought she was well off, but not necessarily rich."

Ty shook her head. "When I was cleaning, I accidentally saw a bank statement. She's damn near a millionaire."

"She doesn't seem like one."

"Exactly. She's quietly rich. Doesn't flash at all," Ty said. "That's how I want to be. I want to have enough money to do whatever I want."

"She's rich, but she chooses to live here with us. Why doesn't she just hire someone to run this place?"

"Girl, I don't know. I think she actually loves this. She loves helping us wretched souls. I've heard her say it's her ministry and God called her to this."

Onika shook her head. "Most of the people I know who say God calls them to something are crazy. I am glad she thinks that, though. If she didn't, I don't know where I'd be."

"Exactly. When my ex was on trial, my attorney referred me here. I was so glad to have somewhere safe."

"If it wasn't for that homeless woman at the Metro station, I don't know how I would've found out about Charmayne."

"The homeless woman who gave you the flyer."

Onika laughed. "You both keep making fun of me about that lady. I tell you she walked straight up to me and gave me a flyer for Safe Harbor."

"I know. I saw the flyer you showed to Charmayne. It's just that she doesn't really advertise. Maybe there's an underground homeless community that knows all about Charmayne."

"That must be it. Some of them stick together like a family. They share things. Like safe places to sleep, and where to get personal items."

"You were homeless, what, all of two days, and you found this out?"

"Well, I was in a hotel first. I heard rumblings of it there. But I don't want to think about that. One of those homeless people at that hotel probably stole my suitcase. I'm still mad about that."

"Why? It's only stuff. And I bet it was one of the hotel employees who stole it."

"You're probably right."

"You know what's funny about you?" Ty asked.

Onika lifted her eyebrows. "Nothing is funny about me."

"Whatever. You don't think you're one of us. It's like in your mind you're on vacation to a homeless shelter. Like this is some kind of social experiment for you. You going out on dates with a guy acting like the socialite you used to be before you wound up *just like me*. You're homeless, Nikki. Stop saying, 'those homeless people,' like they're someone different than you are."

Onika couldn't reply. Ty's words were on point. Onika didn't feel a part of this community of struggling men and women. This felt like an inconvenient detour, but not her actual life. But it was her life. The only home she had was in Goldsboro, North Carolina, and since she wasn't going back there, Ty was right. She was one of them.

"You're not homeless anymore," Onika said. "You have an apartment."

"And I don't plan on getting evicted from it, so don't worry about how I make my money. By the time you figure it all out, I'll probably be buying my own town house."

"You're going to make it rain on the real estate market."

"Yes ma'am. Think I won't?"

Onika laughed, but avoided her feelings about the truth Ty had just dropped in her lap. She'd deal with that later. She couldn't think about it now.

"So do you want my help with this date or not?" Ty asked. "We can really hook it up for Mr. Graham, with his fine self. He looks way better than his homeboy."

Onika laughed. "I don't even think I really paid attention to what his friend looked like."

"You didn't. 'Cause you were mesmerized by that chocolate-covered Graham cracker."

Onika fell back on the bed and had a belly laugh. Graham was definitely fine, and sweet.

"I wouldn't say that I was mesmerized then, but I'm getting there. He's a really special guy."

"So let's hook it up for him. You can deal with your lying spirit later."

"My lying spirit?"

"Yes, chile. You can't even tell anybody your real name. No one has Nikki on their birth certificate."

"It's Onika."

"Look at God!" Ty said, imitating Charmayne's "Praise the Lord!" voice.

Onika grinned, but then realized that what Ty just said wasn't all that funny. Graham was a great guy. Someone she could see having a relationship with. But she couldn't tell him the truth about her situation. What good was falling for someone who might abandon and hurt her again like Aaron had done?

CHAPTER FORTY-ONE

It was a typical Monday morning at work for Graham, except that he was in an extremely good mood after spending Friday and Saturday with Onika. On Sunday, he went to church and praised God for answering his prayers and sending Onika back across his path. And this morning, he'd gotten a text from her, an invitation to dinner on Thursday—at her house. He was in there, and he was glad about it.

"Hello, Graham."

Graham looked up from his computer, and Leslie was standing in front of his desk with both hands on her hips. He'd known this was coming, although he hadn't decided how to handle her.

"Leslie . . ."

"You played the hell out of me, Graham. I thought we were better than that."

"Let me ask you a question."

"What?" Her voice was harsh, but Graham refused to escalate with her.

"When you saw me on Saturday afternoon, did you think I was on a date?"

Her face softened a touch. Not much, but enough that Graham thought he might be able to get through to her.

"I thought that maybe you were on a date. Yes, I thought so."

"So why would you do what you did? Screaming my name like that, sounding all crazy."

Her lip trembled. "I sounded crazy?"

"I mean . . . you did. You and I . . . we're not dating, so that wasn't cool, honestly. If you want us to be friends, you can't do stuff like that."

"It feels like you're scolding me."

"Not at all. I just want us to be cool, you know? I'm sorry things didn't work out the way you wanted them to, but we can still have a good work relationship. I can still see you out in public and be okay."

Leslie sucked her teeth long and hard. "So you laying down the law, huh, Graham? You can't tell me how to act or what to say. I should've told your new girlfriend how you'll flip the script in a heartbeat. How you'll take a girl out on a date and pretend to like her and then all of a sudden want to be just friends. I'm so sick of men like you. Don't want to be Godly at all and find a wife. Just want to go from chick to chick, always looking for an upgrade."

There was such contempt in Leslie's tone that Graham wasn't sure if he should continue the conversation or just chalk it up to a bad experience.

"Leslie, I'm not that guy you just described. To be honest, I just am not attracted to you. I shouldn't have gone out with you that one time. I knew I wasn't interested in anything long-term, and unfortunately, you got the wrong idea."

"You're not interested in me because I'm a real black woman. Because I'm dark and my hair doesn't blow in the wind."

"I love your hair, Leslie. That has nothing to do with it."

"Yes, it does. You are like every other brother out here. Y'all want us to stand up for you, be down for you and have your back, and then when we need you, you're running after the first biracial, light bright chick you see. What is your little friend? She's Latina, isn't she? Anything but black."

Suddenly, the anger that probably had helped Leslie hold her composure changed to grief. She burst into tears and made loud sobbing noises. Graham handed her tissues from the box on his desk, but he didn't move otherwise. What was he supposed to do? Hug her? That would probably make things worse.

Finally, one of Leslie's coworkers ran up to Graham's desk. The girl, Helena, rolled her eyes at Graham.

"What did you do to her?" Helena asked.

"I didn't do anything to her. But y'all should get her together away from my desk, because she's drawing attention over here."

"You're so insensitive, Graham!" Helena fussed. "Don't you see she's heartbroken here?"

"Heartbroken? What? No, she's not. She's tripping."

"It's okay, Helena," Leslie wailed. "I'm okay. Just come to the break room with me, so I can get myself together."

Graham sent Lorne and Craig an instant message and told them to meet him downstairs. As ignorant as his friends were, he needed their help strategizing on this. Leslie was going overboard with her reaction to their non-relationship.

"What's the deal?" Lorne asked once they were out in their courtyard meeting spot. "Did that girl steal your identity?"

"What? No! That part is great. Onika is awesome. We went out again on Saturday. She's fantastic."

"Wait, what have I missed? When did you go on a date? Is Onika Metro girl?" Craig asked.

Graham took a moment to get Craig caught up. Told him about the bar on U Street and how he'd left with Onika right then and there and had their first date.

"You went out with her again on Saturday. Did you hit?"

Graham sighed. "If I did, we wouldn't be having a conversation about it right now."

"He hit," Lorne said as he gave Craig a high five. "This chick was extremely smashable."

"Don't be disrespectful," Graham said.

"Listen to him," Lorne said with a laugh. "Don't be disrespectful. He smashed, and it changed his life."

Graham puffed his cheeks up with air and exhaled loudly. "This is not about Onika. This is about Leslie."

"You smashed her, too?" Lorne asked. "Man, the student has finally graduated."

Craig said, "I think he's trying to tell us something else, Lorne."

"Thanks, Craig. I ran into Leslie when I was out with Onika, and she acted crazy. Chased us down the street screaming my name. When I saw her this morning, she started crying at my desk. Helena came up acting like I had broken up with her or something."

"I told you Leslie was a damn lunatic," Lorne said. "She's going to go to y'all supervisor next."

"That's what I'm trying to avoid."

"Unavoidable, because now she's mad. She put herself out there, and let you know how she felt, and you rejected her. She is going to make a thing out of this," Lorne said.

"Maybe she won't," Craig countered. "She might not want to embarrass herself. Maybe she'll just want it to go away."

Graham wasn't sure which one of them was right. He was worried that it was Lorne, though.

"Have you sent her any questionable e-mails on the work e-mail?" Lorne asked. "We have to do some damage control."

"I've never sent her anything questionable."

"No texts? No pictures of your junk?"

Craig gave himself a face palm, while Graham wanted to choke out his friend.

"No, I haven't sent her any inappropriate pictures. Let's think of this situation as something I am going through, not you. We are wasting time talking about stuff I don't do."

"So I think you should give your boss a heads-up. He's old school, and he probably thinks Leslie is a little thrown off. You need him to have your back when she goes to his office snitching on you," Craig said.

"Or he could break her off, and then she would be happy," Lorne said. "That's all she wants. She needs some vitamin D."

"How about I hook you up with her. You can break her off," Graham said. "I'm not sleeping with her."

"I see that as a win-win situation," Lorne said. "If you do what you're supposed to do, everything will be good. Then if things don't work out with your fairy-tale chick, you've got some real convenient office booty sitting right across the room."

"Dudes like you are the reason I'm in this predicament," Graham said. "I'm just trying to be one of the good guys here."

"Have you just tried telling her why you're not into her?" Craig asked. "Maybe she'll be reasonable."

"She's not reasonable at all, though. She said I don't want her 'cause her hair doesn't blow in the wind. I mean, really. I'm not that guy. I love all the sistas."

"It is hard for chicks like her in DC, though," Lorne said. "There's a lot of competition for the handful of decent guys who would actually settle down with them. You're a hot commodity, and you don't even know it."

"And she's been putting in work," Craig said. "She probably feels like she wasted her time."

"Whose side are y'all on?" Graham asked.

"Yours, but you need to understand your enemy."

Graham sighed. He didn't want Leslie to be his enemy. She was his sister in Christ.

"She's not my enemy."

"She is if she's trying to make you lose your job," Craig said. "Just hold off from saying anything to your boss. She may not say or do anything else."

"He needs to get ahead of it," Lorne said.

"He shouldn't be the one escalating it," Craig argued back.

"Never mind, y'all. I'm gonna pray about it before I do anything. I honestly feel bad that she's upset, but I can't help it that I'm not attracted to her."

"You're gonna wish you followed my advice," Lorne said. "I hope your new boo likes unemployed dudes."

Graham wasn't going to let this thing with Leslie go that far. If worse came to worse, he'd go to his supervisor and defend himself.

CHAPTER FORTY-TWO

Graham looked down at his phone to verify that he had the right address for Onika's home. He did, but there was a sign in front of it that said, "Safe Harbor." Nothing else. What kind of place was this? Was Onika on drugs? Mentally ill?

What had he gotten himself into picking up girls on the Metro platform?

He paid the driver and got out of the cab, but he was still concerned that this had been a bad idea. At least, this was a decent neighborhood on the Northeast side of DC, and the town house was in a row of other well-kept houses. It must've cost Onika a mint, because this area was notoriously expensive due to gentrification.

The door swung open before Graham got up the walkway. Onika stood smiling and waving. She wasn't kidding about him being on time.

"Come on in!" Onika said in a bubbly voice.

"Okay . . ."

Graham followed her inside, and immediately he calmed down. It was just a very nicely decorated town house. Nothing said rehab or home for the mentally ill.

"I made crab cakes, whipped potatoes, and green beans. Sound good?" Onika asked.

Graham's stomach grumbled. He'd come directly from work, "Yes, it does sound good."

"I have to admit, though, I didn't cook it. I ordered in."

Graham laughed out loud. "You just said you made it."

"I made the call."

They both burst into laughter.

"I guess that's good enough."

Onika led him into the dining room, where the entire table was set. It was a really nice setup, with a floral centerpiece. Onika had really gone out of her way to make it nice.

They both sat, and Ty came out wearing an apron and holding a bottle of wine.

"I'm the waitress for the evening," Ty said, "and even though you won't be paying a bill, I do accept tips."

"Hello again, Ty. Did you help Onika put all this together?"

"I did. That's what roomies are for."

"Oh, you're roommates?"

Ty glanced at Onika. "I'll let her explain, but yeah, we're roommates."

Ty poured wine into both their glasses and said that she'd be back later with their dinner. There was bread and salad already on the table.

"Should I bless the food?" Graham asked.

"Sure."

She bowed her head and closed her eyes, and Graham offered a brief prayer. He noticed that she didn't say "amen," but he didn't comment on it. At least she was tolerant of his beliefs.

"So you saw the sign on the way in, right? Safe Harbor," Onika said.

"Yes, I was about to ask you about that."

"This is where I live, but I run a program that houses women in crisis. So sometimes there are single moms here, runaways, addicts, homeless. All of the above. Ty is the only one here now, though, and she's about to move."

"Really? What's her story?"

Onika shook her head. "Not my story to tell, but she was in need, and we helped her."

"We? Do you have grant funding? There may be some government money available if you've got certain licenses."

Onika cleared her throat. "Most of our funding comes from private donors, but I do have a partner. She lives here, too. She's just not here right now."

"So that's why you didn't want to bring me to your home."

"Right. I had to get to know you first. Our residents' safety is important to me."

"But you left Ty with my homeboy, Lorne."

Onika chuckled. "She is a grown woman, plus she liked him. Who am I to block?"

Graham was satisfied with this, and it all made sense. Why she was so secretive, why she didn't call him right away.

Ty brought their food in and placed it on the table.

"Will you two be needing anything else?" she asked.

"No, and if we do, I can get it. Thanks, Ty," Onika said.

"Okay, girl. Y'all enjoy. I'll be upstairs."

Ty left the room, and Onika grinned at Graham. Her good mood made him feel warm inside. He imagined holding her in his arms, and what her lips tasted like. Maybe he'd find out later.

"How has your week been so far?" Onika asked. "Have you seen Leslie at work?"

Graham's warm feeling dissipated. "Yes, and she has been acting crazy. She broke down crying on Monday, like I broke her heart or something."

"Oh no. I feel bad for her."

"Don't feel bad for her. She is tripping."

"You don't know what it's like being a single black woman. It's hard."

Graham nodded. "That's what I've been hearing. I thought I was being nice spending time with her, but it kind of backfired on me."

"Maybe you can still end up being friends."

"Enough about her. What's up with you? Ready to start your new job?"

Onika bit her bottom lip. "No, it fell through. I'm starting this tutoring gig next week until I find something better."

"Will you be able to do everything you need to do to run this place and have another job?"

"Oh, um, yes. This place basically runs itself. I'm actually thinking about moving into an apartment so that we can help more women."

"You would leave here, for an apartment?"

"Well, yes . . . then we could be fully listed as a nonprofit organization and get more grant funding. And of course . . . it would be a nice apartment."

"I see."

The front door to the town house opened, and a middle-aged black woman came inside, her arms full of bags. Graham watched Onika's face go white as a sheet, and she jumped up.

"Charmayne," she said, "do you need help with your bags?"

Onika ran over to Charmayne, and Graham followed. He wasn't going to let Onika carry bags while he sat at the dining room table.

"Well, hello," Charmayne said to Graham.

He extended his hand to shake Charmayne's and then took one of her bags. "Hi. I'm Graham, a friend of Onika's."

"I'm Charmayne Ellis."

"Pleased to meet you. Are you one of the residents here?"

Charmayne gave Onika a look Graham couldn't decipher, but then she smiled. "Yes, I live here."

"I thought you went to your Bible study," Onika said. "Is everything okay?"

"Well, yes. I just decided to bake a cheesecake to celebrate Ty getting her apartment."

"Cheesecake?" Graham asked. "Did someone say cheesecake? That's my favorite dessert."

"Is it? Well, you're welcome to stay if you want," Charmayne said.

"Of course he's welcome. He's here for dinner, silly," Onika said.

Charmayne made her way to the dining room. "You're right. We are one big family here, Graham. I really am happy to meet you."

She looked down at the table. "Oh, crab cakes. Very nice. Romantic."

Charmayne went into the kitchen. Graham and Onika followed with the bags. They started to put things away, but Charmayne stopped them.

"I can handle this. Your dinner is going to get cold," Charmayne said.

Graham and Onika went back into the dining room and sat down. Onika took several rapid bites of food. She seemed nervous and unsettled, so Graham knew something was going on; he just didn't know what.

"Onika . . ."

"What? What's up?" she asked.

"Is this Charmayne's home and you're living here?"

"No! We run this place together, actually."

"Then why are you acting so weird?"

Onika took a huge gulp of water from her glass. "Because I broke one of our cardinal rules. We have it for the residents and ourselves because of some of the issues the women have. We don't entertain at home."

"Oh, and you thought Charmayne was going to be out for a few hours."

"Yes, she left for Bible study like she does every Thursday, but clearly she didn't go. And you were acting like I was being secretive. I wanted you to know where I live . . . what I do."

"All you had to do was tell me," Graham said. "I would've respected the rules."

"Well, now you'll know if I don't ask you to come back. It's not because I don't enjoy you; it'll be because we have someone with a precarious situation. Ty is fine, and she's moving this weekend. We're getting new residents over the weekend, so I don't know what it'll be like then."

"Oh, okay. Well, thank you for breaking the rules just to see me and pretend cook me dinner."

Onika laughed. "Picking up the phone is just as good as cooking if you're not the best in the kitchen."

"What do you know how to cook?"

"Spaghetti, and Hamburger Helper. I can also do quite a few things with a boneless, skinless chicken breast."

"That's enough. I won't starve to death then."

Onika laughed. "So you think I'm going to be cooking for you on a regular basis?"

"Yes. Soon. That's what good girlfriends do for their boyfriends."

"You're going to be my boyfriend?"

He nodded. "I'm already on date number three."

"What do good boyfriends do? Girlfriends cook meals, and boyfriends do what?"

"I'm glad you asked. Boyfriends teach their girlfriends how to swim. So . . ."

"Um, no . . ."

"You have twice-weekly swimming lessons at the recreation center. They're usually seventy-five dollars for ten sessions, but for you, it's free. All you have to do is wear a cute bathing suit."

Onika threw her head back and laughed. "What if I don't want to learn how to swim? Because you know you can't make me learn if I won't get in the water."

"You'll get in, and I'm gonna help you get over your fear. You should know how to swim."

Without warning, Onika got up from the table, ran over to Graham, and kissed him. It wasn't a particularly sexy kiss. It was a loud peck on his cheek next to his mouth, but barely brushing the side of his mouth.

"What was that for?" Graham asked.

"You didn't like it?" Onika whispered, her face still inches from Graham's.

"I did. I just want to know what I did, so I can do it again."

Onika let out a little giggle. "I don't know. I think I like that you're trying to save my life. It's kinda hot."

"Well, we can go down to the Anacostia River if you want me

to really save you. You can jump right in, and I'll pull you out. Then what reward will I get?"

This made Onika's small giggles grow louder. Then she kissed him again, and this one was sexy. He pulled her in closer, wrapped his arms around her, and settled in. It had been a long time since he'd kissed a woman. An even longer time since he'd done more.

He wanted the kiss to last forever. His hand stole into her hair—loosened it so that the curls tumbled over her shoulders and brushed his face. It smelled like coconuts. Finally, when they could no longer breathe, Graham separated, but still held her face close to his. He bit her bottom lip to seal the deal.

CHAPTER FORTY-THREE

Onika looked at the address of the DC community center where she'd be tutoring. It was right near the Eastern Market Metro station, one of her favorite, eclectic parts of Washington, DC. She knew it well, because Aaron's town house was about a thirty-second walk from the station. It was on the southeast side of DC, but near the Capitol, where there were million-dollar residences.

When she emerged from the Metro station, Onika didn't even look in the direction of her former home. She was reminded of a Bible story her grandmother loved about Lot's wife turning into a pillar of salt. Earlene had always said that it wasn't the looking that had killed Lot's wife; it was the longing for everything she'd left behind.

Onika did long for everything she'd left behind, but she couldn't allow herself to think about it. She pushed forward, wondering if the future held a different kind of wealth.

Onika's lip curled at the sight of the dilapidated community center. She'd worn a simple skirt and blouse that she would've worn on the first day of school, but as soon as she walked into the run-down building she wished she'd just worn jeans and a T-shirt.

An elderly woman came out to greet Onika. She had the

brightest of smiles on her face. Onika couldn't help but return the smile.

"You must be Charmayne's friend. I'm Mrs. Grandbury. We don't have any clients yet today, but I think we will later on."

"Okay. Well, what time do they typically show up?" Onika asked.

"Right around dinnertime."

Onika nodded. Her hours were noon until eight o'clock in the evening on Mondays, Wednesdays, and Fridays, and Saturday mornings. Not a lot of hours, but enough to put a few dollars in her checking account.

"Dinnertime isn't for a few hours. Is there anything you'd like me to help with until then?"

Mrs. Grandbury clapped her hands. "I'm so glad you asked, baby. You can help with dinner."

Onika's eyebrows shot up in surprise. "Wait? You mean like help with a meal?"

"Yes, yes, yes. We're having spaghetti and meatballs tonight. That seems to be a hit with everyone."

"I thought the people came for tutoring. You feed them too?"

"We mostly feed them."

Onika chuckled and shook her head. Charmayne knew exactly what this place was, and that it wasn't somewhere Onika wanted to be four days a week. Not that she didn't believe in service. She put in many volunteer hours with her sorority sisters. Epsilon Phi Beta was known for their dedication to service.

But now Onika needed to make real money and build her résumé. She wasn't even able to get a job at a temporary agency. DC was full of contractors looking for talent, but all Onika had was a degree and an in-depth knowledge of table etiquette. No one was hiring for that.

"Spaghetti and meatballs, huh?" Onika asked. "I bet you make a mean plate of spaghetti, Mrs. Grandbury."

"Chicken and dumplings, too. That's what I'm making them on Saturday. That'll really be a treat."

"This type of place is typically staffed by volunteers. How can you afford to pay me?"

"Oh, Ms. Charmayne pays all of the ladies she sends over here. We do have volunteers that come in from the high schools and what not. They will be here in a little while. Mostly, this place runs on faith, love, and donations."

Onika stood staring at Mrs. Grandbury. Charmayne hadn't networked to get her this job. She'd created the job.

"Does Charmayne send many women over here?"

"About once a month we get a new one. They usually last until they get a real job, but Ms. Charmayne gives them a pay-check and sends us food, too. She is a good woman."

Onika followed Mrs. Grandbury wordlessly into the kitchen and got straight to work. With a well-worn apron, she covered her skirt and blouse and chopped onions and bell peppers. It seemed like an endless number of them. She cut so many onions that her eyes were raw from her salty tears.

Onika watched Mrs. Grandbury move around the kitchen, making her spaghetti sauce with swift, nimble motions that be-lied her age. The kitchen seemed to take twenty years off the little lady. While she was cooking, she seemed more like a young grandmother than a great-great grandmother, which is what she probably was.

"Do you have children, Mrs. Grandbury?" Onika asked as Mrs. Grandbury squeezed an entire clove of pressed garlic into a huge skillet containing olive oil.

"I did have a daughter. I gave her up for adoption, though. A nice family got her, and they moved out of town. I didn't see her grow up."

Onika gasped and wished that she hadn't brought it up. "I'm sorry to hear that."

"No need to be sorry. I was only thirteen years old. I didn't have no business trying to raise a baby, and so I didn't."

Mrs. Grandbury kept cooking and didn't elaborate on how she'd ended up pregnant at thirteen but Onika was sure curi-ous. She wondered if it was a rape or if she'd been promiscuous as a girl. Onika couldn't imagine the sweet little lady before her being a bad girl.

Soon the aroma of the garlic, peppers, and onions mingled with the ground beef and ground turkey and had the entire kitchen smelling delicious. Onika watched closely, since she wanted to be able to cook something for Graham that didn't come from a restaurant.

Funny, she'd never wanted to cook for Aaron. He hadn't required it or even requested it. Aaron was happy to hire a chef or eat out at a variety of restaurants. Onika could probably count on her fingers how many home-cooked meals she'd had in the years she was with him.

Graham, though, inspired sweetness and compassion. He made Onika want to bake cakes and give foot rubs. He made Onika value bowling and movies above yacht parties and charity balls.

A relationship with Graham might be more normal compared to what she'd had with Aaron, but at least she felt completely loved and overwhelmingly cherished.

Onika forced herself to stop comparing the two men as she spread butter on long pieces of day-old French loaves. She chided herself for weighing the pros and the cons of the two men again. It was almost as if she was convincing herself that Graham was the better man and that she'd truly won instead of lost.

It wasn't as if she actually had an option anyway. Aaron hadn't given her a choice when he'd said that they were done. The scene replayed in Onika's mind.

She remembered herself sitting still, not panicking, not crying, screaming, or cursing. Her calmness, in hindsight, was shocking. Aaron had told her to get out of his house with only the clothes on her back. That's what it came down to eventually, anyway, when her suitcase was stolen. Onika wondered if Aaron had something to do with that. She wouldn't put it past him. He'd done so much to hurt her.

Mrs. Grandbury took the trays of buttered bread away from Onika and gave her some new pieces to butter. She went to work, unable to answer her mind's questions, and she was grateful for the distraction.

Mrs. Grandbury brought out three huge bags of salad mix and filled two bowls, along with cucumbers, tomatoes, and carrot slivers. This was a pretty hearty meal that people were probably about to eat for free. The little taste of the sauce that Onika had tried was incredible. It tasted like something that should be served in a restaurant.

"Take the plastic ware and the napkins out to that long table set up in the back. I'm going to get these noodles cooked so we can mix them into the sauce. That way when they start rolling in, everything will be ready," Mrs. Grandbury said.

Onika followed the instructions and arranged the items as nicely as possible next to the huge chafing pans that were already set up. It reminded her of Friends and Family Day at Earlene's church. They'd fry a bunch of chicken, but only allow the kids to eat the legs and thighs. Onika hated the slippery, dark meat, so she always threw it in the trash whole. She'd gotten more than a few whippings for wasting what her grandmother called good food.

Onika wondered if Graham's church was anything like Earlene's. Maybe they had dinners after service, too. Graham probably had some woman saving him a good piece of chicken, though. A breast or some wings, and a big slice of cake. He was probably one of their most eligible bachelors, and he'd decided to fall for an agnostic girl.

He barely accepted the truth of Onika's lack of belief, though, because Graham had invited her to his church every week since they'd started dating. Three weeks in a row she'd declined. She'd talk about God with him anytime he wanted, but the conversation always went awry.

It was three o'clock, and the rest of the volunteer staff opened the doors and started to let people in. They began to form a line. Onika went back in the kitchen to let Mrs. Grandbury know.

"Should I get out my tutoring things?" Onika asked. "I was going to set up a little table in the back."

"Yes, baby, go ahead, but first help me serve this spaghetti. That's what they're really here for anyway."

Onika carried out eight trays of spaghetti and garlic bread, because as soon as Mrs. Grandbury left the kitchen she got preoccupied with hugging folks. And it was probably a good thing that she didn't go back into the kitchen after her greetings started, because some of the people she hugged looked covered in dirt and germs.

Onika watched Mrs. Grandbury say hello to her regulars like they were old friends. She flirted with a man who was at least ten years older than her, and she looked like she was around for the birth of Christ. Then a young teenage boy stood in the doorway, looking nervous and afraid. Mrs. Grandbury went straight to him and pulled him all the way in.

"I'm here 'cause I need help on my homework," the boy said.

"You want something to eat, too?"

The boy shrugged and looked over at the table full of food and Onika. "What y'all cooking?"

"We have spaghetti and garlic bread. I just made it today."

The boy touched his stomach, and Mrs. Grandbury brought him right up to the front of the serving line. A few of the people already in line grumbled.

"Now this is a growing boy," Mrs. Grandbury said. "And he's got homework to do. He don't have all night to wait in line."

Mrs. Grandbury got him a plate and motioned for Onika to come sit with him at the tutoring table. They both sat, but the boy looked up at Onika and frowned.

"You're not eating?"

Onika shook her head. "Not yet. I will wait until our guests eat."

The boy laughed. "We're not guests. We're homeless people here for a free dinner."

"What's your name?" Onika asked.

"Mike."

"Well, Mike, I like that Mrs. Grandbury and everybody else who works here thinks of us homeless people as guests."

Mike's jaw dropped open. "You're homeless? You're too pretty to be homeless."

Onika found it so easy to share this little bit of information about herself with Mike because she knew he wouldn't judge her. He wasn't Graham.

"Maybe. I think I used to believe that. But yeah, I'm homeless. I live in a shelter, and I'm here to help you with your homework. What you got?"

"Pre-calculus."

"Pre-calc? I got you."

"For real. Are you really good at math, because sometimes girls aren't good at math."

"Whatever. Girls are great at math. I'll show you. You're taking college-prep mathematics, so where you planning on going to college?"

"I'm not sure. I don't think I'll be able to go unless I get a full scholarship."

"You'll probably get it, right? What are your grades like?"

"Mostly A's and B's, but my attendance is not always the best. My mom disappears, and then I have to go and find her."

"Drugs?" Onika asked.

He shook his head. "Mental illness. I almost wish it was drugs. Then she could go to rehab."

Onika watched Mike devour his food and wondered what his life was like outside of here. She knew she was lucky to have found Charmayne.

"Where do you sleep?" Onika asked.

"In the custodian's area at my high school."

"Wow."

"Yeah, it's good, right? I have someplace safe and warm every night."

"But what about your mom?"

He shook his head. "My mom won't stay anywhere inside. She doesn't trust indoors at all. If she's not sleeping outdoors she thinks someone is putting poison into her food."

"Are you sure you're safe?" Onika asked.

"I am, but there are others who aren't. You can't help them, Ms. Onika, but don't feel bad. You're homeless, too."

Onika heard the reminder and sighed. She couldn't help

but think of herself as separate from these other homeless people she'd seen. Better somehow. But she hadn't been homeless long enough to deteriorate to their level. Hopefully, she'd never have to.

"Just pray for them," Mike said. "That's all you can do."

But she couldn't even do that, because she didn't believe their God answered prayers, or if He did, He was so sporadic and random with whose prayers He answered that it almost didn't make any sense to send the pointless words up.

She couldn't pray, and she couldn't give him a place to live, but Onika could help Mike pass his pre-calculus class. That would have to be enough.

CHAPTER FORTY-FOUR

Graham picked Onika up from her new job so they could go and have a few drinks and listen to music at a cool rooftop bar that he knew of in Eastern Market. As beautiful as she was, Onika looked worn-out and weary, as though she hadn't been tutoring but working on a farm all day.

When Graham hugged her, he could feel her lack of energy.

"What did they have you do in there?" he asked. "I thought you were a tutor."

"I am. I tutored one boy on his homework, but mostly it's just a soup kitchen," Onika said.

"Oh, did you know that? Are they accepting volunteers? Maybe I could . . ."

"No, no. They have way too many volunteers already. Plus you're already doing good work with the kids at the pool. Don't try to hog up all the charity."

"You're being weird," Graham said.

"I think it's because I'm tired. Where are we going? Is it far?"

Graham considered taking her home if she was this tired. "It's not far. It's right down the street. It's walking distance, but I can get a cab if you want."

"No, I can walk."

As Graham led the way, Onika slipped her tiny hand into his.

This always made him feel closer to her. He lightly squeezed and rubbed her hand, then put it up to his lips and kissed it.

Graham had always been an affectionate guy. Some of his previous girlfriends had thought it was too much. But with Onika, he couldn't help himself. He spent all of their dates and outings kissing and touching her in completely unsexual ways.

He was not a eunuch, though. Graham's closeness with Onika had a lot to do with how much he wanted to touch her in completely sexual ways.

It was his goal to not sin and have sex with Onika before he married her. It was probably a lofty goal, especially because Onika had no problem with sinning.

"Your hands smell like onions and garlic," Graham said. "Are you sure you're hungry? We don't have to go out if you're tired."

"I did eat there, but I want to go out with you. It's nice tonight, not too hot and sticky. Are you trying to get rid of me? You got a side piece you want to meet up with?"

Graham shook his head. "Absolutely not. There's no one but you."

"I'm glad I didn't take you away from some girl. I'd never be able to trust you if that was the case. It's almost like you were waiting for me."

"I think I was." Graham waited a moment, enjoying the feeling of holding her hand.

"I'm surprised you were single. Most of the time, women like you aren't single. Some man has scooped them up."

"There are lots of single women like me. As a matter of fact, I'm not even all that special. I know I'm pretty and my body is nice, and I have a degree from an awesome school, but I don't even have a career yet. I'm not the full package."

"You are to me."

Onika smiled at Graham and kissed his hand like he'd done hers. "Would you want me if I had it all together? What if I had a high-powered legal career and stacks upon stacks in the bank? Would you want me then?"

"Of course, I'd want you, but you probably wouldn't have given me the time of day if you had all that."

Graham had come across women exactly like the ones Onika described. Beautiful, fit, no children, education, money, and career. He never had everything on their lists. He had the looks, so some of them simply wanted him as a "maintenance man" to fulfill their sexual needs, but he didn't have the income to become a true partner. His almost six figures didn't mean anything to them in Washington, DC, one of the most expensive places to live in the United States.

The fact that he was a government employee put some of them off. He didn't have a sexy, glamorous job. When he traveled, it was for training or to do a workshop about government contracts and planning. Nothing exciting there, but he had made enough money to pay off his house and travel whenever he wanted.

"Here's the place," Graham said as he led Onika into the tiny bar. "It's small, but the best part is the rooftop."

Graham showed Onika the way up a winding staircase to the beautifully decorated rooftop. They had Christmas lights strung all over that gave it a romantic feel at night. Graham had come by to reserve a table right before he picked Onika up from work, so they had it ready for him.

"Did you plan all this ahead of time?" Onika asked as Graham pushed her chair under the table.

"Not too far in advance. Just before I came to get you. They start to fill up at about nine or so."

"You're so thoughtful. I wouldn't have even cared about waiting for a while. Not if I had a glass of wine in my hand."

Graham laughed. He did plan things out for her, and for all the women he'd dated before. He was a planner and loved for things to run smoothly.

"There was a time when I wouldn't have given you the time of day," Onika said. "You were right about that."

"I know. That's why I can't always take black women seriously when you say there aren't enough brothers."

"There aren't enough, though. That's a true statement."

"Well, no, there aren't enough athletes, entertainers, doctors,

lawyers, and moguls. But there are quite a few fiscally responsible government employees like me."

"Fiscally responsible?" Onika burst into laughter.

While she enjoyed his very serious statement, Graham ordered their wine from the waitress. They both liked sweet white
wine, so he went with a nice Riesling, and a few appetizers.

"Yes, I am fiscally responsible. I have to be to keep my job.
That's a good thing about a lot of the government employees
you'll meet. They have to have a decent credit score."

"That is good to know."

Graham chuckled. "I just sounded so boring and lame right
then. I wouldn't date me either."

"I'm glad we found each other," Onika said. "I wasn't looking
for anyone that day, but you were there."

"I feel like I've been looking for you my whole adult life."

Onika seemed suspended in silence. She simply stared at
Graham as the waitress came back with their wine, opened the
bottle, and poured them two glasses.

Graham meant exactly what he'd said. He had been looking
for her, or his spirit had. It was the reason why certain women
who seemed to have it all weren't appealing to him. They were
not Onika. His spirit knew as soon as it found her.

"When you say things like that, it makes me never want to
leave your side," Onika finally said after having a sip of wine.

"Then don't."

"I don't plan to. It just seems a silly feeling to have after three
weeks."

Graham didn't think it was silly at all. He'd had the same
feeling since their very first conversation. He thought he'd lose
his mind if he never saw her again. And then God had sent her
back to him. He was eternally grateful.

"Would you think I was crazy if I told you that I already know
I want to spend the rest of my life with you?"

She shook her head. "No. Not crazy. But only because of how
I feel. If this was happening to a friend, I'd tell them to run,
and that it is insane."

"Me too."

Onika got very serious and quiet. She took several long drinks from her wineglass. When she set the glass down and looked up at Graham, her eyes were filled with tears.

"Graham, there are things about me you don't know. I don't think you'd feel the same way if you knew these things."

Graham grabbed both of her hands. He squeezed them tightly when he felt her hands tremble in his.

"Tell me. I promise I'll feel the same."

She shook her head and sighed. "Let's just enjoy this time we have, okay?"

Graham slowly released her hands, and she used the table napkin to dab her eyes. He wanted forever with her—even after three weeks, he knew. But she was putting an expiration date on their time together. She was adding conditions without giving him the chance to choose.

The only thing Graham could do was prove her wrong. He could stay, and he would.

CHAPTER FORTY-FIVE

Onika hid in Charmayne's library, searching for somewhere quiet. Renee and her three children were noise makers. Safe Harbor had been quiet before their arrival, and now there was never silence. Someone was always whining, crying, laughing, or fighting. For two weeks, there'd been nothing but nonstop noise. Those children made Onika's uterus want to jump right out of her body and into traffic. They made her never want to give birth.

Onika wasn't just hiding from the noise, though. She needed to be alone to think about what was happening between her and Graham. A month and a week was how long they'd been seeing one another. She'd almost told him she'd lied about Safe Harbor. He had almost connected the dots the night she told the lie. She'd kissed him to try and distract him from his very dangerous line of questioning.

She regretted lying to him as soon as Charmayne had gotten home. It was if Onika could see the judgment in Charmayne's eyes. She didn't want to hear it or deal with it. The lie had already been told; there was no going back without doing irreparable harm.

But then Graham had kissed Onika back. He'd snaked his hand through her hair and gripped her head passionately.

He'd devoured her lips with his full ones. He'd taken her breath away. Made her almost willing to forego oxygen just to maintain contact.

Aaron had never kissed her like that.

And it wasn't just kissing Graham that had her contemplating full honesty; it was his one-track mind. He was completely into *her*. Not just for the evening or until he saw another piece of eye candy. It was like he'd found her and he was done looking for anyone else. She'd shared Aaron for so long that she had no idea what it felt like to be the singular object of a man's passion.

Onika's only reservation about Graham was his regular-sized budget. Of course, she had no idea how much money he had saved or invested, but he spent his money like a man who didn't have enough to last until his next paycheck. Being poor or struggling or even being on a penny-pinching budget was not Onika's idea of romantic. If Aaron hadn't excelled at anything else, he'd been an expert in spoiling her, shopping sprees, vacations, and the like.

Onika felt shallow and superficial letting that one reason give her pause, but she knew too many women who had married for love but who said their next marriage would be for money. Why? Because loving was hard if the lights were out.

Onika had spent her entire childhood dirt-poor and lacking the ability to cover her basic needs. She never wanted to go back to that.

Onika hadn't talked to Charmayne about her dinner date with Graham. She was surprised that Charmayne didn't blow her cover that night and tell Graham her secret. But Charmayne also hadn't said a word to Onika about it.

She pulled up her e-mail, hoping for a job offer. Working at the community center/soup kitchen was emotionally rewarding, but she needed more money. There were none, but there was an e-mail from one of her sorority sisters. She hesitated to look at it, as she did with most e-mails from her DC circle.

It was an invitation, which immediately made Onika frown. She'd been avoiding all sorority events, because until lately she didn't have a date, and of course, Aaron would be there. He was at every DC event, and she didn't want to see him, especially not with his new woman on his arm. How embarrassing would that be?

But this was important. Her line sister, Ari, was having an engagement party, and she was not only inviting her to the party but asking her to be one of her bridesmaids. This wasn't something she could turn down. She couldn't avoid her line sister's engagement party because of a breakup.

Maybe Aaron would be the bigger person and not show up.

Of course, he wouldn't. He was the kind of guy to gloat. He would be there preening with his replacement girlfriend, and it would be a nightmare.

Onika wished Ty was still at Safe Harbor, so she could have someone to talk to about this. Charmayne would just give her Jesus, and she wanted something different right now. Even though they hadn't spoken in months, she pressed Chelsea's number into her phone.

"Hello?"

"Hey, Chelsea, it's me."

"Oh my goodness. Has Jesus come back? Is this Nikki?"

"It's me."

"Or should I say Onika?"

Onika rolled her eyes. "Aaron's been talking? I didn't think he would."

"Aaron? No, my daddy told me your real name. He didn't do it on purpose. He was talking about you, and I had no idea who he meant when he said Onika."

"Well, if it makes you feel any better, I hardly ever went by my name back then. I hated it, so I was Nikki to just about everyone who didn't have access to my tax records and birth certificate. My name wasn't a secret."

"Okay, Nikki. I just thought it was weird that in all those years I never knew that."

There were a lot of things she didn't know and would never know.

"What did your father say about me?"

"He just asked how you were. If I had talked to you lately. Is everything okay with you?"

Onika sighed. "No. Aaron and I split up about six weeks ago."

"What? Why didn't you call me?"

"I'm just trying to deal with it, you know? I guess I didn't really want to talk about it. I didn't want to hear anyone saying that they knew he'd eventually hurt me."

"I wouldn't ever say something like that."

Onika cleared her throat. "Your mama would say it. She's been waiting to say it since we were in Martha's Vineyard the summer of our freshman year."

"Where are you staying? Do you need anything?"

"I'm staying with a friend."

"Oh, okay. Let me know if you need anything. You don't have to go through this on your own. I know you must be hurting."

"I'm actually okay. I think, in some ways, I had been preparing myself for years."

"He's probably gonna be at Ari's party."

"Probably."

"You want me to call her and tell her you might not come?" Chelsea asked. "She'd understand."

"Ari and I aren't really all that cool. She probably only asked me to be in her wedding because we're line sisters. She'll have an attitude about me not showing up."

Ari was one of the few women she knew from Robinson who lived in DC. They didn't go out for brunch or happy hour or share the holidays. She only saw her at society type events when she was on Aaron's arm. Onika suspected that Ari was one of Aaron's side chicks, though she never had any proof or any desire to investigate it further. But now she was going to walk down the aisle at her wedding and dodge the bouquet when it was thrown.

"I'll be at the engagement party," Chelsea said. "Come stay in my hotel room. We can make it a slumber party."

"Where are you staying?"

"The Ritz near Georgetown."

Of course, she was staying at the Ritz. Her husband was a pastor of a megachurch, and they lived in a mansion. She'd stay in nothing less than five stars. Onika forced down her feelings of jealousy.

"Okay, let me know when you get in. I'll come to you."

"And bring some party clothes. When a long relationship like that comes to an end, we need to get wasted."

Party clothes. This was going to be a stretch. She'd have to go into some of her savings to buy something presentable for Ari's party. She'd have to go the thrift store—the vintage route—because she couldn't afford any designers.

"Really, first lady?" Onika asked. "You want to get wasted?"

"Oh, I forgot about that. The church folk might see me, huh?"

"Ya' think?"

"This pastor's wife thing is hard. I mean really hard."

Onika could hear the stress in her friend's voice. She regretted not spending more time with her and keeping up with her life. Too much time had passed without them speaking, especially since the Richards were the only family she chose to acknowledge.

"We'll have our own private session, where the church folk can't see you," Onika said. "You sound like you need to talk as much as I do."

"I do. There's so much to tell you."

Onika wished she could feel as free to divulge her struggles. Her secrets were so very heavy these days. Before, she'd been able to handle keeping Judy a secret, but now, Judy plus joblessness, plus homelessness—it was too much. Too heavy.

"Looking forward to seeing you, girl," Onika said.

"Love you."

"Love you back!"

Onika disconnected the phone, and the tears came in a hurry, before she could blink them back. Hearing Chelsea's voice had reminded her of how alone she truly was. There was not a soul who knew her whole story.

There was a knock on the library door. Probably one of those bad kids wanting to get on the Internet and play games.

"Come in," she said.

It was Charmayne, and she was bearing gifts of tea and cookies. Onika exhaled and relaxed. Snacks always made everything better, according to Charmayne.

Charmayne closed the door right on a scuffle happening in the hallway between Renee's oldest and middle sons. Onika settled herself in for a Charmayne one-on-one. She didn't even consider them to be sneaky anymore. As long as Onika lived here, Charmayne was going to communicate and talk, whether she wanted to or not. The good thing about Charmayne was that Onika only needed to share what she wanted to share. She never pressed for more.

"They are a lot, aren't they?" Charmayne asked.

Onika nodded. "They are making me rethink that teaching career. I may go to grad school, law school, or something."

"That's an excellent idea. Grad school, I mean."

"Yeah, I'm seeing that teaching isn't going to be economically feasible for me. I need a job that can pay bills. Maybe if I ever find a husband, I can teach."

"I stopped waiting for a husband. Not sure if I'll ever have one," Charmayne said.

There was no sadness in her voice when she made this declaration. Just a sense of knowing.

"Is that why you surround yourself with people?" Onika asked. "Is it because you're lonely?"

"I'm not lonely, but I do like to have people around sometimes. I like giving and receiving hugs and encouraging words. People need people."

"I think you're right."

"I just verified that you will get your first check from the tutoring job next week, so that should help you start to put aside money for your apartment."

"That's good. I'm looking forward to a paycheck, even if it is small," Onika said. "I don't like the feeling of helplessness that comes with not having any money and having to rely on you for everything."

"I believe God has you here for a reason. There's something you're supposed to be learning from this situation," Charmayne said with authority. But just because she believed it didn't mean Onika had to believe it, too.

"I think I just ended up in a bad relationship with a jerk, and it's not karma or destiny or any higher power that has me here. It's just bad luck, and it will turn around soon."

Charmayne let out an exasperated sigh. Onika did not care about her exasperation.

"So how are things with you and Graham?" Charmayne asked, changing the subject. "Have you told him yet?"

Onika shook her head. "He is still too new. I'd like to enjoy him for a while before I scare him off."

Because he would be scared off when he found out the truth. When he learned that she wasn't running a homeless shelter but living in one herself, he would take to the hills. He'd think she was a liar—and she was.

"I don't think he'd be scared off by the fact that you're homeless."

"No, not by that. He'd want to save me, I'm sure. He's got a savior complex, like you."

"I don't have a savior complex."

"Oh right," Onika said. "You know a savior. My bad."

"What would scare him off then? Your dishonesty?"

Onika nodded. "I don't think he'd do well with that. He'd take it personally, like I didn't tell him the truth because of me not trusting him. That has nothing to do with it."

"Well, what is it then?"

"It's a habit for me, keeping secrets. Because I know that when people know all of it, all your crap, they treat you differently, no matter what they say. They do."

"You're right. When people found out I married a gay man, they treated me differently. People who I thought were my friends talked about me so bad. It hurt."

"So you know what I mean."

"But I think I needed those people to show themselves. I needed to know who only loved me for superficial reasons. I needed to know who would love me after knowing all my junk."

"How many did you have left, after it all came out?"

Charmayne sighed. "Not many. But why don't you try me. Lighten your load a little bit. Tell me one thing you haven't told anyone else. See if I treat you differently."

Onika laughed. "You already know my biggest secret. I don't have anywhere that's mine, to lay my head. And you treat me differently. If we had met at a charity function, you wouldn't be trying to fix me. Because I'm here in this situation, I am a broken doll for you to fix. You wouldn't be trying to glue me back together otherwise."

"It's hard trying to get through to you," Charmayne said.

"Well then, stop. Stop trying to *get through* to me. If you want to be my friend, then be my friend, but stop trying to fix me. I know this is your ministry. It makes you feel good, but it's not helping me."

Charmayne stood with her cup of tea in her hand. "Okay, but as one friend to another, let me just say this. No one likes being lied to. You should tell Graham the truth."

"You think I don't want to tell him the truth? I want to be able to tell him everything about me and feel secure that nothing will change, but it's not possible."

"It's possible," Charmayne said.

"Thank you for your advice," Onika said.

"But you're not going to take it, are you?"

"I will take it under advisement."

Charmayne shook her head sadly, got up, and walked out of the library, leaving Onika with her thoughts. Onika would deal with Graham if he looked like he was becoming permanent, and by then, there would probably be nothing to tell. She'd have her own place, her own money, and a job that would pay the bills and leave a little over for fun. By then, her lie would be transformed into a little, harmless fib that no one, not even honest Graham, would hold against her.

CHAPTER FORTY-SIX

Onika couldn't believe she'd let Graham talk her into this swimming lesson. Somehow in between all their talk about love and forever, she'd written a check with her mouth that her butt was now having to cash.

"You won't have to get in the deep water at all," Graham said from his position inside the huge, Olympic-size swimming pool. "We can stay in the shallow the whole time. How far can you go into the water before you start to feel uncomfortable?"

Onika sat on the side of the pool with her feet and legs submerged in the warm water. "This is the only place I feel comfortable when it comes to a pool."

"But you aren't even in the water."

"Precisely."

"What can I do to persuade you to get into the water?" Graham asked. "This will only come up to your waist."

"You bribed and persuaded me to come here in the first place with kisses. You tricked me. Got me all flustered and then slipped this swimming lesson mess on me."

A huge smile broke out on Graham's face, but then he already knew he'd flustered her.

"Shall I give you more? Is that what you want as a reward?"

Onika laughed. "No. That sounds like a reward for you."

"We'll both enjoy it. Why don't you slip into the pool, and walk toward me? Just walking. No swimming. When you get to me, I'll kiss you and make you want to strip off that tiny swimsuit."

Onika's suit wasn't particularly revealing, but her curves were not contained by the strips of spandex. The top was made like a sports bra, but her cleavage spilled out, inviting touches. The bottom was full coverage, but not for the hips and behind on Onika's petite frame. On her, the bottom looked like a high-cut thong bikini.

"You want me to slip out of my bathing suit, don't you? Well, we don't have to make me a drowning victim for that to happen. Come on out of the water, and you can make that happen."

Graham shook his head and laughed. "Nope. You're going to be so happy you learned to swim. I can't wait for us to go snorkeling together in the Caribbean."

"You're getting way ahead of yourself. Walking in the shallow end of a swimming pool and going out in the middle of the ocean are two different things."

"I'm just predicting our future. Snorkeling in Aruba on our honeymoon."

If there wasn't a pool full of water between them, Onika would have run and jumped into Graham's arms. His mind was clearly made up, no matter how she tried to warn him to wait until he knew her whole story before he decided on forever.

Onika decided to get it over with and slid into the warm water. It came a little bit over her waist, but she could tell that the water got deeper the closer she got to Graham.

"It's too deep over there," Onika said. "You come to me. I got in, and I want my kiss now."

"It's not too deep right here. The water will just come up to your breasts, and if, when you get down here you get scared, you can jump into my arms."

"Giving you a bird's eye view of my boobs."

"I won't look. I'm only trying to make you a competent swimmer. This has nothing to do with my desires."

"Tell me more about that last part. The desire part."

Graham laughed. "I can't hear you. You're too far away. You'll have to come out farther."

Onika slowly put one foot in front of the next, steadily creeping closer to Graham. The water swirled around her midsection, and then her breasts rested right above the waterline. This was as deep as she could go right now.

"I can't go any more. It's getting too deep."

"Just a few more steps, and I promise I'll come the rest of the way to you."

Onika took two more steps and then wouldn't budge. The water was unnerving her, and it took every bit of her willpower to not turn around and go back to the ladder. Before she got the chance to do that, Graham took a few swim strokes and closed the space between them. He stood up in the water right in front of Onika. Her muscles relaxed, and she felt her heart rate slow. She was calm and safe.

"Even though you didn't come all the way to me, I guess you can have your reward."

He went in for the kiss, and Onika splashed water in his face. He wasn't slick. That reward was for himself.

Graham grabbed each side of Onika's waist and lifted her out of the water. She splashed him some more as he lowered her back in. She wasn't playing with him.

"Do you trust me?" Graham asked.

"I'm not sure. Trust you to do what?"

"Wrap your arms around my neck and your legs around my waist. I want to take you out into the deep."

"Oh, naw. I don't trust you to do that. Nope."

Graham laughed. "I promise I won't let anything happen to you."

"I believe you, Graham, but I almost drowned when I was little. At a church picnic."

Just thinking again about that day made Onika want to walk back to the shallowest end of the pool. She pushed Graham's hands and arms away and started to go where she would feel safe without Graham's help.

"You're done already?" Graham asked.

"You don't know how big this is. I haven't been in water over my waist since I nearly died."

Graham followed Onika, but by the time he caught up, she was climbing out of the pool. She moved incredibly fast for someone who was walking in the water instead of swimming.

"Next time, I'm going to get you to put your face in the water."

"Not unless your Jesus comes back and I get left behind in the rapture."

Graham narrowed his eyes at Onika and shook his head. "My Jesus? He's not just my Jesus."

Onika hated that those words had slipped out of her mouth. She didn't want to ruin their good time. If she was having a good time with Graham at a swimming pool, she could have a good time with him anywhere. Maybe even church, although she chose not to go.

"Oh, I'm just kidding, Graham. Don't take it to heart."

"When you say things like that, it makes me sad."

"Forget I said it."

"I can't, because I know you mean it."

Onika touched his face gently. "Well, then, don't think about it. I will try not to say things like that to you. I don't want to see you sad."

Then she pulled his face closer to hers, so that she could give him the reward he tried to get earlier. She hoped her kisses would erase that look from his face, because she enjoyed being around him, even in a swimming pool. And maybe, just to see him smile, she'd go to one of his church services. She needed more time, though. More time to fall completely in love with Graham, because only her love for him would keep her from mocking the ridiculous side of him that believed in a God who had never once shown up when she needed Him.

CHAPTER FORTY-SEVEN

Chelsea was true to her pampered and privileged roots in her five-star hotel suite. When Onika arrived, there was white wine chilling on ice, and an assortment of fruit, sweets, and appetizers. So much of this would be wasted that it annoyed Onika.

How Chelsea lived had never bothered her before. Onika had lived like this with Aaron. But now, when she thought about how Renee's kids would fight over a grilled cheese sandwich, it bothered her. Being homeless was changing her.

Onika carefully chose a few items that she knew she'd eat and poured herself a glass of wine. She sat down at the room's dining table, across from Chelsea, who looked radiant in her blue silk robe, her hair cascading over her shoulder in soft waves.

"You look fantastic, girl," Onika said. "Being a first lady must not be too bad."

"It's the people. They are constantly vying for my husband's time. It's like they think they own him."

"Right, he's their man of God. They need him for their blessing."

"Correct. And they think if they pray hard enough they'll be blessed like he's blessed. Don't they know he comes from old money? He's got doctor, lawyer, judge, and legislator money. All that didn't come from praying."

"Exactly. My grandmother used to say, folk needed to pray on their way to work."

"I've never heard you talk about your grandmother before."

Onika didn't know what made her bring Earlene up. Probably the talk about church and church people. Onika associated Earlene with church.

"She was a piece of work. Pretty much raised me, and loved her church."

Chelsea smiled. "I'd like to meet her."

"No, you really wouldn't," Onika said. "She's not a nice lady."

"So you get it honest, huh?"

"What? I am nice."

"You're nicety. Nice, but can turn nasty in a heartbeat."

Onika considered this. "I'll own that. Don't mess with me, and all you get is nice."

"Is that what happened with Aaron? Did he bring out that other side of you?"

Onika scoffed. "He broke up with me."

"Did he say why? Did you know it was coming? Talk to me."

"He says it was because I had an abortion."

"Oh . . . he wants kids? But not a wife."

"I think if polygamy was legal, he'd have twenty wives. He just doesn't want to be chained to one woman."

"You don't sound . . . angry at him."

"Oh, I'm angry at him. I'm angry at how he decided to end things suddenly, leaving me scrambling. That's what I'm mad about."

Chelsea poured herself another glass of wine. She'd downed the first one when Onika said abortion.

"You know, I think I'd have an abortion too if I got pregnant right now. I don't want any babies," Chelsea said.

"Then don't get pregnant if you can help it. I'm still not over that."

"Are you bringing a date to Ari's party? You know he'll be there."

Onika had started to ask Graham, but didn't. She didn't know that he would fit in with this group, with his government job, associate's degree, and lack of familiarity with all things Greek. They'd probably seem pretentious to him, because they were, and if he started talking about God, they'd probably laugh at him behind his back.

"I'm seeing someone, but we're not there yet for me to showcase him."

"What if Aaron has someone?"

This made Onika finish her wine and pour herself another glass. "He does have someone else. He had her before I left. I came across her wearing one of my outfits. That did not go well."

"What happened?"

"I accidentally spilled red wine all over her. Ruined a pretty good piece of couture."

"Ugh. Who would wear another woman's clothes?"

"He found her at Robinson, so I guess a Robinette."

Chelsea shook her head and stared out of the window. "I don't think this is how our lives are supposed to be playing out."

Onika wanted to scream. Chelsea knew nothing about struggle or pain or hardship. She'd left her daddy's mansion for her husband's mansion. She knew nothing except excess and abundance.

"What do you mean? Your life is playing out just fine. You have whatever you want."

"Life isn't just about things, you know? I want something more than possessions."

"I'll take the possessions first and figure the rest out later." Onika was so serious about this. She'd trade with Chelsea in a heartbeat and would never look back.

"I know I sound like a spoiled, pampered princess."

"You do. Sorry."

"Well, think about it for a second. How much shopping can one person do? How many times can you go to the beach? I want to do something important. I want to leave something behind that's my creation. I want a legacy."

"Children can do that. Maybe you do want some babies."

Chelsea shook her head. "Any woman who is healthy and has the right body parts can have a baby. I want to do something unique."

Onika didn't know that her friend *was* unique. Maybe she hadn't discovered her special gift to the world yet, but Onika had no idea what Chelsea could offer to the world, other than being a consumer.

"Do you understand what I mean?" Chelsea asked when Onika didn't reply.

"It sounds like first world problems to me," Onika said with a chuckle. "Maybe go to one of those Oprah transform your life conferences or something."

"I can't stand you."

Onika laughed. "I'm just saying. You've got it all, girl. I can't be concerned with your little issues right now."

"You're right, I guess. Did you . . . did you know that my father was sleeping with girls at Robinson? Was he doing it while we were there?"

Onika's jaw dropped. "That came from out of left field."

"A girl sent my mother a letter about her five-year-long affair with my dad."

"What did Mrs. Richard do?"

"Nothing," Chelsea said. "She did nothing, except show me the letter and then burn it. The girl was someone my mother had mentored."

"That's a shame that Dr. Richard would do that to her."

"My mother insisted that it wasn't the first time, and she said that it wouldn't be the last. Were you one of the girls?"

"No! Why would you think that?"

"It just occurred to me that my father knows more about you than anyone. He knew your name. What else did he know?"

"Chelsea, I would never have hurt you or Mrs. Richard by sleeping with Dr. Richard. He was a mentor to me as well. We never had that sort of relationship."

"Maybe he was planning on it, though. He brought you to Martha's Vineyard that time. He was probably working his way up to getting with you, and then you shocked him by linking up with Aaron."

Onika had never considered that Dr. Richard had wanted anything from her. He'd never made a pass at her, had never said anything inappropriate.

"I don't think your dad was looking at me, but your brother, Jaime, tried to rape me freshman year."

"Is there more wine in that bottle?" Chelsea asked. "We need to open another one. Get the hell out of here. Jaime?"

"He was drunk. Luckily, I wasn't. Remember that party we went to in Buckhead where you puked everywhere?"

"Oh, yes, how could I ever forget that?"

"That was the night it happened. He didn't come for me again, though."

Chelsea shook her head as she opened the second bottle of wine with the wine opener. "You're just telling all the secrets tonight."

"Not all."

Onika could never tell Chelsea how she'd threatened Dr. Richard over his indiscretions. And that Dr. Richard had been with several of their sorority sisters. If she found out one day, it wouldn't be from Onika.

"Why are we talking about such horrible things?" Onika asked. "We're going to be completely useless at this engagement party tonight if we drink any more wine. Will we even be able to give a toast?"

Chelsea shook her head. "You're right. Let's talk about what we're wearing. Or about what you're not wearing. That outfit you hung up in the closet is not going to cut it."

"There's nothing wrong with that dress. It's vintage."

Onika had combed through rack after rack of dresses in just about every thrift store she could reach on the Metro. And she'd come across a cream-colored lace minidress that was probably made in the sixties. It fit perfectly, and after Charmayne helped her clean it with white vinegar, baking soda, and Woolite, it was stain-free.

"It's a beautiful dress. I love it," Chelsea said. "But it's not going to make Aaron regret the day he kicked you out of his bed."

"He didn't kick me . . . well, yes he did. You're right."

"I've got something perfect for you to wear."

It was a white jumpsuit with a top whose opening plunged all the way to the waist. Onika would need bra tape to wear it, but it was perfect. And the right size.

"Did you bring this on purpose for me?" Onika asked. "I am a size two, and you're like a six. Why would you even be traveling with my size?"

"Because I'm your sister. I'm here to help. You never want anyone to help you, but you should lean on someone from time to time."

"I've been hearing that a lot lately."

"You should listen. Let me be there for you in this."

Onika smiled and hugged Chelsea. "Okay, well, what am I supposed to do about shoes, accessories, hair, and makeup?"

"I thought you'd never ask."

Chelsea got up and made a phone call, and then clapped her hands together.

"We're going to make Aaron wish he'd never lost you."

Even though Onika didn't want Aaron back—at all—she wanted him to want her. She needed that feeling of vindication. So she was about to pour her body into that pantsuit and rock whatever shoes Chelsea and her great fashion sense had chosen. She was going to slay any girlfriend Aaron had on his arm. And maybe she'd feel good about it all and be able to move on with her life.

CHAPTER FORTY-EIGHT

Onika was glad she'd listened to Chelsea about her outfit. It was beautiful, but the couture at this event was on another level entirely. She would've felt out of place in her vintage, thrift-store lace. Because of Chelsea, Onika was feeling a bit like her old self. She didn't feel like her home was a shelter for women. She felt like the socialite she'd intended to be when she left Goldsboro.

Onika was also glad that Chelsea had left her husband home. The husband would've kept them from sticking together like glue. Chelsea had rescued Onika from multiple conversations that night already, and she'd rescued Chelsea as well.

It seemed like Onika was worried for nothing, because Aaron didn't seem to be coming to the party. That was a good thing, because Onika had a few glasses of wine, and if he brought that girl to this party, things might turn ugly. Not on purpose, of course. Onika would blame it on the alcohol the next day.

"Did you hear Ari's going to have the bridesmaids wear turquoise?" Chelsea asked. "She would pick a crazy color."

"I like turquoise," Onika said. "It looks beautiful on me. I'm going to flow in like the ocean."

"You can't upstage the bride, now."

"No woman upstages the bride on her day. I've never seen a homely bride."

"Yes, you have. We've been to a few weddings that had homely brides."

Onika and Chelsea laughed hard, partially from the jokes, but more from the wine.

"Is someone going to tell me the joke?"

Onika snapped to attention when she heard Aaron's voice. Chelsea's eyes widened, and she stumbled a bit from the shock of him sneaking up on them.

"So you decided to show up," Onika said.

"Did you think I wouldn't?" Aaron hugged Chelsea and kissed her cheek. "It's been a long time since I've seen you, Chelsea. How are your parents?"

"They're good."

"I need to call your dad next week. He and I are supposed to get together in Atlanta before the school year starts."

"Okay," Chelsea said with a shrug.

"Chelsea, can I talk to Nikki alone for a minute?" Aaron asked.

Chelsea narrowed her eyes to little slits. "Why do you need to talk to her? She doesn't have anything to talk to you about."

"It's okay, Chelsea. Give us a second," Onika said.

Onika was curious. She noticed that Aaron didn't have his girlfriend with him. She wondered if that was because they weren't together or because he knew she'd be there. Either way, she wanted to hear him out.

"Okay," Chelsea said, "but I'll be right over there if you need me."

Aaron reached in for a hug, and Onika stepped back. She was nosy about what he wanted, but she had no desire to touch or hug him.

"Don't go there, Aaron. What do you want from me now?"

"How have you been?"

"Man, don't even try to stand up here and act like you care

about my well-being. If it was up to you, I'd be back at that shack in North Carolina."

"With your grandmother. Right. You know, I'm sorry about that. I shouldn't have gone there. That's your life and your history. I didn't have a right."

Onika sighed. This felt like an apology, but she wasn't open to it. She didn't want to hear any apologies from Aaron. He was a deliberate kind of man. Everything he did was planned and plotted. Nothing was accidental, so even this apology had hidden layers of meaning.

"I do care how you've been, though. How are you getting by?" Aaron asked.

"I know how to survive. Worse things have happened in my life than you."

He shook his head and chuckled. "Wow."

"I know you find that hard to believe, Aaron, but I lived a few years before I met you."

Aaron grabbed the hand that Onika hadn't even realized was poking a finger in his face. He lowered it slowly and gently.

"Nikki, I came over here to give you this."

He reached in his pocket and pulled out a folded-up piece of paper.

"What's this?"

"It's help, Nikki. I was hurt when I found out what you did, but I am not a cruel man."

Onika looked down at a check for twenty-five thousand dollars. It was enough for her to get an apartment and carry her over for a few months until she found a teaching job.

As much as she wanted to take the money, she folded the check up and handed it back to him.

"What are you doing? Don't act like you don't need it."

"Why are you doing this now? Why couldn't you leave me with any dignity when we broke up? You didn't even let me take my clothes and shoes. Your new chick was wearing my clothes, Aaron."

"Hey, I would've never let her do that. I didn't know she'd

been through your things. You can come and get them if you want."

Onika's mouth watered at the idea of having her shoes. He could keep all the clothes, but if she could have her Louboutins and Jimmy Choos, she might feel like things were looking up again.

"You can come and get them," Aaron said. "But where would you put them? I know you're living in a shelter, Onika. It's not a secret."

Onika swallowed hard. How did he know? Worse, who else knew? She felt nauseous at the thought of their entire social circle in DC knowing that she was homeless.

"It's not the talk of the town," Aaron said, "but a few key individuals know. Just take the check. It makes me look bad, too, that you're in this situation. This isn't just about you."

"If I take this money from you, do you have any expectations of me?"

"What do you mean?"

"You know exactly what I mean, Aaron. I'm not sleeping with you."

Aaron shook his head. "Come on, Nikki. You know that I don't need sex from you."

"Correct. You've got enough receptacles. Enough depositories."

"You don't have to be vulgar."

"I'm being truthful."

Aaron put the check in her hand again. "Take it. No matter what you think, I care what happens to you. I honestly thought you would go back to North Carolina."

"If you knew what was waiting for me there, you never would've thought that."

"Maybe if you'd told me about your life before Robinson, I would've known."

Onika shook her head and tucked the check into her purse. She was glad she'd never told Aaron about her childhood. He didn't deserve to know. He was proof that secrets needed to stay secrets.

"I'm only taking this check because I need it. Not because I need you."

"Okay, good. You still have my number? Let me put it in your phone."

Onika felt frozen in time as Aaron took her phone and typed his number into the contacts. He flipped the phone over in his hand but didn't comment on it, although Onika was sure he wanted to. She snatched her phone back and put it in her purse. He had no right to judge her lack of the newest technology when he'd taken everything from her.

"Are you finished? You done?" Onika asked.

"Almost."

He tipped her chin back and kissed her passionately. Or as passionately as he could muster. And it didn't come close to any of Graham's kisses. Graham made her feel like she was the only woman in the world that he wanted. With Aaron, she was one of many that could turn him on.

"We don't have to get back together, but don't close the door on us," Aaron said. "I reacted badly, but I miss you. We're good together. You understand me like no other woman."

"I may understand you, but we don't want the same things out of life."

"Let me ask you a question, Nikki. This has been bugging me since I found out about what you did to our child."

Onika's lip curled angrily. Every time he brought up that abortion, she felt like he absolved himself of any responsibility in their relationship's demise. He acted like the decision for her to end their child's life was the determining factor in everything being over. Not his infidelity or lack of commitment.

"What is your question, Aaron?"

"If we had been married, if you had the big wedding and the rock on your finger, would I be a father right now?"

"You mean if you were committed enough to not have sex with every woman who catches your fancy? You mean if you looked at me and said, 'You're all that I need'?" Onika shook her head. "This is a stupid hypothetical question, because you were never committed, and there isn't one woman alive who is all you need."

"I was so broken when I found out what you had done."

"How did you find out anyway?"

He shook his head. "There's not much you can do in this city that doesn't make its way back to me. I have friends all over. One of my friends donates to the home you live in now. DC is a big city and a small town."

Onika was surprised that he didn't say anything about Graham. If he had all this other intel, then he must know that she'd moved on.

"It's too late to ask those questions. I can't go back in time and make a different choice. Something tells me you would've found another way to dismiss me. Maybe if I had your child I would have a child-support check coming in."

"Do you think I'd ever let you walk away with my child?" Aaron said.

"So you would've gotten full custody and put me out on the street, then. How could I have gotten that story wrong as well as I know you."

"I don't think we would be apart if we had a child together. I think we would've made wonderful parents."

The conversation was wearing Onika down a bit, but not enough to accept anything other than Aaron's money.

"Thank you for this. I do need it, and I will use it."

"All right, Nikki. Don't lose my number. Call me when you need me."

He said when, not if, and that made Onika want to delete his number right then and there. He didn't believe in her at all. He didn't think she could make it without him.

While she was definitely going to cash the check, he could keep the clothes and the shoes. Onika didn't want any other reminders of their life together.

If she needed another human being, she had one. She had Graham, who would gladly put a ring on it and forsake all others just for her.

So she was done with Aaron. As soon as the check cleared.

CHAPTER FORTY-NINE

Graham sat in Sunday morning service feeling defeated. He'd been feeling this way ever since that Saturday morning at the pool with Onika. Everything had been going well until she'd made that comment—until she'd called Jesus *his* Jesus.

Why would God send him a woman who was perfect in every way except this one thing? And she wasn't even content to just be agnostic and not bother him about his faith. She had to keep picking and making snide remarks, like she thought less of him for believing in God the way he did.

As far as he could tell, she had almost every characteristic that he wanted. She was beautiful, smart, funny, and sarcastic. She even cared about helping people in need. He enjoyed her company, and she enjoyed him, but anytime faith came up, she turned away.

While the pastor preached, Graham scanned the church full of women. There had to be at least fifteen women to every one man. And some of those men were married, gay, or too old to be searching for a woman. Why couldn't Graham just pick one of them to be his wife?

Leslie was there, wearing a lime-green suit. There was something about the color that Graham didn't like on her, but it definitely complimented her shape. The skirt seemed to be some kind of stretchy material that was pulled taut across her behind and hips. The jacket was snug and cinched at the waist. As she lifted her hands to praise God, every man sitting behind her was treated to a nice view, but Graham looked away. He wasn't interested.

Graham was falling in love with a heathen. A woman who used to go to church when she was a little girl but changed her mind when she grew up. He wanted to change it back. Graham wanted her to sit next to him in the pew and raise her hands in worship right alongside him.

Graham remembered all of the sermons he'd heard, mostly in the men's bible study group, about dealing with women who weren't saved. The minister had said that the men were like the sons of Israel, and women outside the church were like the Philistines, Edomites, and Samaritans—all groups the Israelites didn't marry.

That minister had told them all that they should choose a sister from within their congregation or at least another church, so that they could be equals. Back then, Graham had agreed and thought that it was a good idea to believe the same as his potential wife.

But now, since he was falling for someone who didn't profess to be a Christian, he didn't know where he still stood on that, especially since he felt God put Onika in his path for the first and then the second time.

After the service was over, he hurried out of the church to take Onika to brunch. He'd driven to church, because it was Sunday and the traffic would be easy.

He pulled up in front of Safe Harbor and jumped out of the car. Before he could even make it up the walkway, Onika had opened the front door, emerged, and then closed it behind her.

"Come on. We've got a houseful, and I want to leave and come back," Onika said.

Her hair was in a bun on the top of her head, showing off

her sexy neck. It looked so smooth and creamy that Graham wanted to kiss it, but since he'd just come from church, he kissed her cheek instead.

"Is it okay for you to leave this way? Who's in charge while you're gone?"

"Oh, it's Charmayne," Onika said as she got into the car. "Everything is fine."

Graham went around to his side of the car and jumped inside. Onika was examining the wood panel dashboard on his older-model Honda. He hoped she didn't have anything negative to say about it, because he absolutely loved his car. He'd bought it at an auction and fixed it up.

"Where are we going?" she asked.

"Do you want to have brunch at my place? I was thinking of making you my famous apple pancakes."

"Famous? With all the girls you loved before?"

Were there really any girls before Onika? He'd had a girlfriend in high school, a couple in college that weren't serious. As an adult, he had friends that he occasionally slept with but didn't consider marrying. But there was no one he'd loved before.

"They're famous in my family. My mom loves them, and so do my cousins."

"You have a big family? Lots of cousins?"

Graham nodded. "Yes. My mother has five sisters and two brothers, so there are a bunch of us."

"Do they all live nearby?"

"Not all, but many of them do. We don't get to see each other as much as we like, but they are here in DC and Maryland."

"I always wanted cousins. I didn't have any. My mama was an only child, and I'm not sure about my father. Actually, I bet I have some cousins on my father's side."

"So why don't you start looking for them. It's always good to find your family, if you can."

"My family on my father's side speaks Spanish. I don't even know how to go about communicating with them or contacting them," Onika said.

"You want me to help you look for them? I love doing that kind of stuff."

Onika shook her head. "No, I'm good. They aren't looking for me, and I ain't looking for them. That's actually kind of a good thing."

"So, to my house for pancakes, or do you want me to take you out somewhere?"

"It doesn't make me a difference. Whatever you want to do is fine."

"I've seen where you live. I want you to see where I live."

"Okay."

Something wasn't right. Graham couldn't put his finger on what felt funny, but something did. Onika felt distant, like on their first date when he'd kept saying the wrong thing. Except today he hadn't said anything that could be offensive.

"Are you okay?" Graham asked. "You seem a little distracted, like you left part of yourself back at home."

"Maybe I did leave part of myself at home. I was out really late last night at my friend's engagement party."

An engagement party. Wasn't that the kind of event when girls wanted to have a date? Why hadn't she asked him to go with her?

"It's one of my line sisters that I don't really like," Onika said. "I'm in the wedding, so I'll be stuck being near her on her wedding day. That is no bueno."

"I didn't get to go to the engagement party with you, but I'll go to the wedding if you want me to."

"It's a ways off, but thank you."

Wait. What if she hadn't invited him because her ex was going to be there?

"You don't think your friends will like me?" Graham asked.

"Of course not. My friends are going to love you."

"Ohhh. So you're just not ready to show me off then."

Onika smiled. "I just want to keep you to myself for now. I am a private person. I don't like everyone in my business."

Graham liked to think that he was a private person as well, but he had his two homeboys that he told everything to, and they were it. Lorne was a bottomless pit of secrets, and so was Craig. He never needed anything to go beyond the two of them.

Onika took her privacy even more seriously than Graham, though if she couldn't take him to an engagement party, it probably wasn't privacy at all. There was most likely an old boyfriend who was going to be there, and she wanted everyone to think that she was still single. Maybe not everyone, but just that one guy.

"Do you have eggs and bacon, too? What about some smoked sausage?" Onika asked, snatching Graham's attention back on her and away from his suspicions.

"Oh, yeah, I have everything."

"Graham, is something wrong?" Onika asked.

Graham almost said nothing, but denial when something was wrong was not a good precedent to set. Plus, the more he thought about it, the more he *needed* to know the answer to the question nagging at him.

"I would've gone to the engagement party with you if you'd asked. Why didn't you?"

She nodded, maybe understanding his sudden change of tone. It was a simple question, and her pause was a bit too long for Graham's liking.

"This is a pretentious group, Graham, and I honestly haven't dealt with any of them in months. I had a bad breakup, and he kept custody of the friends. I didn't want to put you in an awkward situation."

He knew it had something to do with a man. An ex. The only ex, if she was being truthful about the number of guys she'd dated.

"Was it your first time seeing him since you broke up?"

"I didn't say he was there."

"You didn't. I assumed."

"Don't do that."

Graham tapped his index fingers on the steering wheel, trying to think of how to counter. He felt like he was being a jerk, but he couldn't help it. He'd never felt this kind of jealousy.

Questions pummeled his mind like actual blows. When she'd seen her ex, had she hugged him? Kissed him?

Graham wanted to know if their new, fledgling love had doused her old flame.

"I'm sorry," Graham said.

He could only offer an apology for his rudeness, but not for his feelings.

"I forgive you."

Graham didn't want forgiveness; he wanted an explanation, but she clearly did not intend to give him that.

While he drove, Onika slid her hand over Graham's knee. She squeezed a little, massaged and caressed the same spot. He almost let her touch distract him again, like it had done at the swimming pool. This time he focused.

"I'd like to say that we're exclusive. Are you okay with that?" Graham asked.

"We are. Okay. I'm more than fine with it."

That felt easy. Too easy.

"I didn't mean to come across like a caveman or anything. I just want you to know that I'm not kidding around, even though it's only been five weeks."

"Well, to be honest, I'm not seeing anyone else, and I wasn't when we met. So being exclusive is pretty easy. Plus, I like where this thing is going so far. I want to see where we end up."

"Okay."

While not conclusive, this was enough for now. It was okay that her passion didn't match his. He was the one dreaming of her when she came along.

One of Graham's favorite gospel songs played on the car radio. It started, "Be not dismayed." It was his favorite because of the chorus, "God will take care of you." He believed that over everything in life. No matter what, God had him.

He was caught up for a moment in the beauty of the singing, and in his thoughts. But then he noticed that Onika was singing along.

Graham said nothing, he just let her sing, and marveled at her pretty soprano voice. Then she chuckled.

"My grandmother used to sing this song all the time. I'm surprised I still remember the words."

Graham wasn't surprised at all. He said a prayer of thanks for what he considered a sign. If Onika still remembered a gospel song, then maybe she still remembered God. And if she still remembered Him, she could one day believe again.

CHAPTER FIFTY

Onika felt a sense of comfort looking at a five-figure balance in her bank account, even though every apartment she called had minimum-income requirements that she couldn't meet. Or they'd ask for four pay stubs when she only had three. So even though she had the cash, she had to remain under Charmayne's roof just a little longer.

She logged off her bank account and logged onto a few job sites, uploading her résumé anytime she thought she was qualified to do the work. She applied for bank teller jobs, restaurant gigs, and government jobs. She was closing in on two months at Safe Harbor. It was too long, especially with her new roommate, who was nothing like Ty.

Graham wasn't even around to keep her company and take her on fun, albeit cheap, dates. He was out of town with his job for a training class. Would be gone for four days. Onika had gotten so used to seeing him every other day that she missed him.

After applying for dozens of jobs, Onika went onto Graham's Facebook page. She liked looking at his pictures, especially from when he was younger. And he had a couple of workout photos where his ripped, chocolate-dipped chest was exposed and covered in sweat. Those were her favorites.

Graham had new photos on his page, apparently from the training class. He was smiling from ear to ear in all of them, and some of the photos were group pictures. Onika narrowed her eyes at the screen to make sure her suspicions were correct. Yes, Graham's coworker, Leslie, was posing near Graham in just about all the pictures.

Everyone looked like they were having fun—especially Graham. She wondered what his church friends thought about the multiple empty cocktail glasses near Graham in the photos. Not that they were all his, but the glazed-over look in his eyes, along with his bright smile, made Onika think that several of them were.

Onika clicked through the photos until she saw one that really irritated her. Leslie had taken a selfie with Graham, and although he wasn't smiling in this one, she was. Onika folded her arms across her chest and glared at the computer screen. Leslie needed to back up off her man.

She chided herself for this thought at first. They were still new, but he's the one who asked her for exclusivity. And she had agreed. So . . . he needed to get that woman off of him. Immediately.

Onika sent him a text. YOU AND LESLIE ARE HAVING BIG FUN.

Then she waited for a response. It came quicker than she expected.

NO WE'RE NOT. SHE GETS ON MY NERVES.

This made Onika laugh, because she knew that, regardless of what Leslie put on social media, he was telling the truth. The nerve of Leslie, though, when Graham had told her multiple times that he wasn't interested.

Onika felt like being petty and stirring the pot, so she typed a comment under the non-cute selfie. IS THIS WORK OR PLAY? ☺

Leslie must've been feeling equally petty, because she responded almost immediately with one word: BOTH.

Onika stared at the screen, wanting to reply, but not replying, because she didn't want to impact Graham's job. Plus, she'd started it, posting on a picture Leslie had put up. Graham needed to handle Leslie, though, because Onika didn't have a problem handling the desperate woman herself.

"Your little girlfriend is posting on my Facebook page," Leslie said to Graham in front of all their coworkers at the dinner table.

Graham fumed, not just because of Leslie's announcement, but because of the picture in the first place. He'd watched her go around the room taking selfies with everyone, deep down knowing that she only wanted the selfie with him. Lorne had told her to get the heck out of his face with her camera, and Craig had disappeared at the last second. She'd only caught Graham, because he'd just had a glass of wine and was feeling friendly. Almost as soon as she clicked, he realized she was going to post it on social media.

She had, and Onika had seen it. Onika never posted on his page. He had inspirational quotes up daily, but she never responded to those. But one tagged photo with a woman she knew he didn't want, and she was online commenting. Women.

"Graham's little girlfriend just might come see you," Lorne said. "She seems like the rowdy type. If I was you, I'd leave her alone."

"She's not the rowdy type, but she's *my* type," Graham said in response. "She doesn't have anything to worry about. She probably genuinely liked the picture."

Leslie frowned, probably not liking getting a comeuppance, but she deserved it, since she wanted to start stuff.

"I'm turning in, y'all," Graham said. "We have class in the morning, so I want to get some rest."

"Party pooper," Lorne mumbled.

He might have been a party pooper, but he wasn't going to spend another minute at the table with Leslie, giving her time to think up more lies or attacks on Onika.

"Good night, Graham," Leslie said in a very seductive tone.

Everyone laughed. Everyone except Graham.

"She'll be on her way up later," Helena said, getting a roar of laughter from the group.

Graham didn't think that was funny at all, but if he commented, then of course he would be the villain. So he left the table without responding. He could see that eventually, whether he wanted to or not, he was going to have to do something about Leslie, and he didn't see it ending well.

CHAPTER FIFTY-ONE

Onika jumped up from the desk in Charmayne's office and shouted with joy. It was too early for all that noise, but she couldn't help herself. She had a job offer—for a real job. It was as a legal secretary, and it paid fifty-eight thousand dollars a year. Even though it wasn't even close to how much she needed to make in expensive DC, it was better than what she had now, and she would be able to move.

She looked at the communication again and realized she didn't recognize the company's name. She didn't remember applying for the job, but that's not to say that she hadn't. She was pretty much mindlessly applying for any and every job she saw online. She definitely hadn't interviewed for it, so they were giving her an offer sight unseen.

"Everything okay in there?" Charmayne asked from outside the door.

Onika should've known Charmayne would wake up and come down there with her nosy self. She wanted all the scoop at all times.

Onika opened the office door. "Yes, everything is incredible. I got a job offer. I start next week. It's as a legal secretary."

Charmayne jumped up and down and clapped. "Look at

God! Didn't you say you might want to go to law school? Maybe this will lead you to that. What a blessing."

The joy went right out of Onika's face. Why was Charmayne giving credit to God? Onika hadn't prayed about her jobless-ness and homelessness. She hadn't asked Him for anything. She'd asked God for one thing a long time ago—a sober mother. He hadn't helped then, so why give Him any credit now?

"This is not a blessing. This is me attracting interest with what I'm putting out there. I am putting out positive energy and receiving positivity in response to that."

Charmayne looked confused. "Okay, well, I prayed for you, so I'm going to thank God. You can say it's whatever you want it to be."

"I'm saying what it is."

"Well, what's positive about lying to your boyfriend? He still doesn't even know why you live in a women's shelter. So what happens with that? When you put lies out into the universe, what happens then?"

Onika narrowed her eyes angrily at Charmayne. "How dare you try to make fun of what I believe?"

"I am actually surprised to hear that you believe in anything. That is a start. That's a way to get you back to God."

"I never said I didn't believe anything. I just said I'm not going back to any of your churches, and I'm not asking Jesus for anything. If there is a higher power, it has enabled all of us to attain exactly what we can have. Reaping and sowing is a law of the universe."

Charmayne merely stared at Onika. She didn't react, even though Onika was screaming now. Onika checked herself and calmed down. She still lived here, under Charmayne's roof. She was grateful to her, even if she was a Christian.

"I'm sorry," Onika said. "I didn't mean to scream."

"It's okay. I rather like you showing some emotion. Do you realize that you hold everything in? I've only seen you break down once, and in your situation, that is hard to imagine."

"Why do you think I have to let you see me break down? You don't know what happens with me in my private time. You don't know what kinds of personal reflections I have about all this. I just haven't let you see it."

"That's fair," Charmayne said. "And I don't have to see you break down. As long as you are examining what went wrong with your choices and are planning to make different ones. If you continue to live the same way, you're going to have the same outcomes."

"Thank you."

Charmayne shook her head, probably because of Onika's stony facial expression. Onika wasn't going to give her anything else. She refused to feed Charmayne's need to feel other people's suffering. There was a whole house full of women who had buckets of pain. She could go and listen to them wailing and moaning and praying. They wanted the breakthroughs that Charmayne prayed about, so she could go and talk to them.

"You're going to regret not telling Graham the truth."

"Your warning is duly noted. I will be moving in a couple of weeks. That will free up a spot for another woman. I appreciate you being here and doing what you do. I don't know where I would be if it wasn't for your kindness."

"I suppose the universe dropped you at my front door."

Onika laughed and didn't bring up the homeless lady and the flyer anymore. She was just going to have to remain a mystery.

The doorbell rang, and Charmayne furrowed her eyebrows.

"It's only eight o'clock in the morning. Who is visiting this early?"

Onika followed Charmayne to the door. She opened it, and there was a moving truck outside. The driver stood at the door.

"How can I help you?" Charmayne asked.

"I have some personal belongings to deliver to Nikki Lewis."

Charmayne turned to look at Onika, and she shrugged with confusion. She had no idea what was going on.

The driver started back to the truck, but then ran back to the door like he had forgotten something.

"There's a note for Ms. Lewis," he said as he handed the card to Charmayne.

Charmayne passed it to Onika. Thinking that this might be a surprise from Graham, she opened it with a smile. It said, *Since you now have a new job, you'll need your clothes and shoes. Dress to impress. Xoxo, Aaron.*

Onika looked up to see racks of her clothing and shoes being brought up to the front door. At Aaron's town house, her closet had been larger than her bedroom at Safe Harbor.

"Where is all this stuff gonna go?" Onika groaned. "I can't believe this."

"Who is it from? Your ex-boyfriend?"

Onika nodded. "When I left, he wouldn't let me take anything he bought me while we were together. He said that the designer clothes were listed as his assets."

"Well, we could put what won't fit in your bedroom in the basement. It's waterproofed and finished down there."

Onika imagined her snakeskin shoes and soft leather skirts in the basement and cringed. Aaron knew exactly what he was doing. He was making her uncomfortable at Safe Harbor. It would be nothing to him to send movers out the very next day to pack Onika up and bring her to his town house. What would she look like living in a homeless shelter with two-thousand-dollar shoes? Absolutely foolish.

"You could keep some of it, and we could have an estate sale," Charmayne said. "I know some very elite women who would pay top dollar for designer shoes and handbags."

"Let's think about how to set that up. I can definitely use the money."

"How did he know where to send your things?" Charmayne asked.

"That is a very long story. I think he wants me to come back to him, but I won't. I refuse."

Charmayne said nothing, although Onika expected to hear much more. Onika was happy for Charmayne's silence, though. She was already feeling irritated enough that Aaron was inserting himself into her life again. First, with the check, then pulling strings to get her a job, and now sending thousands of dollars' worth of clothing to a homeless women's shelter.

Onika had a feeling that she'd opened a Pandora's box by accepting that check, but she couldn't silence the voice in her mind that told her she deserved it. She deserved to walk away with something instead of being empty-handed.

That's why she couldn't stop the movers from bringing in box after box of clothes and shoes. And because she'd accepted this kindness, and she'd accepted the job and Aaron's check, he wouldn't stop.

This was just the beginning. Aaron liked to win, and wouldn't stop until he did.

CHAPTER FIFTY-TWO

Graham enjoyed watching Onika sprawled across his couch eating a bowl of popcorn. Well, they were supposed to be eating the popcorn while they watched a marathon of X-Men movies. He'd let her pick, and that was what she'd come up with. Superheroes. He wasn't mad about it, though.

"I thought we'd be watching either foreign language films or Tyler Perry movies today."

"Eww to both. I hate movies where I have to read the screen, because I don't completely pay attention to movies. My brain likes to multitask."

"What does that mean?"

"It means I am incapable of just sitting in front of a TV watching a movie from start to finish without thinking of something else."

"What do you do when you go to the movies?"

"That's probably the only time I see an entire movie, because I can't do anything else but watch it."

"Note to self, if I want Onika to really watch the movie, take her out to the theater."

"Correct, unless you take me to one of those places where they have wine and food. Then I'm paying more attention to my snacks than the movie."

Graham laughed. "And what's the reason for not choosing the Tyler Perry movies?"

"Not my type of hype."

"I haven't heard that in . . . ever. I've never heard someone say that. Maybe in a movie. An old-school movie about the nineties."

Onika giggled. "I love nineties hip-hop. Now you know. I like superheroes and nineties hip-hop."

"I love that."

"I start a new job on Monday, so I won't be at the soup kitchen anymore."

"A new job? You don't sound excited. Tell me about it. Does it pay well?"

She nodded. "It pays better than the soup kitchen, and it's full-time with benefits. I'm happy about it."

Her actions didn't fit her words. She didn't seem happy about it. She seemed indifferent.

"Well, how will this impact your work at Safe Harbor? The community center was part-time, right? Will you be able to do both?"

Onika sighed and sat up on the couch. She set the bowl of popcorn on the table.

"Graham, I need to tell you something, but before I do, just know that I never meant for it to happen. And after I tell you, please know that the only reason I did it is because I like you so much."

Graham got worried. What was she about to say? Would it change everything?

"Okay . . ."

"I don't really run Safe Harbor. I do live there . . . because I don't have anywhere else to live."

"Wait, what do you mean? You're homeless? You don't seem homeless."

Onika shrugged. "I know, but that's only because Charmayne took me in."

Graham didn't know what he thought she was going to reveal, but it certainly wasn't this. The girl he loved was homeless. Damn.

"I mean . . . how long have you been homeless? When I met you at the Metro station? Were you then?"

She nodded. "I was on my way to Safe Harbor that day. The night before I spent at the Gallery Place Metro station."

"That's the reason you didn't call."

"That's exactly the reason I didn't call. And then when I saw you again, I thought, just like you did, that it was the universe putting us together."

"I didn't think that."

"You know what I mean. You thought God sent me to you. I felt the universe did. Same thing."

"Not the same thing."

"Graham, you are missing the point. I lied to you, but only because I thought you wouldn't want me if you knew that I was homeless. I didn't think anyone wanted me. My ex threw me out on the street. I was not in a good place."

"Where are you now?"

"I'm in the best place ever, that's why I'm telling you this. I feel so much love for you, and I don't want to go any further without knowing whether or not you'll accept me."

She felt love for him. Was this the same as loving him, or was it some destination on the way to being in love with him?

"I don't care about you being homeless, Onika. You can live here if you want. You don't have to stay there."

The look of shock on Onika's face let him know that maybe he'd gone too far telling her she could move in, but he meant it.

"I have two bedrooms. I'm just saying you don't have to live in a place you have to share with other people."

Onika jumped up from the couch and threw herself into his arms. She kissed his face and neck and finally his mouth. He kissed her back and wrapped his arms around her lower back.

"I hate that your ex threw you out and that you didn't have anywhere to live, but if he hadn't done that to you, I wouldn't have you. So, being homeless brought you to me."

"You're too good for me, Graham."

He wasn't too good. Because while Onika was in his arms, Graham was thinking about how hard Leslie would laugh if he knew he was dating a homeless woman. Lorne and Craig would be completely insufferable if they found out. They couldn't find out.

As proud as he was to have Onika on his arm, he was as embarrassed as she was about her homelessness.

And that wasn't the worst part. Now Graham was starting to question everything. If she wasn't homeless, maybe she wouldn't have ever looked his way. He only had a chance because she was at her rock-bottom. What would she do when she wasn't struggling anymore?

"Thank you for offering me a place to live," Onika said, "but I will be moving into my own place soon. I just need a pay stub."

"You've got the money to move?"

Onika said nothing. She untangled herself from his arms, went back to the couch, and sat down.

"What?" Graham asked, not understanding what he'd done wrong.

"This is why I didn't want to tell you. You're asking too many questions now. I don't need you to manage the situation, Graham. I am just correcting a lie that I told you."

Graham sat down next to her. "I'm not trying to manage the situation. I just want to help."

"I appreciate you for that. I just want to go through this piece of it myself. Depending on a man is what got me homeless in the first place. I'm going to handle this on my own."

"Okay, but you don't have to worry about me judging you, Onika."

She smiled sadly. "I know you think you wouldn't, but let me ask you this. If I had told you on the Metro station that I was homeless, would you have wanted to see me again?"

Graham would be lying to himself if he said he would. He would've seen her completely differently. He probably would've given her money, but not his business card. She was right—even he was judgmental.

"I'm glad I didn't know then, because I would've missed out."

"You would've, because I'm incredible."

Graham slipped his arm around Onika and pulled her close. He buried his face in her hair and inhaled. He loved that coconut scent. He kissed her forehead affectionately.

"You are."

It was just that now Graham was worried. No matter how incredible she was, Graham didn't know if he could handle being with a woman who had a secret life.

CHAPTER FIFTY-THREE

Graham sat across from Leslie in a conference room. She glared at him, but he didn't care. He wanted her foolishness to stop. Which was why the alternative dispute resolution representative, Shelly, and their boss, Roger, were both in the room.

"Just so that everyone is aware, what is said here is confidential," Shelly said. "It won't be shared outside of this meeting and won't be used for any further action against you—disciplinary or otherwise."

"Can we just get this over with?" Leslie asked. "I don't even know why we're here."

"Graham reported what he considers to be a hostile working environment," Roger said. "I have to say I was alarmed about his allegations. We won't tolerate anyone feeling harassed in our department."

Leslie looked at Graham like if she wouldn't lose her job for it, she'd leap across the table and gouge his eyes out. Graham wasn't concerned about her, or even about her harassment. He just wanted to draw first blood in case Leslie got mad enough to flip it on him.

"Has Roger accurately described your claim?" Shelly asked.

Graham nodded. "The truth is, she can't take no for an answer. I tried to let Leslie down easily."

"Let me down easy? You act like I'm crying over you or something."

"I don't know whether you're crying or not. I just know that I've told you that I'm not interested in dating you, and you won't stop making advances."

Leslie narrowed her eyes to tiny slits. "You should feel privileged that someone is looking at you. The way you have your head up Lorne's behind, I should've known that you wouldn't be interested in me. I'm not your type."

Graham closed his eyes and shook his head. He wasn't going to respond to this. She wanted him to flip out on her, and he wasn't going to give her the satisfaction.

"Are you implying that Graham is homosexual?" Roger asked. "That is uncalled for, Leslie. We're not going to get anywhere trading insults."

"I don't consider that to be an insult," Graham said, "but I'm not gay, and she knows it."

"These allegations further state that Leslie and her friend, another coworker, implied that Graham was going to have sexual relations with Leslie at a recent training," Shelly said. "What do you have to say about that, Leslie?"

"First of all, that was a joke. Second of all, am I on trial here? I thought this was a mediation."

"What would you like as a resolution, Graham?" Roger asked, clearly deciding to side with Graham.

"I would just like her to stop, that's all. I don't want anything else."

"And you couldn't just ask me to stop?" Leslie asked. "Your grown ass had to pull me into a meeting with our boss to tell me to stop bothering you?"

"Leslie, do you agree to stop pestering this man?" Roger asked.

"Wait a minute. Graham took me out on a date. He's up here trying to act like I'm a crazy person or something. He led me on, and then started acting up when he moved on to another woman."

Graham sighed. "We never went on a date. She called it a date, but it wasn't a date."

"Just because a man goes on one date with you, it doesn't mean he has to enter into a relationship with you," Shelly said. "It's okay for him to change his mind."

"It wasn't a date, and I haven't changed my mind. I didn't date her. I don't want to date her. I'm never going to date her," Graham said.

He didn't mean for his voice to sound as harsh as it did, but it was too late. The words were already out. Of course, Leslie burst into tears, but to Graham's surprise neither Shelly nor Roger moved to comfort her. After almost a minute-long performance, she just stopped.

"Can we go on now?" Shelly asked.

Leslie nodded.

"I believe that what Graham is saying is that if you simply stopped your advances, he would no longer feel that the workplace was hostile," Roger said. "Am I correct, Graham?"

"Yes."

"Leslie, this means that you don't make jokes about dating Graham, and you don't ask him out again. You will also not harass him on social media or outside the workplace as a part of this agreement," Shelly said.

"Why doesn't he just get a restraining order then?" Leslie said.

Her voice sounded so defeated and pained that Graham almost wanted to take it all back. He didn't, though. Being nice was what got him here in the first place.

"Graham can get a restraining order if he finds it necessary. We're hoping that he doesn't," Roger said. "If he does, it could impact your public trust clearance for the federal government."

Leslie's shoulders slumped. Graham had probably won. It didn't feel like it, though. Both Roger and Shelly were white, and Leslie's eyes told him this betrayal went deeper than two coworkers having a disagreement.

"Do you understand?" Shelly asked. "Can we consider this matter closed?"

"It's closed," Leslie said.

"Graham?" Roger asked.

"Yes. I consider it closed."

"Great," Roger said. "Now, let's get back to work, folks."

Roger and Shelly rushed out of the conference room, leaving Graham and Leslie behind. They must've had another fire to put out. Probably going to counsel two more employees to try to keep them from filing a lawsuit.

When they left the room, Leslie glared at Graham again, then glanced up at the surveillance camera in the corner of the room. She stopped glaring.

"I'm sorry, Leslie," Graham said. For some reason, he felt like apologizing.

"You sure are."

Leslie pushed past Graham out of the conference room. He hoped she found a man soon. One who wanted her.

Graham needed a break after this meeting, so he went outside the building. He was going to find Starbucks or a snack.

"Graham!"

He heard a man's loud voice calling him, but he didn't recognize it. He looked around until his gaze stopped on a man in a three-piece suit. The man was staring at him, so he must've been the one who called his name.

"Who are you?" Graham called.

"Someone who knows Onika better than you ever will."

Graham felt his muscles tense. He flexed, ready to fight the man if he had to, although the man was clearly not dressed to fight.

"What do you want?" Graham asked.

The man walked toward Graham, and Graham didn't move an inch. If the brother wanted to talk to him, he could come to where he was standing.

"I was just about to leave my business card at the security desk and ask you to give me a call," Aaron said. "This is better. I'd rather see you face-to-face."

"See me face-to-face for what?"

"To introduce myself. I'm Aaron. Just letting you know that your girlfriend lives in a homeless shelter."

"You're the ex-boyfriend, right? You put her in that shelter."

"Actually, I bought her a plane ticket to North Carolina to see her people."

Graham tried not to look confused. He failed.

"Oh, she didn't tell you about them?" Aaron said.

"She doesn't have to tell me everything about herself. We haven't been dating long," Graham said.

He nodded. "You're right. At least you do know her name is Onika. She introduced herself to me as Nikki. She always has secrets. She'll never tell you the entire truth."

Aaron's words echoed Graham's fears. Onika's reveal about being homeless made him wonder what else she was hiding.

"Are you still in contact with her?" Graham asked, not really wanting to know the answer.

Aaron smiled. "You'll have to ask her, but just know that we were together for a very long time. I was her first, so she'll probably always still carry a torch for me."

Graham slowly clenched and unclenched his fists. "Yeah, I'm pretty sure I helped her put that torch out."

"Pretty sure or positive? I know you're not positive, because the look in your eye says you're worried about what I'm doing here. You're probably going to call Onika as soon as you go back up to your cubicle. You're going to ask about me, and she's going to give you vague answers."

"I'm not worried about anything. When Onika gets ready to share, I'll be ready to listen. I'm treating her with respect, which is obviously something you never did."

"No need to insult me, brother. I'm not your enemy. See you around."

Aaron turned to walk back to his car—a silver Jaguar. Graham would have to save for years to have a whip like that. Apparently, they shared the same taste in women and in cars, but Graham disagreed with Aaron on one thing.

Aaron was, without question, Graham's enemy.

CHAPTER FIFTY-FOUR

The day after he sent all of Onika's clothes and shoes to Safe Harbor, Aaron showed up in person. Onika saw him pull up in the Jaguar, his out-and-about car. Seeing him again so soon was irritating. She wished she hadn't been desperate enough to cash his check.

"Who is out there now?" Charmayne asked.

"My ex."

Charmayne fumed. "The nerve of him showing up here. Get rid of him."

Onika nodded and went outside to meet him, even though she wished she could stay inside and hide.

He was, as usual, dressed to the nines in blue linen pants and a casual, short-sleeved shirt. He was wearing sunglasses, and little dots of sweat peppered his head.

"Why aren't you at Martha's Vineyard? Why are you here stalking me all summer?"

"You think I am the only one impacted by our breakup? You think I want the Richards to know that I was forced to throw you out?"

Onika couldn't help it. She laughed, and it sounded like a holler.

"You were forced to throw me out? I have never seen the victim role played out so well."

"My dignity forced my hand. How could I be with a woman who wasn't honored to bear my child?"

Onika knew he was insulted by her decision. She'd gotten to the point that she didn't care.

"Can you please not belabor the point about the pregnancy?" Onika said.

"Can you come closer so that the entire neighborhood doesn't have to hear our conversation?"

"Or you could just leave, and the conversation would be over."

"So rude to your benefactor. So rude."

"Dropping designer clothes off at a homeless shelter does not make you my benefactor."

"What about that $25,000 check?"

"You gave me more than that to shop with in Paris."

Aaron smiled. "Do you not miss that?"

Onika took too long to reply. Their rapid back-and-forth banter had suddenly paused.

"You do miss it. No need to lie about that."

He was right. Onika missed the money, clothes, vacations, and shopping sprees. She missed almost every part of their life. It was the part she didn't miss that gave her strength to rebuff his advances.

"Come sit in my car and talk. We have hurt each other. You don't have to come back. I get that. But let me put you in your own place."

Onika knew Aaron was poisonous, and she wasn't quite sure she was immune.

"I'm not going to bite, Onika. You act like you don't know me," Aaron said.

Not fully trusting him, but wanting to hear what he had to say, Onika followed Aaron to his car. Ever the gentleman, he opened the passenger-side door for her to get in.

"You could invite me into the shelter," Aaron said when he got in on his side.

Onika rolled her eyes. "Or not."

"I get it. I don't really want to see you living like that anyway."

"It's actually nice on the inside. It's not what you think."

Aaron nodded. "So you don't mind staying here, then?"

Onika sucked her teeth. "Man, are you playing games or what? You said something about helping me get a place to live."

"I can give you keys to an apartment tomorrow. I can send the movers to pick up your things, but you'll have to make a choice."

"What choice?"

"To allow me to come and see you when I need to see you."

Onika felt her stomach turn. He wanted her to become one of the women she had always loathed. He wanted to leave his live-in girlfriend, her replacement, to lay up in her bed.

"It would be like old times. Just that you'd have your own space, away from me. You can even keep your boyfriend if you want. I visited him at his job today. He's quite the traditional macho man. I thought he was going to take a swing at me."

Onika wanted to choke him. She had never wanted to do physical harm to him before, but she wanted to wrap her hands around his throat and squeeze the life out of him.

"Why were you at his job? Why do you know where he works? Stop stalking me."

"You're mine, Onika."

"You put me out!"

"I've reconsidered. It was a mistake."

Onika couldn't believe that she'd stayed with this narcissist for so long. He really felt like he was entitled to her.

"I created who you are right now," Aaron said. "Your boyfriend should thank me. He only looked at you because of my grooming."

Except that Graham hadn't met a groomed version of her. He'd met Onika at rock-bottom when she no longer had access to Aaron's money, power, or influence.

"Thank you for the offer, but I don't want the apartment from you. The price is too high."

"But you'll accept the clothes, the shoes, and the job?"

"You can take that back, too, Aaron. I don't need anything from you if it comes with sex."

Aaron chuckled slowly. "But you sure as hell cashed that check already."

"Sure did."

Onika got out of the car, slammed the door, and turned her back on Aaron. She never wanted to see him again. If he didn't stop his stalking, she'd get a restraining order. She was turning the page on this relationship. No, that was too mild. She was burning it down to the ground, collecting the ashes, and spreading them to the four corners of the earth. She was done. She didn't desire him anymore, nor did she need him.

The place in her heart where Aaron had lived had a new resident—Graham. And hopefully he'd want to stay a long, long while.

CHAPTER FIFTY-FIVE

She got in his car.

Graham had left work early and gone straight over on the Metro to surprise Onika. To let her know that nothing she'd said could change how he felt about her. He had flowers and wine, and was going to take her out for the Thai food that she loved.

But when he got halfway down her street, Graham saw the car. The same silver Jaguar that had pulled up outside his job earlier. The car that held her ex-boyfriend. The ex-boyfriend who had come with warnings about Onika and her secrets.

Seeing the car didn't bother Graham at first. It just made him walk faster. Clearly this guy wasn't done with Onika. He'd thrown her away like a bag of trash and now he was mad that Graham had scooped her up and identified her as treasure.

He saw Onika storm down the walkway. It looked as if they were arguing. They were definitely going back and forth. Graham almost called out Onika's name, but he wanted to see how she would handle the situation on her own. He definitely wanted to see what she would do.

After a few moments of talking, she got in his car. What had he said to make her do that? When she didn't get out right away, Graham scowled. Why was she in there? Were they kissing or rekindling their flame?

Graham found that he didn't want to know the answer, so he didn't stick around to find out. He dropped the bouquet of flowers on the ground. Turned and walked away.

This girl had one secret too many.

CHAPTER FIFTY-SIX

Graham stared at his phone. There were multiple text messages from Onika. Asking questions. What was he doing? Was he done teaching his swimming class? Did he want to get together?

He didn't reply to any of them.

Then he realized if he didn't reply, then she'd think his silence had something to do with her big reveal. She needed to know that if they were broken, it was because of her shenanigans and not any judgments on his part.

He replied to all her texts with one line. Super busy. Let's get together next week to celebrate your new job.

It was a cop-out that bought him more time. Graham didn't plan on getting together with her at all. He was going to cut his losses before he was in too deeply.

But he was already in too deeply.

Seeing Onika get in Aaron's car hurt him badly. True enough, it could've been innocent, even though Aaron insisted that Onika carried a torch for him.

Why would she get in his car or even talk to him at all after what he'd done? What kind of game were they playing?

Graham had too many questions, and he didn't want to have Onika give him scripted, well-thought-out answers, or none at all. That's what she liked to do when she didn't want to tell the whole truth—she went silent.

Then his phone rang. He should've known she would call. He hesitated. Let the phone ring a few times.

Finally, he gave in. "Hello."

"Hi, Graham cracker. What's going on? I haven't seen you all weekend."

"I know. I just have a lot going on."

Onika was quiet for a moment. Maybe she caught his tone. He didn't care.

"What's wrong, Graham? Why are you being short with me?"

Graham sighed. He was a communicator. Keeping his feelings bottled up wasn't in his DNA.

"Why were you in the car with him?"

"Huh?"

Graham's head felt close to exploding. He just realized that Onika was just like a dude with her secrets and evasiveness. Every guy he knew said, "Huh?" when trying to avoid being interrogated by their woman. And Graham's woman had just given him the "huh" treatment.

"I can't believe this. You know what I'm talking about, Onika. You were in the silver Jaguar. Your ex-boyfriend's car. Why?"

The silence on the line went on for too long. He knew she was trying to quickly formulate a response to his question.

"Graham, it's not what you think. He made an indecent request of me, and I turned him down. That's all."

"But you got in his car. I saw you talking to him; then you got in. Why couldn't you turn him down from the sidewalk?"

"I wanted to . . . I don't know . . . hear him out. He said he would help me get my own apartment."

"And you thought he would do it out of the kindness of his heart?"

"Not out of kindness. Out of guilt. Just like he sent over my clothes and shoes and got me a job."

"If you're tired of that shelter, you can move in here. I already offered you that."

"Graham, I've never had my own place. I wanted space for

myself. If Aaron was going to give me that with no strings attached, I was going to take it."

"He's a man, Onika. There're always strings."

"Were there strings when you offered your place? Were there conditions? Were you gonna make me go to church every Sunday morning?"

"No. None of that."

"You should've asked me before, Graham. You should've walked right up to the car and asked what was going on. But you decided to assume and get all butt hurt."

"I'm not all butt hurt."

"You are. And all you had to do was ask. You don't trust me."

"It's hard to trust a person who tells you lies from the very first day."

Onika was so silent that Graham thought she'd hung up the phone. Then he heard her breathing.

"Is that what your God teaches you?" Onika asked. "To throw someone's mistakes up in their face when they've asked you to forgive them?"

This had nothing to do with God, but, of course, Onika took it there.

"I'm not throwing anything up in your face. I just find it hard to believe that what I saw was innocent."

"I don't know what to tell you then. Maybe you should go pray about it. How about you fast *and* pray. Ask God to reveal the truth to you."

Sarcasm and mockery dripped from her tone, but even though she meant it as an affront to what he believed, Graham agreed with her. He did need to ask God about the situation and about her.

"Onika, I meant it when I said I want to get together next week. I just need some time to process this."

"Take all the time you need."

Onika didn't wait until he said good-bye to disconnect the call. She'd told him to take all the time he needed, like she didn't care if he took forever to process and decide whether she was telling the truth.

The crazy part was that Graham believed her. He knew she was telling the truth about what had happened in the car. Her voice had sounded sincere and authentic before she spread on the sarcasm.

But he didn't want to go through this every time she said or did something suspicious. He didn't want his heart breaking every time she lied or every time he discovered another one of her secrets. He would only survive this relationship if she promised to tell the truth and he promised to believe her.

CHAPTER FIFTY-SEVEN

Onika's first day at her new job was awesome. Her boss was an older white woman who'd been practicing law since she graduated from law school in the seventies. She was going to mentor Onika and had promised to help her get into law school.

And even though she and Graham were in the throes of their first argument, he had sent her a text letting her know that he was praying for her on her first day. It had warmed her heart, even though she'd only replied with "Thanks."

It was a good day.

Out of habit, Onika checked her e-mail in the library. She had spoken with more than one apartment complex about renting a unit. She was waiting for responses.

Instead of receiving a notification from one of the apartment complexes, Onika had received an e-mail from Dr. Richard. She stared at it in disbelief. He wanted her to call him, but she was afraid. What could he want? She hadn't talked to him in years, and she didn't owe him any favors. As a matter of fact, she was mad that he'd told Aaron about her family in North Carolina. Even though Aaron never admitted it was Dr. Richard, it couldn't have been anyone else.

But Onika's curiosity got the best of her. Although she didn't want to talk to him, she needed to know what he wanted.

"Hello." Dr. Richard's rich baritone sounded the same as it had nearly ten years ago when she was a college freshman.

"Dr. Richard, this is Onika. I got your e-mail. How can I help you?"

"Onika, I hope you're doing well. I wish my e-mail was good news. Unfortunately, it's not."

His voice sounded so grave that Onika started to worry. "Is it Mrs. Richard? Chelsea?"

"Oh no, they're fine. It's about your mother. She's dying."

Onika was speechless. She took the phone from her ear and sat it down on the kitchen counter. She looked at it like it was a foreign object. She didn't want to pick it back up, although she could hear Dr. Richard talking.

Finally, she picked the phone up and put it to her ear. "Dr. Richard, I need you to repeat what you just said. I'm sorry, but I had to put the phone down for a minute."

"Your mother is dying."

"Did she have a drug overdose? Does she have AIDS? What is she dying from?" Onika asked.

"I'm sorry. I don't know the details. Your grandmother called the college and asked that someone get a message to you since she didn't know how to reach you. She said that she's unable to take care of your mother. She has cancer and only has a few weeks to live."

It was crazy hearing that Judy was dying, truly on her death-bed, when she'd been dead to Onika years before.

"Is that all you know about it, Dr. Richard?"

"Yes, I'm afraid that's all. If I might give you a word of advice, you should go. You'll regret it forever if she dies without you seeing her again."

"Thank you."

Onika disconnected the call and set the phone down again. Then it started buzzing. Was that Dr. Richard calling her back? She hurried and pressed the button to answer the call.

"Yes, hello?"

"It's me."

It was Graham. "Oh, hi."

"What's wrong?" Graham asked.

Onika burst into tears when she realized that she couldn't tell him. She couldn't tell her boyfriend that her mother was dying, because her boyfriend thought that she was already dead. There was that heavy feeling again.

"Graham, I just need you here. Can you come over?"

"Are you okay?"

"No. I'm not okay. Not at all. Please come."

"I'm on my way."

Onika was overloaded and carrying too much. She had to tell Graham about Judy, and if he thought she was an unapologetic liar, then so be it. At least she wouldn't be dragging that last secret around. It would be out, with all of the rest of her lies. She didn't have enough energy to keep hiding. She needed all of her strength to deal with Earlene . . . and Judy.

Charmayne knocked on the office door. "Nikki, what's wrong? Are you okay?"

Onika opened the door and nearly collapsed into Charmayne's arms.

"My mother is dying," she sobbed. "S-she has cancer."

"Oh, baby, don't cry. Maybe it's just her appointed time."

Onika shook her head. She wasn't crying about Judy's illness. She'd grieved the loss of her mother years before.

"I'm crying, b-because I lied and told Graham she was already dead. He's not gonna want me anymore. He's gonna think I'm a pathological liar."

"My sweet Jesus," Charmayne said. "Well, you never know. Maybe he'll still love you."

This made Onika sob harder. He did love her. He was the first man to love her for unselfish reasons, and she had ruined it with her secrets. She wished she'd told him everything from the first time she decided to be truthful. Now it was probably too late.

"You think he might?" Onika asked, her voice sounding small and pitiful.

"Maybe. But I'm going to go to my room and pray for your mother. If you've been telling people she's dead, and she's yet living, you have more to worry about than a man."

Onika knew Charmayne was right, and even though she didn't want prayers, Onika was too distraught to ask Charmayne to keep her prayers to herself.

CHAPTER FIFTY-EIGHT

It was going to be a long five and a half hours.

When Graham had heard Onika crying on the phone, he'd dropped everything and run to her side, only to hear that her mother was on her deathbed in North Carolina. The mother she'd told him was dead.

This was the family in North Carolina that Aaron had been hinting about. He could've said it was her mother. Graham would've moved on from Onika right then and there if Aaron had told him. What kind of person lied about their mother? How sick, depraved, and broken did a person have to be to lie about that?

Yet he was driving her to her mother's bedside, because she was distraught and in need. But it didn't change the way he felt. He was done with this relationship.

"I didn't have a normal life," Onika said after they'd been driving for an hour.

Graham didn't reply. The air in the car felt stale and thick, and made Graham cough. Or maybe it was being in close proximity to Onika that made him uncomfortable. She wanted his understanding. She only had his pity. He couldn't relate to someone who chose lying over the truth. Every time.

"I am deeply ashamed of my mother. That's why I lied," Onika said. "It's a lie I've been telling since I left Goldsboro."

He wanted to interrogate her about her reasons, but he just didn't trust that anything that came out of her mouth was the truth. If she didn't want anyone to know about her past, all she had to do was not talk about it. No one was entitled to know anything a person didn't want to share.

"I grew up going down the street to get her from a shack where she was turning tricks. My grandmother would make me bring her home for dinner," Onika said.

Graham still said nothing. He drove and listened, but didn't comment.

"When she wasn't turning tricks, she was smoking crack," Onika said. "My daddy got her hooked and also turned her on to being a prostitute."

It sounded like a bad movie, and Graham didn't know how much of it he could even believe. She'd lied so much already that she could tell him Rosa Parks rode on a bus, and he'd have to fact-check it in a history book.

"So how many boyfriends have you actually had? You said one," Graham asked, wanting to make sure, while she was telling the "truth," that he had the whole story.

"That was the truth. I met Aaron when my mentor and his wife took me to Martha's Vineyard with their family."

"Hmm . . ."

"You really think I'm just lying about everything, huh?"

"What would you think if you were me?"

Onika sighed heavily. "I would think you were lying about everything."

"So you understand then."

"Yes."

Graham became quiet again. He was partially angry at himself, because even with the lies, his heart went out to her. If she did really grow up with a crack-smoking prostitute, she was probably irreparably damaged. He couldn't fix her. Didn't want to even try. That was God's work, and she didn't believe in Him.

"I'm here because I don't think you have anyone else," Graham said. "Not because I still want to be your man."

Another sigh from Onika.

"Thank you. You're right, too. I don't have anyone else, except Charmayne. My sorority sisters, my mentors, and everyone thinks my mother is dead."

"Even the ex you lived with?"

"Yep, and he did an investigation, apparently. I don't know what he knows, but I don't think he knows about my mother, because he would've thrown it up in my face."

Graham would try very hard not to do the same while he was with her in North Carolina. He wouldn't remind her of her lies anymore, because he didn't have to live with them.

"She has cancer," Onika said. "I never thought she'd live long enough to have cancer. I thought she'd have an overdose or a heart attack, or maybe even go how my daddy went."

Onika paused and seemed to wait for an interaction from Graham. He didn't have anything to say, so he remained quiet. He damn sure wasn't asking her any more questions, because he didn't trust the answers anyway. But he wouldn't stop her from talking if she wanted to hear herself speak.

"He died of complications from AIDS. Some sort of rare cancer."

With each additional bit of knowledge from Onika's childhood, Graham felt his wall weaken. How could she have survived this? And not just survived—gone to a prestigious college and graduated.

"Your sorority sisters would probably look at you differently," Graham said, remembering the Epsilon Phi Beta women he'd seen in DC at their conference. He didn't think they took members with drug addicts for mothers.

"Probably? Of course they would."

"But does it mean anything to be in the sorority if they wouldn't accept you for who you are?"

"I didn't want to *be* the daughter of a crackhead. In my mind I wasn't her. I'm *not* her," Onika said. "I'm aware that my mother gave birth to me, but I don't belong to her. I have no mother. I have no father."

"But your mother is dying right now. She apparently wants to see you, since your grandmother made sure to find you. After all these years, what do you want to say to her?"

This seemed to stump Onika. She shook her head back and forth like the question was unbelievable.

"I don't know what she could want with me now. Maybe she just wants to see me one more time before she transitions."

"Maybe," Graham said. "But wait. What do you mean by transition? You think she's going to heaven?"

"I see what you did there," Onika said. "I mean we all transition when we die. We transition back into the earth and feed the planet. Nothing spiritual about it. Simply biology."

"I am going to respectfully disagree. Even people who don't go to church believe that we are spiritual creatures, housed in our bodies. When people die, their spirit goes out."

"These are your beliefs, not facts."

"Okay, Onika. I thought it would give you comfort to know that a part of your mother will live on after she's gone."

"Truth and facts give me comfort. You know, my grandmother prayed for one thing my whole, entire life. I prayed with her when I was little. Prayed for my mother to get clean."

"And she never did," Graham said.

"She never did. You can't know what that does to a child. I believed harder than anyone. I begged God to make my mother like one of the mothers on TV. Or if not like one of them, then just a mother who would be there when I got home from school, cooking dinner. Shoot, I would've even taken a mother who drank forties and smoked cigarettes on the front porch while scratching her dirty behind. I would've taken almost anything other than what I got. Do you understand that?"

"At least you had your grandmother."

"I had a grandmother who had two obsessions, the Church of God in Christ and my mother. She didn't have room for another one."

Onika was in tears now—big, fat, juicy tears that poured down her face. Graham's wall was gone, but he wasn't ready to restore the love. That was another matter entirely.

"You're sitting here judging me, like anyone else would if they heard these things," Onika said.

"I'm not judging you, but if I were, it wouldn't be about your childhood. It would be about what you could control. No one made you lie. You could've owned your tragedies."

Onika laughed a bitter laugh. "Listen to you. Reasoning like someone who had an upbringing and home training. You're thinking about what you would do if you were in my shoes. The truth is, you don't know what you would do in my place. You're not seeing things the way they are; you're seeing them through your own eyes. If you could look through my eyes, maybe you could understand my choices."

Onika must've been tired of talking, because she turned her back to Graham and pulled her knees up to her chest. She pulled her sweater around her body—it was hot outside, but cold in the car. She drifted off to a restless sleep, leaving Graham alone with his thoughts.

Onika had pegged him truly and accurately. He was seeing her situation through the lens of his solid, faith-based upbringing. He wasn't seeing things the way they were.

Graham couldn't even comprehend the gravity of Onika's life's trials, but he was interested to meet the grandmother. They were almost to her house, and Graham was sure he'd be able to gain insight from one of Onika's elders. Whether she knew it or not, Onika was lucky to have her grandmother.

CHAPTER FIFTY-NINE

"We're here," Graham whispered as he woke Onika. "We're at your grandmother's house."

Onika didn't look excited or happy. She had an expression of resignation that she coupled with a huge sigh.

"Let's get this over with," Onika said.

They both got out of the car, Onika not waiting on Graham to open her door before she jumped out and started trudging toward the dilapidated front porch. He almost couldn't even call the house a house. It was a shack with a porch.

A woman came out of the house and onto the porch. She was small, but it looked like she'd shrunken to that size with age. Graham thought she might've been a taller woman when she was younger.

"Who are you?" the woman asked Graham.

"I'm Onika's friend Graham, and you must be Onika's grandmother."

"Ms. Earlene to you. Last time she came down here, she came alone. This time she brought reinforcements. Guess she got tired of lying and saying we don't exist."

All of this was said to Graham without even acknowledging that Onika was alive and standing right before her grandmother.

Onika didn't wait to be acknowledged. She walked up the stairs, past her grandmother, and into the house.

"Come on, Graham," Onika yelled from inside the house.

Graham and Earlene locked eyes. He wasn't afraid to walk past her but felt that it would be incredibly rude to do so. He would wait for an invitation.

"You might as well come on in, since she insists on being ornery."

Graham didn't think she was being ornery. He thought she was upset because she'd gotten word that her mother was dying.

Graham followed Earlene into the house. His eyes immediately began to water at the stench. It smelled like an outhouse or a cesspool. Or maybe like someone was boiling manure.

Graham gagged. Earlene laughed.

"You ain't never smelled chitlins before, have you? Well, I'm cooking up fifteen buckets of them. We've got family coming to town."

"Why is family coming?" Onika asked.

"Didn't you get my message? You ain't been to the hospital yet, have you? Your mama is about to leave this world. She ain't got but a few more days, maybe hours. Doctors think she's waiting on you."

"I can't believe you invited the family to start coming while she's still alive."

"Shole did. Who in the hell else is gonna help me pay to bury her? She ain't got no life insurance."

Graham could see Onika's anger rising. He'd never seen her angry, so this was new.

"Come on. Let me take you to the hospital," Graham said. "You'll never forgive yourself if you don't get to say good-bye."

"Oh, she said good-bye when she left for college. Never did come back and visit for a holiday or nothing. She started running with those rich people at that college, and we never heard from her again. Exceptin' that one time . . ."

Onika gave the woman a look that would freeze a boiling pot of water. "Come on, Graham."

"When y'all come back, bring a bucket of chicken or something to eat. I shole hope y'all don't plan on staying here, too. Only got one spare bed, and no man and woman lay up together under my roof without being married."

Graham opened his mouth to respond, but Onika shook her head. He followed her lead. When they got into the car, he punched the address of the hospital into his GPS.

"I came to see her on the worst day of my life," Onika said.

"When Aaron put you out?"

"No. The day I had an abortion, I got on the road and drove here. She turned me away and said she didn't have a granddaughter."

"You had an abortion. Wow."

"It was Aaron's baby, of course. I wasn't ready, because *he* wasn't committed."

Even though Graham was fiercely opposed to abortion because of his faith, he remembered what Onika had said earlier. He tried not to view this through his experiences. He refused to judge her.

"Maybe your grandmother was hurt that you didn't visit her while you were in college."

Onika shrugged. "Maybe she was. Or maybe she's just mean and evil."

"She raised you, though. Got you to adulthood in one piece. You could've starved. Could've been left outside."

Onika glared at Graham as he started the car, but he didn't care.

"I get she's not going to win the best grandmother award," Graham said, "but you need to show some respect."

"Oh, okay. Well, just for that you get a whole big bowl of chitlins with your weak stomach having self."

They both laughed, although the sounds Onika made were louder and more obnoxious than they needed to be. It sounded forced.

"It's okay for you to feel sad about your mother dying," Graham said in a quiet voice after the laughter stopped. "You don't have to laugh and joke for my benefit."

"Thank you. I appreciate that."

Now the only voice in the car was the GPS, and Graham was okay with that. Even though he knew Onika would never let him if she knew he was doing it, he sent up a prayer for her. She'd need the power of God to handle what awaited her at the hospital.

CHAPTER SIXTY

Onika stared at Judy in the hospital bed. Graham had offered to come upstairs with her, and now she was glad she had declined his offer. Judy looked like something out of a horror movie. It was worse than Onika had expected.

She remembered her mother being big, with hair that was kinky but groomed. She was never ashy, no matter how many days she went without moisturizing.

But this Judy was another person. She was so small. She couldn't have weighed more than eighty pounds. If the nurse hadn't told Onika that this was her mother, Onika would not have believed it. All of her mother's kinky hair that she'd always been ashamed of was gone, save for a few patches.

"She's been waiting for you," the nurse said. "She asks about you every time she's conscious."

"Is she conscious now?" Onika asked. She couldn't tell if Judy's eyes were shut or not due to the swelling and puffiness around her eyes. "Why are her lips so dry? Is she dehydrated?"

The nurse walked over from the side of the bed and touched Onika's arm. "Baby, her lips are dry because she doesn't eat or drink anything anymore. Not even water. I rub ice and Vaseline on her lips when she lets me."

"What do you mean she doesn't eat or drink anymore? Can't

y'all give her an IV? Isn't this a hospital? Y'all in here letting her kill herself."

All of Onika's refinement, etiquette, and proper speech went out the window when she saw the shell of a woman lying in the hospital bed. She looked like a brisk wind would blow her away, while Earlene looked as hearty as ever, even with her cane.

"Her organs are shutting down, sweetheart. She doesn't need food. That's how we know when someone isn't going to be much longer on this side."

In spite of making a million promises to herself not to cry, Onika broke down. She cried because Judy had never really lived. She'd been on drugs since she was a teenager and probably hadn't gone more than a few feet from her mother's house since she got addicted. She'd never traveled the world, worn an expensive gown, or even gone to the beach. Judy's was a life wasted. There was no salvaging it.

Suddenly the eyes flickered open. The scary figure on the bed grabbed the nurse's arm. "Ah . . . ni . . . ka."

Judy slowly pronounced Onika's name twice.

"I think she wants to talk to you," the nurse said.

Onika stood next to the bed and touched her mother's hand. It felt like a collection of bones.

"Tae . . . mah . . . bayyy . . . guh," Judy said in a gravelly, unintelligible voice.

Onika looked at the nurse and shook her head. She didn't understand what Judy was saying.

"T-tae mah . . . bayyy guh." This time the nurse shook her head. "She had two strokes last week. After that, I couldn't understand anything she said."

Judy touched her lower abdomen and rubbed slightly. "Mah . . . bayyy beeee."

Onika's mouth fell open and then clamped shut again. Judy had another baby?

"Your baby? A baby girl?" Onika asked.

Judy's hand slumped to the side, and she relaxed. Her head slightly nodded.

"My mother has a baby?"

"I don't know," the nurse said. "I just started taking care of her a month ago."

Suddenly, one of machines that Judy was attached to started making loud beeping noises. The nurse pushed Onika out of the room, to make room for the doctors and nurses who swarmed the area. Onika tried to see what was happening but could not.

Then she heard one of the doctors say, "Time of death . . ."

Onika fainted in the hospital hallway.

CHAPTER SIXTY-ONE

Graham tried to make himself useful by helping Onika plan her mother's funeral. The smell of the chitlins wasn't as bad once they were cooked, but every now and then he had a wave of nausea. When Earlene had offered him a plate, he'd politely declined.

He'd brought Onika home from the hospital after her mother died. Apparently, her mother had been waiting for her, because Judy died only a few minutes after Onika arrived. Onika had chosen to sit a few hours with the body before going back down to the waiting area. Maybe she'd gotten all of her tears out then, but when she came back to Graham, she wasn't crying at all. She didn't say a word on the way back to Earlene's house, but she seemed okay.

Graham sat with Onika at Earlene's dining room table going through a box of photographs.

"This is a good one. Is that you when you were little?" Graham asked as he handed a picture to Onika.

She shook her head and handed him the picture back. "Judy was on her way to the corner on that one. That was her favorite man-catching outfit. We can't put a picture of her in her prostitute outfit on the cover of her obituary."

"There's no such thing as a prostitute outfit. These look like regular clothes to me," Graham said.

"Body ain't even cold yet, and you already planning the funeral," Earlene said. "It ain't proper."

Onika put the picture that was in her hand down and stared at Earlene. "This coming from the woman who already started inviting family. I'm doing this to keep from going crazy."

"Ain't even shed a tear for your mama!" Earlene hissed. "I know why you don't believe in the Lord our Savior. It's because of your devil daddy. He killed my baby and left me with the spawn."

Onika rose from the table. "Graham. Let's go. We can finish this later."

Graham quickly jumped up from his seat before Onika made a sudden move. She was quickly out the door, though, as if she was just as aware of herself being on edge and needing to escape from that house.

"I can't go back there," Onika said when they were in the car. "Just drive. I wanna show you something."

Graham followed Onika's directions until they were at a huge lake. There were well-used picnic tables and a huge brick barbeque pit. Onika didn't wait for Graham to get out of the car or barely even put it in park. She jumped out and ran across the grass, then sat on one of the benches and stared out over the water.

"Did you come here when you were little?" Graham asked.

"This is where I almost died."

"Where you nearly drowned?"

Onika nodded. "Yep. My grandmother was sitting right where I'm sitting now, and my mother was standing next to her. They sat, this close to the edge of the water, and almost let me die."

"Maybe they thought you'd start swimming."

"To this day, I think I remember my mother being high at that church picnic and my grandmother being embarrassed about it. But my grandmother was good and sober. She didn't try to save me, though."

"Country people have some strange ways sometimes."

Onika stared at the ground. "Before my mother died, she said something about having a baby girl. I think she had another baby."

"She did? Did you ask your grandmother about it?"

Onika shook her head. "For some reason, I get the feeling that she doesn't know. No matter how evil my grandmother is, she believes in being obligated to family. If my mother had another baby it would be living at her house."

"Is she really evil, though?"

"What grandmother takes in their grandchild and then raises that child without so much as a hug or a kiss. Definitely not an 'I love you.' She told me Jesus loved me, and that was supposed to be enough."

"It wasn't enough," Graham said sadly.

"Of course it wasn't."

Graham walked over and sat next to Onika on the bench. He put his arm around her and hugged her. He didn't kiss her or do anything that she might think was sexual. This was purely affection, because she needed it, even if she didn't know how to ask for it.

"Let's get a hotel room. We have to go a ways down the road to find any decent ones," Onika finally said.

"You're sure you don't want to stay over at your grandmother's house? I'm okay with driving you back there and going to get a hotel room for myself."

"You trying to leave me in the chitlin house?" Onika asked.

"Does the smell get on you? It felt heavy enough to get on me."

Onika sniffed him. "You do smell a little bit like raw chitlins."

"Oh my goodness. You're right."

"You know, I think my mother wants me to take her daughter. She said 'tae mah bay guh.' Doesn't that sound like 'take my baby girl'?"

Graham nodded. "It does, but if your grandmother doesn't know about her, how in the world are you gonna find her? Do you know how old she is?"

"She can't be no more than nine or ten."

"We can start looking for her tonight if you want."

Onika kissed Graham full on the lips, letting her tongue trace the inside of his mouth. This kiss was more than affectionate.

"We can start looking tomorrow," she said.

Graham knew that Onika's kiss was a promise of a night of pleasure, but he refused to accept the offer. Even though he wanted it just as badly as she did, he didn't want the first time they made love to be right smack in the middle of her pain.

There would be another chance. There would be joy attached to their moment instead of sorrow.

CHAPTER SIXTY-TWO

Judy's funeral was a circus, and Onika hated every second of it. Earlene had wanted to cremate the body, still embarrassed for anyone to see how Judy had wasted away. But Onika refused to allow it. She paid for everything out of her money from Aaron. Spent seven thousand dollars of her apartment fund for a nice casket, dress, wig, and makeup.

Judy's body looked nothing like any memory Onika had of her, and it definitely didn't look like the poster-sized photo on the easel next to the casket. She'd decided on a rare picture of Judy going to church. She was very young, probably nineteen, and she was holding Onika in her arms. Onika'd never seen that picture before. Earlene had put it away.

It would've been nice to know what Judy had been like before she was on drugs.

Even though Onika had paid for everything, Earlene insisted on being in charge of the funeral program. Judy had been baptized COGIC, and even though they probably wouldn't have let her have communion while she was alive, they were going to give her a good send-off in death.

After the first soloist sang "Order My Steps," Earlene stood from her seat on the front row and wobbled up to the microphone.

"Most of y'all here knew my Judy her whole life. She had a lot of demons. She suffered all her days. From the time she was in the cradle 'til they stretched her out on that hospital bed. I know God coulda saved her if He wanted to, but I do believe that my Judy went into that hospital tired. She held on until that prodigal daughter showed her face in town again. And then, my God, my God, Jesus gave her the rest she desired. But before she took leave of this earthly realm, I did hear her repent from her sins and call on the name of Jesus, the name above all other names, the sweetest name I know. Hey glory! Me and Onika used to pray for Judy, right here on this altar. You remember?"

Onika stared straight ahead. She refused to get caught up in Earlene's frenzy.

"She might not remember, but I do. Jesus be a balm, a balm in Gilead. That's what we prayed, and my God, sweet Jesus, He is comforting my Judy right now. Hallelujah!"

Earlene's speech had the majority of her fellow church-goers on their feet. Even though it was a funeral, if folk started to shout in this church, shouting music was played.

Onika didn't lift her hands, she didn't stand, she didn't dance. She sat unmoving in her seat, unless you counted the tear trickling down her face.

Earlene, though, hobbled up and down in front of the church, trying to do a little dance. When her knees started to buckle, Onika gasped.

She nudged Graham in the ribs. "Go help her before I have to bury her, too."

The funeral service went on, but the shouting didn't stop. They sang, preached, sang, testified, read resolutions, sang, and preached.

Onika was over it. She got up, walked down the center aisle, unnoticed, because the performance was happening straight ahead.

Onika walked outside to the parking lot. She was headed to the car but wasn't sure what she was going to do after that.

A short distance away, at the edge of the parking lot, stood an older woman and a little girl who, judging from her size, was about five years old.

As the woman got closer, Onika squinted, thinking she saw something familiar about the woman. She couldn't get a good look at her, because she had on a huge hat.

The duo stopped in front of Onika. The little girl smiled up at her and handed her the flower she was clutching in her hands.

"Can you put this in my mama's casket? She dead, right?"

Onika cleared her throat. "That's my mama in there, and yes she's dead."

The little girl looked up at the woman with a mask of confusion on her face.

"It's her mama, too," the woman said.

Onika looked hard at the little girl. This must be her little sister, Judy's other daughter. The little girl looked just like Judy. Dark skin, thick kinky hair, and huge expressive eyes. She was beautiful.

Onika stooped down and hugged the girl. "I think we might have the same mama."

"We do? You're pretty."

Onika looked back up at the woman. The recognition hit her like a sack of boulders. It was Joyce, the woman from the Metro station with the flyer for Safe Harbor. She was cleaner, and dressed well, for a funeral.

"How are you here?" Onika asked.

Joyce, or whatever her name was, only smiled.

"She's always here," the little girl said.

Onika turned her attention back to the child. "What's your name?"

"Seraiah."

"Where were you before you came here? Where do you live?"

Seraiah looked up at Joyce, perhaps for an answer. When she got none, she gazed into Onika's eyes.

"I was nowhere, and then here, but I was safe before. Now I'm not so sure."

Onika hugged the little girl tightly. She kissed her little face until it was covered in her lipstick.

"She's coming with me," Onika said, but when she looked up for Joyce to confirm her request, Joyce was gone.

"Where'd she go?" Onika asked.

"Sometimes she disappears, but she always comes back."

Onika glanced back over her shoulder at the church. This scene outside was too spooky for her liking. A mystery child, and a big old woman who appeared and disappeared at will.

Onika took Seraiah's hand and led her back to the church.

"You think she's an angel?" Onika asked.

Seraiah shook her head. "I think she's my auntie, from a long, long, long time ago."

Onika said nothing, because she knew she couldn't explain any of this, and no one would believe her if she tried. But for some reason, which she also couldn't explain, she believed that Seraiah was right. Joyce was some sort of protector. A gift.

But from whom? Onika wondered if the God she'd stopped believing in a long time ago was still trying to get her attention. And if He was, what did He want with her?

EPILOGUE

Graham watched Onika and Seraiah play their little hand-clapping game before Onika tucked Seraiah into the twin bed situated in the corner of Onika's room. They were so much alike, it was scary. They had the same laugh, and the same expressive eyes.

Although no one knew where the girl had come from or why, a DNA test confirmed that Seraiah was indeed Onika's little sister. There were also records that Judy gave her child to a woman passing through, as an adoption. She'd wanted to get her baby out of Goldsboro.

Apparently, Onika's mother had more sense than Onika gave her credit for, because she didn't let Earlene even know that the child or the pregnancy existed.

"Can I call you daddy?" Seraiah asked Graham as he stood in the doorway. "You can come in if you want."

Graham did come forward to the bed. "I'm not your daddy. I'm your friend, and you can always call me that."

"Can I call you Graham Daddy?" Seraiah asked.

Graham and Onika laughed. Seraiah had such a way of tickling them both and making them feel joy.

"Good night, sweetie," Onika said, and they left the room and closed the door.

Graham handed Onika a glass of wine he'd poured for her before he realized Seraiah was still awake. Onika eagerly took the glass and sat on the couch.

"She wears me out in that little time I have her after I pick her up at the end of my workday. Those day-care directors must have superpowers."

"They probably do."

"I think I may have found me and Seraiah an apartment."

Graham was offended. He'd moved them both in with him after the funeral. He'd stood by her when the social worker gave Onika the DNA test results. He didn't know why she kept talking about moving.

They never had to leave as far as he was concerned.

"Save your money and stay here."

"I can't. You're not asking for it now, but one day you're going to feel like I owe you something for rent that goes beyond writing a check."

"I would never."

Onika laughed. "You are a boy. You will."

"I am a grown man. I know how to exercise restraint."

"Oh, okay," Onika said, not really sounding convinced.

"You're going to mess around and miss out on the best man you've ever had," Graham said. "There are plenty of women out here who want to cuddle with me."

"But you're sitting up here waiting on me?" Onika asked.

He smiled. "Of course I'm waiting on you."

Graham was waiting. And while he tarried, he was falling in love with Onika and the little one who wanted to call him Graham Daddy. They were starting to feel like a family. Graham didn't want to lose the feeling, but there was just a tiny bit of fear in the pit of his stomach.

Onika never did tell Graham what happened the day of her mother's funeral. When she'd gone outside for fresh air and come back with a child. He did know that after it happened, she still didn't want to go to church, but she didn't make him stay quiet about his faith anymore.

He wondered if she'd had an experience with God. If so, he would let it marinate.

Some people went to church and had an experience with God there. But some other people—and he suspected Onika was a member of this group—had God meet them somewhere else. Graham didn't mind. Inside and outside the church, God was the same. He was no respecter of buildings and couldn't be contained in one, anyway.

The God that Graham met on Sunday mornings at his church service was the same one who'd nudged Graham on a Metro station and who'd planted Onika in his path, not once but twice. He was also the God who whispered His peace in Graham's ear when Graham thought of loving Onika for the rest of his life. Graham's God was omnipresent. He was even present in the desolate and dark corners of Onika's heart and spirit.

Where He was present, He lived. And where He lived, He let there be light.